W9-AWF-565

relativity

relativity

To Gracie —

CRISTIN BISHARA

WALKER BOOKS
AN IMPRINT OF BLOOMSBURY
NEW YORK   LONDON   NEW DELHI   SYDNEY

Copyright © 2013 by Cristin Bishara
All rights reserved. No part of this book may be reproduced or transmitted in any form
or by any means, electronic or mechanical, including photocopying, recording, or by any
information storage and retrieval system, without permission in writing from the publisher.

First published in the United States of America in September 2013
by Walker Books for Young Readers, an imprint of Bloomsbury Publishing, Inc.
www.bloomsbury.com

For information about permission to reproduce selections from this book, write to
Permissions, Walker BFYR, 1385 Broadway, New York, New York 10018
Bloomsbury books may be purchased for business or promotional use. For information
on bulk purchases please contact Macmillan Corporate and Premium Sales Department
at specialmarkets@macmillan.com

Library of Congress Cataloging-in-Publication Data
Bishara, Cristin.
Relativity / by Cristin Bishara.
pages   cm
Summary: If Ruby Wright could have her way, her dad would never have met and married
her stepmother, Willow, her best friend George would be more than a friend, and her mom
would still be alive. Then she discovers a tree in the middle of an Ohio cornfield with a
wormhole to nine alternative realities. But is there such a thing as a perfect world?
What is Ruby willing to give up to find out?
Includes bibliographical references.
ISBN 978-0-8027-3468-6 (hardcover) • ISBN 978-0-8027-3469-3 (e-book)
[1. Reality—Fiction. 2. Families—Fiction. 3. Science fiction.]   I. Title.
PZ7.B5239Re 2013   [Fic]—dc23   2013007834

Book design by Regina Flath
Typeset by Westchester Book Composition
Printed and bound in the U.S.A. by Thomson-Shore Inc., Dexter, Michigan
2 4 6 8 10 9 7 5 3 1

All papers used by Bloomsbury Publishing, Inc., are natural, recyclable products
made from wood grown in well-managed forests. The manufacturing processes
conform to the environmental regulations of the country of origin.

In memory of my father,
John Bishara

The truth may be puzzling. It may take some work to grapple with. It may be counterintuitive. It may contradict deeply held prejudices. It may not be consonant with what we desperately want to be true. But our preferences do not determine what's true.

—*Carl Sagan, American astronomer (1934–1996)*

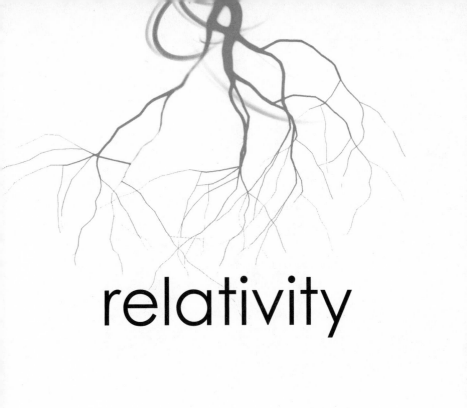

relativity

chapter one

I hold up my phone and snap a photo of the windowless cafeteria, then close-ups of the gory details: paper wedged underneath uneven table legs, yellowed ceiling panels sagging with water damage, deep gouges scarring the linoleum floor.

I thumb the words Rescue me and hit send.

Mr. Burton, the guidance counselor, emerges from the men's room, wiping his damp hands on his pants, leaving dark streaks across the khaki fabric. I tuck my phone into my back pocket and manage a smile.

"Okay," he says. "Where were we?"

"You were just explaining the themed lunches," I offer, since I'm the only one here, the only new student enduring orientation. And why would that be? Perhaps because you'd need an IQ of 40 to move to this total nowhere, to think Ennis, Ohio, is a great place to call home. Seriously. There's a McDonald's, a library that screams 1970, a bunch of half-vacant strip malls.

Hiking trails? Nope.

Movie theater? Two towns north.

Rapid transit system to a thriving metropolis? Yeah, right.

Look, I'm not saying Dad's IQ is deficient. He's not stupid. But he is stupid-in-love, and that's what fueled the moving vans.

"Right. Themed lunches." Mr. Burton seems to have this habit of rubbing the top of his bald head. It's like he keeps checking for hair. "On Mexican Day they set up a taco bar. Italian Day is spaghetti and meatballs."

Authentic ethnic cuisine, right? I swallow the sarcasm and try to sound sincere. Really, I do, because it's not Mr. Burton's fault I'm here, and he seems genuinely excited about the food. "I like tacos," I say.

He nods and motions for me to follow him. "We have a variety of extracurriculars," he says as we walk, counting them off on his stubby fingers. "Soccer, drama, cheerleading."

He glances at me when he says "cheerleading," like he's embarrassed he mentioned it. Yeah, I don't exactly fit the bill, with my super-short hair and black-rimmed glasses.

"Crafts?" Mr. Burton points to a fluorescent-yellow poster pinned to a bulletin board. LEARN TO QUILT AND SEW. He's already shaking his head; he knows my answer is a serious negative.

"No thank you," I manage.

Mr. Burton continues to tick off extracurriculars, and he's running out of fingers. "Fast-pitch softball is a big deal here. Some kids are trying to start an organic gardening club. I don't know what you were accustomed to doing in California."

"What about a science club, or math?"

"Sorry, Ruby." Mr. Burton rubs his head. "You could try to start one."

"Try?"

"Yes, try. If you can find enough interest." He opens a thick metal door, and we walk outside, across the parking lot, stepping over disintegrating curbs.

"New goalposts, and a fresh coat of paint on the stadium." Mr. Burton spreads his arms, introducing the Home of the Bears. The football field reminds me of Hyperion.

"What?" he asks.

I didn't realize I was talking out loud. "Hyperion. One of Saturn's moons. It's totally pockmarked by craters, kind of like the football field."

"I see."

"Never mind," I say. "It's nice. I mean, it's . . . you know."

My phone vibrates in my back pocket, and I fight the urge to check it. It's probably George, his response to the cafeteria photos and my plea to be rescued.

"Well," Mr. Burton says, forcing a smile. "That about does it." He looks at his watch, then me.

"I'm sorry." I know he's picked up on my sour mood. "It's just that it's pretty different here. For me, anyway. I'll get used to it."

Mr. Burton nods. "You'll adjust."

"There's my dad now." I point to our black Jeep pulling into the parking lot, going too fast. Dad dodges a pothole and swerves around a pile of broken glass before stopping.

"How'd it go? Fine?" Dad leans out the window, his two-day beard uneven, his eyes rimmed with red. I climb in the passenger side and pull my door closed.

"Ruby will find her place," Mr. Burton says, shaking Dad's hand.

I slide my phone out of my pocket and unlock the screen. Yep. It's a text from George. Rescuer at your service. Attached is a picture of a kid, front teeth missing, flexing his little biceps in a Superman costume.

I quickly type, Is that u? and hit send.

Mr. Burton is still talking to Dad. "I'm available if there are questions or problems."

"There won't be any problems," Dad says, smiling. "She's got Kandinsky to show her the ropes. Kandy."

Right. My stepsister. Who, according to Dad, will soon be my new best friend. So far, she's been outstanding at ignoring me. If she bothers to make eye contact, it's only for the sake of driving home an insult. Such as: Ruby, those glasses make you look so . . . smart? Anytime you want to borrow my clothes . . . um, don't?

Mr. Burton shifts nervously. He rubs the top of his head. Nope, still no hair. "Mr. Wright," he says. "I don't want you to take this the wrong way, since Kandy is now family and all. But she's made a few visits to the principal's office for fighting."

"Arguing?" Dad asks.

"Fist fighting."

"Oh."

Mr. Burton lets that hang in the air for a minute. "Getting back to Ruby here," he says. "I need to mention that tattoos are against the dress code. She'll have to cover hers."

My hand goes to the nape of my neck.

"I didn't get a good look," Mr. Burton says, squinting into the Jeep. "What does it say?"

"It's an equation. The Einstein tensor." I turn my head to show him.

"It's not gang related?"

Dad lets out an exaggerated laugh, then adds a horselike snort. "Of course not. It's just a math equation. Ruby likes that kind of stuff."

"The Einstein tensor is used to calculate the curvature of a Riemannian manifold," I say before I can stop myself.

Mr. Burton's face is blank.

"Sorry," I say. "I mean, it's not just a math equation. It's used for describing space-time."

Dad tries to help. "It's geometry."

"You could tutor other kids." Mr. Burton smiles, seeming relieved he finally thought of something I could do outside of class. He pats the roof of the Jeep. "Okay, then. See you Monday, Ruby." He waves goodbye and heads for a dented pickup truck.

My phone vibrates, and George's response appears. Yep. That's me. 6 yrs old.

Luv it, I write back.

What I want to write is Luv *u* and send myself as an attachment. I'd whiz across the continent bit by bit, byte by byte. Ruby particles flying through the atmosphere, a jumble of my deconstructed self. He'd open his messages, and I'd buzz out of his phone, reassembling, downloading 60 percent . . . 70 percent . . . Within seconds—with George—I'd be perfectly whole again.

I cross my arms over my chest, which feels heavy, full of loss. I've left so much behind, thirty-five highway hours away. "Honestly, Dad. How do you expect me to like this place?"

He puts the Jeep in drive, navigating around the shards of glass, the pothole. "Give it a chance."

That's Dad's new line. Give Willow a chance, give Kandy a chance, give Ohio a chance. We just moved last week. He just got married last month. Give it a chance.

"The library is the size of a bathroom stall," I say. "The chem lab is totally outdated."

"What can I do to cheer you up?"

"Move us back to California?" I give him a winning smile, and he laughs.

"How about ice cream?"

"No thanks. I'm not five years old."

"With all this pouting, you sound like it." Dad stops at a red light, one of the few traffic signals in Ennis. He rubs his temples. "I did some hunting around on the Internet. The Cleveland Museum of Natural History looks promising. Want to go tomorrow?"

"Yeah, sure."

"Although," Dad says. There's always an *although*, some caveat. "I've got to finalize a copywriting project first."

"Of course."

The copywriting is numero uno. That's just the way it is. Oh well, who wants to go to a museum with Dad anyway, after what happened the last time? We were at the de Young in San Francisco, on a Saturday night in April. Behold the disastrous chain of events that ensued: (1) Dad spilled his wine on Willow's Birkenstocks, (2) she laughed, (3) she wrote her phone number on the program, (4) after a couple of months of long-distance dating, Dad tried to convince her to move to California, and (5) Willow refused, making us move here.

"Did you know about Kandy?" I ask, putting my fists in front of my face and jabbing into the air. A one-two punch.

"No," Dad says, watching the traffic light, still red. "But I'm not going to judge until I know the whole story. She might have been fending off the school bully."

"I'm kinda thinking she *is* the school bully."

Dad looks at me sideways. "Give her a chance," he says. "It's only been seven days."

It's just not possible. Seven days ago—that's all?—I was drinking coffee shakes with George, in the back of the East Bay Café, in our usual spot on the leather couch. When I got there, he was hunched over his sketch pad, his colored pencils scattered across the coffee table. And when he saw me, he patted the couch, like always.

He'd been pissed. About Dad's sudden marriage, the impulsive move. About me being told rather than asked that we were packing up and heading out.

And he couldn't understand why Dad and I weren't driving cross-country together. Why I was taking a flight by myself to Cleveland, while Dad was driving alone. A twenty-five-hundred-mile drive. Nine states.

"Holy crap. The photographs you could take!" George had thrown his hands in the air, exasperated. "To have a sketch pad in Nebraska. Are you kidding?"

"Utah's got a couple of dinosaur quarries," I'd said. "And we'd go right around Chicago and the Adler Planetarium."

I knew I sounded nerdy, as usual, but George didn't give me a hard time about it that day—or ever. Which is why I love him.

"Your dad's clinical," George decided.

"Bonkers."

"Daffy."

George pulled his iPhone from his pocket. "Thesaurus app," he'd said. "He's a lunatic, demented, cracked, brainsick, *non compos mentis.*"

"He's got deadlines, so he can't take a week off. He's driving fourteen-hour days so he can get to Ohio by Monday."

"No fun."

"None of it."

The traffic light turns green, and Ennis High recedes in my side-view mirror. Mr. Burton's pickup bounces out of the parking lot and heads in the opposite direction. I stare at the photo of George in his Superman costume, while Dad yawns and strums his fingers on the Jeep's steering wheel.

We drive in silence the rest of the way home. Home? It's Willow's home and Kandy's home, but not mine, not Dad's. Our home is across the bay from San Francisco, a little apartment in Walnut Creek with blue carpet, an always-cold swimming pool, and a Thai grocery store across the street.

I slam the Jeep door a little too hard. The house looms over me.

Three stories of peeling paint, shutters that hang by rusted screws. Dense ivy strangles the porch columns. The front door is swollen with rot and age.

"Let me get that." Dad gives the door a hard shove and it opens.

Inside, it's quiet. Dad makes a beeline for his laptop, which is perched on the coffee table in the living room. Above the couch is one of Willow's enormous oil paintings, gray with streaks of black and navy. It looks like a threatening rain cloud. I'm half tempted to get Dad an umbrella, but I suppose that would support his theory that I'm acting like a child.

"Where is everyone?"

"Kandy's off somewhere getting her nails done," Dad says. "Willow's in her studio."

"Looks like you're busy too," I say, motioning to the piles of paperwork.

He nods. "The label for the spinach-artichoke sauce is killing me."

"A delicious source of iron?" I try. "A heart-healthy pasta topping?"

Dad wrinkles his nose. "That's all been done before. I'm trying to create a story, something fresh." He deepens his voice. "In the year 1864, an Italian farmer planted his first tomato plant."

"When was the last time you slept? That's a question for you, not a suggestion for the sauce label."

"I tried last night." He winks at me and starts shuffling through a stack of file folders.

"You should get some fresh air. Go for a walk or something."

Dad gazes at the computer screen. "Hmm."

"I'm going to unpack some more," I tell Dad, though I know he's just tuned me out. Click. Off. He's in spinach-artichoke land, in Italy, in the year 1864. So I head upstairs to my room. At some point—maybe—it won't feel horrible to call it my room. Right now it's just walls, ceiling, and floor, in the wrong city, in the wrong state.

There are stacks of boxes labeled RUBY'S. I use a pair of scissors to slice through the tape on a smaller box. It's crammed with DVDs and my old iPod. Plastic hangers go in the closet, and a lace-collared dress I should've never packed goes in the trash.

Under my suitcase, I find *Physics of the Impossible*, so I put it on the bookshelf, next to Kaku's other books. Then I sort through a stack of laundry on my bed, and an unfamiliar hoodie surfaces. I hold it up to examine it, and a plastic drugstore bag—full of lipstick and eye shadow—spills onto the tangled sheets of my unmade bed. It must be Kandy's.

I sift through the goo tubes. Several are red, and I have to laugh. I'm sure Kandy has no idea they make the red coloring from pulverized beetle shells. Yeah, you're wearing a scale insect in the suborder Sternorrhyncha on your lips.

I walk across the hall to Kandy's room and flinch at the sign on the door: GET LOST, GO AWAY, DIE. It wasn't there yesterday, so I can only assume it's for me. Gosh, I feel all warm and fuzzy inside. I listen for a moment, trying to hear footsteps or voices coming from downstairs. Silence. No sign that Kandy's home yet, so I open the door.

In contrast to the rest of the house, her room is bright with color. Three walls are red, the fourth silver. The red walls are covered with clippings from magazines. Mostly celebrity red-carpet photos. On the silver wall is a framed Wassily Kandinsky print. That's who Kandy's named after, which is just plain wacky. I mean, the guy was a Russian painter, no relation. He just happened to be the subject of Willow's MFA thesis when she got pregnant.

I toss the hoodie and the bag of makeup on Kandy's bed, then go to the window to look at an astounding oak tree that's on the property behind us, about a half mile away. Kandy's got a better view than I do, the best in the house. I'm guessing the tree's eighty feet tall, maybe more. It's crooked and magnificent, surrounded by acres of cornfields. I don't believe in magic, but I do believe in jaw-droppers conjured up by Mother Nature. The Northern Lights, for one. Brachiosaurus standing forty feet tall, volcanoes spewing 2000-degree lava, the Milky Way containing 100 billion planets. All of it seems otherworldly, the stuff of pure imagination.

There's something about this ancient oak tree that's startling in that same otherworldly way. I find myself stopping at any window that allows even a glimpse of it. It's got this presence, a vibe. It almost seems like it's watching me back. For a long time—maybe longer than I realize—I'm glued to Kandy's window. Mesmerized.

I shudder, shake off the feeling.

Get a grip, Ruby. It's just a tree. Go finish unpacking.

I head across the hallway back into my room just as Kandy reaches the top of the stairs. I smile. She glowers.

"How was the manicure?" I ask, trying to sound light and casual. My heart is pounding. If she'd come upstairs thirty seconds sooner, she'd have caught me. . . .

"Were you in my room?"

"Um, yeah?" I say. She narrows her eyes, so I hurry to explain. "I found some of your makeup, and I put it on your bed."

She looks startled. "You found makeup?"

"It was mixed up in some laundry—"

"Whatever." She points to the sign on her door. "You can read, right?"

"Sorry," I say, taking a step back. She's a little too close; I can smell her mint gum.

She puts her hands on her hips and sizes me up. "You should've kept the bag for yourself. You need, like, a total makeover," she says with a look of sheer repulsion. "That shade of denim? It is so bad. And those shoes."

I look down at my frayed jeans and olive sneakers. "Thanks for the tip." I sidestep around her and head downstairs.

Yep, we'll be best friends in no time.

Dad's laptop is still on the coffee table, but he's nowhere around. I find Willow in her studio, perched on a stool, paintbrush in hand. She's working on a painting of bare winter trees. Gray branches set against a gray sky with a gray barn in the background. Super-cheerful.

"Have you seen my dad?"

"He ran to the grocery store to get some frozen pizzas and a rotisserie chicken for dinner." She turns to look at me, black paint in her curly blond hair. "You okay?"

"Fine," I say.

"Really?"

I half nod. Hardly convincing. At least she cares enough to ask.

"Is there something you need or can't find?" She puts her paint-brush down, ready to help. So far Willow seems like a decent human being. Then again, I have to wonder what she's really like, under-neath, because there has to be a reason Kandy's the way she is. Gene-tics. Her upbringing.

Willow searches my face. "If you give me a list of your favorite food, I'll make sure I stock up the next time I shop. Doritos? Cheetos?"

I sigh. "I'm not much of a junk-food person."

Her eyes ask, *Then what's wrong?*

I can't exactly say that her dilapidated house is depressing, that Ennis will never compare to Walnut Creek, that I miss George, that her daughter is sharpening her freshly painted talons so I'm afraid to go back upstairs. I can't tell her that since she's become my stepmother, I've suddenly been missing my real mom. That I'm wondering how different my life would be at this very moment if Mom had survived that car crash eleven years ago, when I was four. She got hit hard, but her dependable Volvo weathered the impact. She had her seat belt on. It wasn't an airbag malfunction or anything else that might make sense. No. It was an airborne windshield wiper—propelled with arrow accuracy and speed—that skewered her esophagus.

If it hadn't been for that windshield wiper, I wouldn't have a step-mother or stepsister. We wouldn't have moved to Ohio. I wouldn't be standing in this room right now. Action and reaction. Cause and effect. One event triggers another, one path stems to another, and eventually you end up standing in the middle of Somewhere Unrecognizable without a compass or map. You get there one increment at a time, with movements so subtle that you don't even notice until it's too late to find your way back.

"That bookstore in the shopping strip," I say, trying to distract myself before I get emotional in front of Willow. "Could I borrow someone's bike and go? I saw a magazine there yesterday."

"I'm sorry, Ruby." Willow sighs, sincere in her disappointment. "We only have one bike, and it's in bad shape. I'll drive you tomorrow, okay?"

I nod. "I'll just go for a walk, then." I turn to leave the studio but notice a canvas propped against the wall. A chill runs through me. "That's the oak tree that's off in the cornfields."

Willow follows my gaze. She looks at the painting with a weary smile. "You've noticed it too?"

"It's hard not to."

"I know what you mean. After we first moved into this house, I couldn't stop painting it. The second Kandy left for school, I'd go upstairs and sit at her window and work. I must have twenty oils and watercolors, and a notebook full of sketches."

"There's something about it. Definitely." True to Willow's style, the painting is dark. The oak tree looms, its branches reaching out with sinister, clawlike leaves. "You made it look pretty menacing."

"Well, that's because of the legend." She leans forward to tell me. "Apparently someone tried to hack it down with an ax sometime in the late 1800s, and he was said to have burst into flames."

"He caught fire?"

"So the story goes."

I cock my head and consider the lightning-lit clouds that Willow painted behind the oak. "You know, human bodies contain electrical fields, as well as flammable gases. Put the two together, and you've got flames."

"You're talking about spontaneous combustion?"

"Yeah, but there's never been any scientific proof it actually happens." I wave my hand to dismiss the idea. "Usually it's just a dropped cigarette."

"There's more to the story," Willow says. "About fifty years ago, a couple of professional loggers tried to cut it down with industrial chain saws. They were both electrocuted."

"Dead?"

Willow shrugs. "Who knows. But after I found that out, I stopped using it as a subject. I felt like I was painting a serial killer. I like my palette dark these days, but not that dark."

"Did you ever look it all up?" I ask. "They sound like campfire stories someone made up to scare kids."

"No, I never did any research to find out if it was fact or fiction," Willow admits. "I walked all the way to it one day, and there was nothing out of the ordinary. For all I know, the tree just marks a property line, and it probably provided good shade for cattle at one time. But just the idea of those crazy stories was enough to turn me off." She points her brush at the canvas in front of her. "I found other trees to paint."

"Innocent trees without blood on their branches."

"Do me a favor and don't tell Kandy." Willow winks at me. "About me painting in her room? She's doesn't like me setting foot in there.

She calls it 'trespassing,' and that if I'm not careful, I'll be 'cited and fined.'"

She laughs, but I'm not so sure it's funny. What would a "fine" from Kandy consist of? If she actually caught me in her room, would she expect me to do her math homework for a month? Clean her hairbrushes? Organize her purses by color? Of course not. It would be by brand, then color.

"Gotcha," I say, pretending to lock my lips with a key. "Your secret's safe with me."

"Enjoy your walk. We'll eat around six," Willow says, dipping her brush in water.

"Sounds good."

I grab a soda from the fridge and venture into the backyard. A few hundred feet from the house, the grass ends and the cornfields begin. The stalks are dense, in tight rows, but there's one wider alley at the corner of the yard, like they skipped half a row. A mistake when they planted.

I can see into the field far enough. It looks like a navigable path, and it's aimed in the right direction, so I decide to walk to the oak tree. I've been wanting to get a closer look, and after hearing Willow's stories, I'm more curious than ever. Besides, let's face it: there's nothing better to do.

Five minutes into my trek, reality check. This is not easy. Leaves lash my face, dust and dirt invade my sinuses. I'm sweating. And sneezing. My entire body itches. A humongous insect orbits my head, and I spin around, swatting and ducking.

"Get away!" It dodges the palm of my hand and slowly drifts off, unimpressed.

I'm left wondering: Was I going this way, or that way, or . . . ? There are no landmarks in a cornfield.

"Crap." I walk a little more, then stop to gulp the last of my soda, wishing I'd chosen water instead. Sucrose and caramel color aren't exactly quenching my thirst.

Relax, Ruby. You've only been walking five minutes. How lost can you be?

Okay, maybe it's been ten minutes, though as far as I can tell, I've stayed within the confines of a single row, which means I'm walking in a straight line. I jump, stretching my neck, trying to glimpse the third floor of Willow's house. No use. The corn is eight feet tall. Add the tassels on top, maybe it's ten. And I suck at jumping.

Ridiculous? Yes, indeed.

I can navigate BART all over San Francisco, to and from the East Bay, south to the airport, and anywhere in between. The maps are easy to read; the lines are color-coded. I never feel intimidated. I'm never lost. But then again, I'm never alone. I'm either with Dad or George.

George. I picture him at the café, in our usual spot, on the leather couch. I should be next to him, scooping whipped cream off the top of my shake, then his. I should not be dripping with sweat in the middle of a cornfield. Last week should not have been the end. It shouldn't have been our last time together, our good-bye.

"Your going-away present," he'd said, handing me a wrapped gift.

"Thanks!" I'd taken the opportunity to move closer. Our thighs were touching; we were shoulder to shoulder. I could smell his skin, a hint of the sandalwood soap his mother stocks the bathrooms with. "Let's see," I said, though it was obvious it was a book. A big one.

"Try not to squeal with excitement."

I snorted with sarcasm. "I wouldn't know how to squeal, even if I wanted to."

"You'd squeal if your dad told you he'd changed his mind, and you weren't moving."

"I might attempt a cartwheel," I admitted. "Which would be ugly."

I peeled the wrapping paper off and held the book in my hands, grinning. It was a collection of photos from the Hubble telescope. Amazing, full-color pictures of impossible things. Star clusters, the Crab Nebula, spiral galaxies. New stars emerging from molecular clouds. Storms on Jupiter.

I'd wanted to kiss George, but things weren't like that. Couldn't be like that. He and Jamie had just broken up, so he was still off-limits. She would've killed both of us in a jealous rage. Maybe after a few months, it would've been okay. After she'd moved on to the next boy-friend, and if I hadn't moved three time zones east. Then George and I would've had a chance to become more than just flirty friends. Eventually, I'm pretty sure. Like a 90 percent shot. But now I'll never know.

Because I'm going to die from corn asphyxiation. Honestly. If one more leaf smacks me across the neck or ends up in my mouth . . . gag.

Finally, the upper branches of the oak tree emerge, sending shadows over the tall cornstalks. Yes! All along I was perfectly on track. After another hundred feet or so the field ends abruptly, and I'm standing in an open patch of grass, shaking off corn silk and claustrophobia. I breathe. A very deep breath. So far, the only good thing about Ennis is the smell of fresh air.

And the tree!

It's enormous, majestic. It casts its shade thick and wide, blocking the sun, and the cool air is a kiss of relief after sweating through the cornfield. I walk carefully, stepping over roots that erupt through the earth at intervals, like knuckles, fingers gripping the ground. To think this tree started as an acorn—a seed you could hold in the palm of your hand. How long ago? It shot roots into the soil, spread branches into the sky, feeding on carbon dioxide and rainwater. It thickened and stretched, cells multiplying, pulling itself up, straightening its spine like an evolving primate.

"You're beautiful," I whisper. It's almost human in its presence. A breathing, living thing.

I hit the web browser on my phone and type in *how old are oak trees* in the search field. I scroll through the site listings and find an oak in England that's a thousand years old, and one in California that's two thousand. Most sites say they live closer to four hundred years. So this tree could predate the American Revolution, or even the Pilgrims.

I wish George could see this. I pull out my phone and try to frame the tree for a photo, but of course it doesn't fit in the viewfinder. I step back, but it's no use. There's no way to capture its size and grandeur. If he were here, he'd pull out his sketchbook, and we'd sit quietly for hours while he worked his pencil magic.

I step closer to the trunk, reaching out to press my hands against the bark, layered and gray like stone. But I pull back, suddenly remembering Willow's stories of electrocution, death by fire.

I put my hands on my hips. "You're not going to fry me up for dinner, right?" I ask.

You're an idiot, Ruby. It's a tree. A bunch of xylem cells and phloem tissue. Plant matter. Not a serial killer.

It doesn't answer my question. "Didn't think so," I say. At the base of the trunk there's an even nook, almost like a small front porch. With some lingering apprehension, I sit cross-legged there, leaning lightly, hesitantly, against the trunk. Nothing bad happens. The methane in my intestines doesn't erupt into flames. I don't spontaneously combust.

In the distance, I hear the hum of a lawnmower. A soothing buzz. I close my eyes and relax, daydreaming. My mind skips through memories and settles on one of George singing happy birthday to me in the school parking lot, the way he jumped onto the hood of his car and ended with an operatic flourish: "And many more!" I feel happy in this moment, and sleepy. I'm just nodding off—destined for sweet dreams, for sure—when something hits the top of my head and bounces into my lap.

"Hey!" I say, startled and annoyed. It's a piece of bark. I twist around to look up and behind me. Maybe a squirrel knocked it loose. I pick it up and chuck it toward the cornfield.

I lean against the tree again, trying to pick up where I left off. George singing happy birthday. I'm dozing off when another piece hits. This time I stand up and accuse the tree. "A break, please? That's all I want!"

I shake my head. What am I doing here? Stranded in the middle of nowhere, at the bottom of Dad's priorities. I'm not going to cry. But if I do, at least no one will see me here. I look up at the tree, its branches outstretched like it would give me a reassuring pat on the back, if only it could. That's when I notice, about ten feet up, a bare spot.

A lot of bark has fallen off, and now I see that the ground is littered with chunks. Odd. I wonder if a tree disease, a parasite, is at work. And then I hear the buzz again. The hum I thought was a distant lawnmower is neither: it's not distant, not a lawnmower.

It's the tree. Tentatively, I press my hands flat against the trunk. It's vibrating. From within.

I pull away, my hands tingling slightly. Are the stories true? The only thing I can hear is my heart, and the voice in my head: *They're just stories to scare kids.* There must be a reasonable explanation for the vibrating. Something's going on here that makes sense.

Insects. Yes, that's it. The entire oak is full of them, infested. See? It took a whopping thirty seconds to come up with a logical hypothesis. There's no reason to panic. But then I think about how many insects there must be. Are they boring holes into the outer bark, and at any moment they'll break through, and I'll be surrounded by swarms, angry and with stingers?

Come on, Ruby. Don't go jumping to conclusions.

I put both hands on the trunk again, then lean in and press my ear against the rough bark. It sounds like an engine.

I step back, stumbling away from the tree. I grab my empty soda can from the ground and hurry back into the cornfield. What was blue sky half an hour ago is now half-covered in inky clouds. And more are rolling in.

Trees don't rumble. It's thunder. It's about to rain.

I attempt a nonchalant laugh at myself, but it comes out as a high-pitched giggle. I think of George and his iPhone thesaurus app. Bananas, loco, out to lunch, mad as a hatter.

As I jog into the cornfield, I take one last look over my shoulder at the tree. And that's when—for a split second, I swear—it seems to be glowing.

chapter two

The rotisserie chicken is greasy, the pepperoni pizza worse, making dinner delicious-disgusting. Dad also bought the token iceberg salad with approximately three carrot shavings. A glob of ranch dressing is its only hope. I'm seeing a pattern here. Last night was fried chicken with a side of mayo—I mean coleslaw. The night before was ribs from Pig-Out. Dad could cook if he tried, but he can't pry himself away from work long enough to boil an egg. At least back in California, we had top-notch takeout. Burmese noodles, eggplant rollatini, burritos with fresh guacamole.

I sit at the kitchen table, armed with a stack of napkins, expecting someone to join me. But Willow and Dad flop down on the family room couch to watch the news, and Kandy takes her plate upstairs.

Fun times.

I send George my tenth text of the day (BORING! Tho there's

mystery tree in backyard. Buzzes. Full of locusts) and immediately begin checking for his response.

Are there locusts in Ohio, or some kind of termite that eats a tree
from the inside out? I don't know. It's more likely there's something
underground nearby, like a generator or transformer, and the vibrations are resonating enough to shake the tree. I think of the dozens of
minor tremors I felt in California; there could be a seismic zone running through Ennis. I'm not sure about locusts, but I know there are
fault lines all over the Midwest.

If it weren't so late, I could have Dad drive me to the library. I could
check to see if the electric company has an underground hub near the
tree, or if any sinkholes have collapsed. Maybe there's an underground
river.

And if people really did die trying to cut the oak down, there must
be something in the library archives about it. There would be newspaper articles and obituaries. Those clues would provide a way into the
research. But I'll have to wait until morning when the library opens,
probably at nine.

Dad slides over toward Willow to make room for me on the couch,
so I settle in to watch TV with them for a while. It's annoying. They're
both channel surfers, stealing the remote from each other at every
opportunity. My phone vibrates and I eagerly read George's text: At
movie. Trning phone off. Srry.

Bummer. He's putting on 3-D glasses without me, at the movie we
were supposed to see together. Which makes me wonder who he's
with. Maybe his brother, but what if it's Jamie? What if they're getting
back together? I send Jamie a text that says Whatcha up 2 2nite?

then toss the phone onto the coffee table. She hasn't been keeping in touch, so she might not even respond. So far the only contact she's made was when she posted a message on my Facebook wall: How's it going in Cowville?

Dad eats the last of his chicken, leans forward, and scribbles on a piece of paper. Copywriting inspiration has struck. Even when he's not working, he's thinking about it. It's like constant background noise.

"Did you figure out the spinach-artichoke label?" I ask.

He nods, holds up a finger for me to give him a second. He scratches out what he just wrote, then writes something else. "I'm on to the gnocchi packaging now."

"Squishy pasta-potato things, only good with buttery sauce."

"I'll try to remember that," he says, smiling.

"It's catchy," Willow agrees. She pulls the cheese off her pizza and rolls it into a ball before popping it into her mouth.

"That's kinda gross," I say.

"Ruby," Dad warns.

"She's right." Willow winks at me. She stacks her pepperoni slices, one on top of the other, and eats them all at once. "I've been eating pizza this way since I was a kid. Bad habit."

"It's cute," Dad says, squeezing Willow's knee. "Adorable."

Ugh! I move away from them, pressing up against the armrest. There's nothing worse than parental PDA.

"I walked out to the oak tree today," I tell Willow, trying to ignore the dreamy look in Dad's eye.

Willow raises an eyebrow. "That was brave of you. I see you survived."

"Yeah. It's weird, you know? There's this sort of humming noise around it, or in it. Maybe it's bugs, or maybe it was just thunder rumbling. I'm not sure. But I was wondering if there are any underground caves around here."

She thinks for a moment. "There are some in Bellevue. They're called the Seneca Caverns, or something like that. Why?"

I shrug. "I get the feeling there's something underneath the tree."

Willow frowns. "I'm not sure I like you going near that thing."

"What tree?" Dad asks. He grabs the remote from Willow's lap and changes the channel again.

"An oak off in the cornfields," I say. "There must be an easy way to explain the noise it makes. I just need to collect some data, come up with a hypothesis."

Dad taps his finger against his temple. "She's got a science noggin," he says to Willow. "Let her figure it out. It'll give her something to do until school starts."

"I thought you were going to the Natural History Museum tomorrow," Willow says.

"Oh," Dad says with a sigh and an apologetic cringe on his face. "About that." Yep, here we go: the clearing of the throat, followed by the repentant tone of voice. "Even though I finished the sauce label, now I'm on deadline for this. They moved everything up on the production schedule."

"It's okay, Dad." For once, I'm actually glad he's ditching me. Because now I've got my own agenda for tomorrow. A trip to Cleveland would eat the entire day, and I wouldn't have the chance to get back to the tree.

Willow pats me on the knee. "I'll take you to that bookstore you wanted to go to."

"Sure," I say. "Thanks." I can hit the library first thing, the tree next, then go with Willow after lunch. If the bookstore has a local history and geography section, I might find some useful info there too.

Willow snatches the remote, and just as we're settling into a show about poisonous snakes in Africa, Dad steals it back. After two hours of watching sixty shows, two minutes each, I go upstairs and tiptoe past Kandy's door. It's open, but the room is quiet and dark, except for a dim light, like a night-light. I sigh, relieved. The dragon slumbers. At the hour of 8:30. Why not, I guess, when there's nowhere to go, nothing to do. So far I haven't met any of Kandy's friends, and it occurs to me that she might not have any. Gee, shocker.

I unpack the last of my clothes, organize my bookshelf some more, and arrange a lamp, a wedge of amber with an insect inclusion, a meteorite chunk, and a few framed photos on my dresser.

First, George. He's smiling, holding a bottle of water, wearing a backpack. The blue of the sky behind him matches the blue of his eyes. That was the day we hiked Mount Diablo. From the summit, we could see the Golden Gate Bridge.

Next to that, the photo of my old dogs, Isaac and Galileo. They're outside our apartment in Walnut Creek, looking through the sliding-glass door. Their ears are straight up, mischief in their eyes. When the dogs both died of cancer within a year of each other, I kept that photo under my pillow. Dad bought a frame for it before it got completely wrinkled and ruined.

And finally, the faded, out-of-focus photo of Mom and me. My only photo of her, after our roof leaked years ago and ruined a closet full of keepsakes. I'm about three years old, sitting on her lap, wearing a red-gingham blouse with denim overalls. Mom's hair is long and black; the Cherokee in her blood also asserts itself in her cheekbones. She's looking off to the side, like something has caught her attention. She seems not quite sad. Maybe wistful is the word. I know the feeling.

" 'Night, Mom," I say, settling into bed with the Hubble book from George. I flip through the thick, glossy pages, stopping at 30 Doradus #016, a heavyweight star in the Tarantula Nebula. It's ninety times bigger than the sun, and it's zooming across space so fast it could travel from the Earth to the moon in an hour.

Next page, a titanic collision of galaxy clusters. Followed by a photo of galaxies aligning to form an "Einstein ring," which could help us understand dark matter and the curvature of the universe. I rub the tattoo on the back of my neck. $R_{\mu\nu} - \frac{1}{2}g_{\mu\nu}R = -\kappa T_{\mu\nu}$. The Einstein tensor.

I read for I don't know how many hours. Dad and Willow have both ducked their heads into my room to say good night. The house is quiet when there's a flash of light outside my window, then *crack*! Thunder. The room goes dark, the electricity out. I slide a metal ruler between the pages as a bookmark and flip my book shut. Nothing to do now but sleep.

But I can't. For hours, I turn from stomach to side, trying to get to REM, but every time I'm half dreaming, the thunder startles me awake. I let out a frustrated growl, push the sheets back. I listen for Dad or Willow, but the house is silent. Hurray for everyone else, snoozing through the storm.

The pounding rain suddenly subsides to a rhythmic *drip-drop-drip*.

The storm is tapering off. I press my face against my bedroom window, trying to catch a glimpse of the tree, but there's nothing but darkness. As black as outer space.

I press my forehead harder against the glass, wishing I had a better angle. Because that's the tree . . . glowing! Light purple, like a pale neon sign. So it wasn't my imagination.

First it hums from within, and now it lights up? Forget locusts or underground caverns. Something more is going on here. I need to get a better look, so I pad across the hallway. Luckily, Kandy's door is still ajar. I gently press my fingers against it, pushing it open wide enough for me to sneak in. She's snoring.

A battery-operated book light illuminates her desk, creating a dim glow throughout the room, just enough for me to safely dodge furniture. I'm shaking—anxious to see the tree and afraid that Kandy will catch me in her lair.

The windowpane is cold under the palms of my hands, and my breath leaves a fog of condensation across the glass. There it is. The magnificent oak, illuminated by an eerie incandescence.

Crack! I jump back from the glass, shielding my face. For a split second, I think the window has shattered. But it's just the crack of nasty thunder—thunder that's penetrated Kandy's sleep. She thrashes in bed, and a surge of adrenaline rushes through me. Time to get out.

I creep back past the desk and now notice that the book light is attached to an open journal. Handwriting on lined pages. I know, I know! I should keep walking. Instead, I pause and listen to Kandy's breathing. It's steady; she's settled back into sleep. Besides, I'm already holding the diary. Think of Sir Isaac Newton's first law of motion. You know—an object in motion will remain in motion in a straight line with constant speed unless acted upon by an external and unbalanced force. There's no external force keeping me back.

So I'm reading. For two seconds. Ten seconds tops.

Kandy's handwriting is all loops and bubbles. She dots her *i*'s with little circles, sometimes hearts. All over the margins, she's written the name Maddy.

> *Ennis (aka Pissville), Ohio, day 694. Could we be about halfway through the bleak period??? Mom's bright period lasted four years, so maybe. But by the time she gets through this stupid phase, I might be moved out anyway.*

There are a couple of sheets of loose paper folded together, so I carefully pull them apart and see that it's an application for admission to the Miami International University of Art & Design, about half filled out. Kandy has checked the box for an associate's degree in fashion design. Question number twenty-one is: Have you ever been convicted of, or pleaded guilty to, a crime other than a traffic offense? Kandy has checked the box marked "yes."

Lightning gives the brief impression that every lamp and chandelier in the house is on. A roll of thunder follows.

Kandy committed a crime? Nobody mentioned that juicy tidbit. I'm dying to read more of her journal, but Kandy mumbles something in her sleep, which sends a fresh jolt of panic through me. Really, I'm pushing my luck here. I silently put the journal back on the desk, book light still flipped on, as it was. I sidestep through the doorway and pull the door shut to exactly where I'd found it, glancing up at the GET LOST, GO AWAY, DIE sign.

Then I remember to breathe.

Back in bed, I burrow into my pillows and start counting backward from one hundred. If I could just stop thinking about the tree. Eighty-seven, eighty-six, eighty-five. If I could forget about Kandy's journal and the university application. Sixty-three, sixty-two . . .

I'm asleep for what seems like two minutes. Daylight is suddenly streaming through my windows. The house's electricity is back on. I feel like my electricity is back on too. I'm amped up, and I know exactly what I need to do today. First the library, then the oak. I slide out of bed and head to the bathroom, locking the door behind me.

The shower gauge is cranked to hot, but nothing's happening in the heat department. If I wait twenty minutes, it might happen. But this house was built in 1876, back in the days of outhouses. It was never meant to have indoor plumbing. I keep testing the temperature. Frigid . . . icy . . . hopeless. I hop in and make it fast. It was somewhere around eighty degrees outside yesterday. What's going to happen when the pipes are cold, when it's zero degrees in January? Yeah, tune in for more tales of torture here in Ennis, Ohio.

After drying off, I throw on the usual—jeans and a T-shirt. I make three scrambled eggs for myself and a big glass of orange juice, which I practically choke on when I notice the wall clock. It says it's 1:15! How could I have slept so late? I hurry back upstairs to decide what I should take with me: notebook, digital camera. I've just finished tying my shoes when Kandy appears in my doorway.

" 'Morning," I say. "I mean, afternoon."

"What's this?" She holds up a metal ruler. I recognize it as my bookmark. "I found it in my room."

Busted.

It must have been caught in my pajamas, and it fell out while I was at the window. Or worse, while I was at her desk. I can just imagine my bookmark sitting next to her diary.

"Kandy, I'm sorry, I—" I fumble for the right words. "I was just—"

Remember what I said about Newton's first law of motion? Well here's where the external and unbalanced force comes in. Unbalanced, as in mentally. Kandy lunges on top of me, and we both crash to the floor. She pounds my sides, smacks my face. Her long fingernails bite into my skin. I curl into the fetal position, thinking she'll be done any second. But she's not letting up, and it dawns on me that she doesn't want to get one good punch in; she wants to beat the living crap out of me. I try to roll away, but she easily pins my arms to the floor and sits across my abdomen. Trapped.

"Are you kidding?" I sputter, trying to breathe under her weight. "Get off!"

"What did you read?" She leans into my face, her burgundy lip liner and overwhitened teeth an inch from my nose.

"Nothing!" I flip and crawl for the door, but Kandy grabs my legs and pulls me back into the room. "Dad!" I sound like a pathetic little kid.

"He's outside," Kandy says. "They went for a walk."

Then she smiles this really evil, creepy smile.

"What?" I say, watching her eyes.

"Run," she whispers.

So I do. I jump to my feet, bolt down the stairs, and crash into the glass-top coffee table, knocking Dad's laptop onto the floor.

"Ouch!" I scream. Did I just break my shin? I guess not, because I'm still running. You can't run with a broken leg, right?

I'm out the back door. Within seconds, my lungs tighten and I feel nauseated. I haven't sprinted since phys ed in June, and on top of that, I hold my breath when I run. Brilliant.

Kandy, on the other hand, is graceful, and she's gaining ground. I abruptly change direction and look back again. She hasn't missed a beat, but I do notice something—her bare feet.

I need gravel. Broken glass. Anything nasty to run across. That would stop her cold.

Fill your lungs with fresh air, Ruby. N_2 and O_2 in, carbon dioxide out. Breathe. Breathe before you pass out.

Kandy is ten feet away, then five. Now I can hear her breathing—her easy, steady, in-great-shape breathing. My shin burns like hell, and my right pant leg is wet. Is that sweat or blood soaking through the denim? It might be rain, because the grass is wet from last night's storm. Soaked and slippery.

That's when I trip, spectacularly. Hands forward, I try to break my fall, but my chin smacks the ground. The iron taste of blood fills my mouth.

Kandy stands over me. I push my glasses back up my nose, gulping air like a suffocating fish.

"Leave me alone," I manage between breaths. "You've made your point."

"Aw," she says. "Your leg is bleeding. I bet you need stitches."

I scan the rows of corn at the edge of the yard, then make a sudden break for the opening I found yesterday.

"Get back here!" Kandy shouts, diving at me. She has my shirt sleeve, but I yank away, ripping the seam.

The broad leaves are coated with rainwater, and soon I am too. The ground is a muddy mess; the water has unearthed rocks, worms, dried-out corncobs. Tough going for someone without shoes. I press through the towering corn, as fast as I can manage. Barefooted Kandy doesn't follow.

She calls calmly after me, "You've gotta come home sometime." When I don't respond, she goes berserk. "You snooping bitch!"

I yell over my shoulder, "You're one planet short of a solar system!"

Kandy gives the F-word a serious workout. Her voice fades as I keep walking. Once I feel like I'm at a safe distance, I collapse to the ground, a shaking mess. Did she mean to kill me? She's crazy, but she can't be homicidal, can she? No. I mean, it's possible, but probably not. She just meant to scare me. Badly. Same as Willa Mason, in fifth grade. A kid full of hate. For everyone. Instead of packed lunches, she brought other things from home: bruises under her shirt, a knife in her back-pack. She got caught before she could use it.

I lie in the mud, waiting for my heart to stop banging, for the veins in my forehead to quit throbbing. Mr. Burton said that Kandy had been in fistfights at school. So it's not just me. It's anyone. For some reason, she's angry. Really, insanely angry.

I swat at a persistent fly and wipe the sweat from my forehead. I'm not used to this kind of humidity. The air is thick with moisture, and the sun makes it boil. If I lie here much longer, I'll be UV-fried and peppered with insect bites. I take a deep breath and stand, telling myself I'm fine, just fine.

Same as yesterday, I walk in a straight line until I'm worried that I'm lost. The rainwater slides off the leaves as I pass, wetting my head, sending muddy trickles down my arms. I push forward, always looking skyward, until I see the upper branches of the oak—the leafy crown of the tree.

Minutes later, I'm out of the cornfield and in fresh air, under the tree's canopy of cool shade. It seems taller, more splendid than yesterday. Ancient, alive. I take my glasses off and wipe the water from the lenses.

Now, in daylight, the purple glow is hardly detectable. But the humming is louder. And the trunk has changed. Significantly.

A layer of bark has been shed, in the shape of a large, perfect rectangle. Jabs of fear, quick and strong like voltage spikes, tell me I'm in danger, that I should go back. At the same time, I'm pulled forward by a force that feels inescapable, gravitational. Push and pull. Goose bumps spring up along my arms.

"Hello again," I whisper. The ground beneath me feels charged, a steady thrum of power.

I take a few steps closer and see that it's not just a rectangle of smooth trunk. There are etchings all over it, and in the middle, near the right edge, there's a metal knob.

It's a door.

chapter three

I stand in front of the door, frozen with excitement and disbelief.

Calm down, Ruby. There's no way it's a functional door. It's just a tree carving, more elaborate than *John-n-Jane 4-ever*, but the same idea.

Tentatively, I run my fingers over the etched surface, a complex work of fine chiseling. This was all hidden underneath a layer of bark. The twisted lines remind me of illustrations from my physics books— grid patterns depicting the fabric of space. At the top of the door, about eight feet above my head, there's a carved sign. Only I can't read it.

ᴄʀy Ʞᴅo iye ᴄoousꭓꝗ?

Like Kandy said, I'm a geek. But this isn't in my repertoire. I can read Latin and three words in Sanskrit—the result of an eighth-grade project. This? Nope. What kind of language has consonants pushed together into unpronounceable combinations? Maybe Russian, or maybe letters have been dropped, like in a text message.

It feels absurd to knock on the door, but I do. "Anybody home?"

I wait a minute, honestly wondering if someone—or something—will answer. A talking white rabbit, right? A three-headed alien? I look up at the oak's vast network of thick branches, the canopy of leaves.

It's a tree, Ruby, a tree. That's all.

But it's a tree with a doorknob, probably copper or bronze, with a green patina. Why put a doorknob on a door? To make it possible to open and close said door. Am I wrong? It would only make sense to try it. Give it a little wiggle, twist it, you know. Just to see what happens.

My fingertips meet the metal knob, triggering a sudden snap of static electricity; a spark leaps from the charge exchange. "Whoa," I say under my breath, shaking the sting from my hand. That's all I have to do—just touch the knob—and the door creaks open a few inches.

Gasping, I lurch backward, trip over a root, and sit down hard. A cold sweat overtakes me; my entire body quivers. It's a functional door.

"Anyone in there?" My mouth is dry, my voice weak. I clear my throat and try again. "Hello?"

My pounding heart counts off the seconds, or, more likely, quarter seconds. Ten, twenty, thirty. No answer.

I try again. "Anyone?" Finally, I pull myself to my feet, nerves jangling, hardly able to walk. Deep breath, Ruby. I press my hands against the door and push. A rush of stale air escapes the inside of the tree, giving the impression that it's exhaling. I exhale too, standing at the threshold, ready to step inside the hollowed-out tree.

Should I? I linger in the doorway, wishing for a flashlight. The engine-like hum is louder now that the door is open, and I can feel the vibrations penetrating my entire body.

A sharp pain shoots through my leg. Damn. My shin. My blood-soaked jeans. I need antibiotic ointment and a bandage. I need something that numbs. I should go home.

I look over my shoulder, surveying the cornfields, thinking of Dad trying to meet his latest deadline, of Willow absorbed in a canvas, of Kandy at the bathroom mirror with a flatiron and hairspray. I think of Ennis High's pitted football field, the fluorescent-yellow poster: LEARN TO QUILT AND SEW.

"What's to lose?" I ask, then steel myself and take a step forward. And then another, deeper into the trunk of the tree. The smell of decaying wood—damp and decomposing organic matter—gags me. I press my nose to my shoulder, breathing in the smell of my T-shirt. The perfumed residue of a Downy dryer sheet. Another step forward and my shoes sink into a shallow puddle, completely soaking my feet, socks and all.

"Perfect," I grumble.

Behind me, the light diminishes—the door is closing!

"No! Wait!"

I do a quick one-eighty and thrust my arm into the receding space. But the door keeps closing and I pull my arm back inside before it gets crushed. The inside knob—where is it? There's nothing but a smooth surface on the backside of the door. The last ray of sunlight filters around the door, and then with an air-tight finality, it's closed.

I'm locked inside.

Fear bubbles through me until I'm dizzy, panicked. It's impossibly dark in here. How could the door have sealed shut so perfectly? There should be a seam of light along the top or bottom.

"You're okay," I tell myself aloud, but I don't sound okay. I sound terrified. The tree's internal engine pulsates, and in this complete darkness, the idea of locusts takes shape again. There was that behemoth insect stalking me in the cornfield yesterday; now I imagine swarms of them covering my clothes, burrowing into my hair.

I press my trembling hands along the wet tree walls, patting the damp circumference, finding nothing. No knob, no lever, no buttons.

"Seriously? Come on!"

Is there no way out of this thing? I start to crisscross the center of the hollowed-out trunk, making lines back and forth, groping into the blackness, tentatively tapping a foot forward, and then another. I stretch my arms in both directions, and my fingertips meet with nothing but air. The sound of my breathing fills the void.

Then I run into something. It's waist level, and it feels like metal. A disk, about the size of a steering wheel. I run my hands along its cold surface. It's solid with intermittent little grooves. Along the edge my finger catches on something sharp, triangular. In the center, there's a thick pole that extends upward.

There is no knob, or lever, but there's this.

Please work. Please be a way out.

I grab it with both hands and turn. It gives, a little. But it's damp and slippery and I can't get a firm grip.

"Come on, come on, come on," I chant, wiping my hands on my jeans. With every beat of my heart, my leg throbs in time, and I wonder if I could bleed to death in here. Ironic, because the inside of a tree is, well, coffin-like. That thought is enough to energize me, and I give the wheel a firm twist. It advances, and seems to click into a preset position. There's a single clank that sounds like an out-of-tune bell. And miraculously—finally!—the door slowly swings open, and I'm blinded by sunlight.

Blinking back tears, squinting, I stumble away from the tree. When my pupils finally adjust, I take a good look around. "What the . . . ?" I whisper.

I'm not in the midst of cornfields. I'm standing on a hill, on the outskirts of what looks like a college campus. There's a four-story building made of quarried stone, with a slate roof and central spire. Just ahead, there are tennis courts, and beyond I can see towering lights, probably for a football field. Dark clouds are convening in the distance.

For a long time, I stand in the shade of the tree, trying to get my bearings. The door is closed, though I have no recollection of shutting it behind myself. There's got to be a reasonable explanation—for all of this. Maybe applying the scientific method will help.

First, define the question. That's easy. Where the hell am I?

Second, gather information and resources. Third, form a hypothesis. Here's a theory: I'm dead, and this is the afterlife. I mean, maybe Kandy actually strangled me to death when she caught up with me. I look down at my shin, which is still oozing. Blood-soaked jeans somehow don't compute with the Great Beyond. Aren't you supposed to be wearing white and sporting wings?

Logic, Ruby, logic. You can figure this out.

A bell rings. Suddenly, a metal door on the back of the stone building bangs open, and dozens of students rush out. They're wearing backpacks, carrying books. I hear school bus engines, and I catch a glimpse of one rounding the side of the building. This must be a high school, not a college.

Though it's certainly not dingy, dinky Ennis High, Home of the Bears.

I have two choices: go back into the oak or explore the school grounds. But if I try the tree again, what if I won't be able to turn the slippery steering wheel? I'll be trapped, doomed to starve to death inside a rotting tree trunk. Really.

Decision made.

I head toward the four-story building. I'm not sure what I'm looking for. A street address, a phone book, any geographic clue. A glass of water would be nice. I'll have to avoid coaches and teachers. I don't want anyone asking me, "Who are you, and what are you doing here?" Uh, yeah, I'd love to know.

A pebble sidewalk traces the side of the building. I pass a courtyard with a fountain and orange mums blooming, my wet shoes making a squishing sound as I walk. About a dozen kids are sitting on the ground, rehearsing something. Sounds like Shakespeare.

A group of cheerleaders walk past, giggling conspiratorially. They pay no attention to me, even as I stand in my bare feet, wringing my socks out and picking a corn leaf out of my back pocket.

Finally, I round a corner and find the front of the main building. Near the road, a sign says: Ó DIREÁIN HIGH SCHOOL. WELCOME BACK! YEARBOOK PHOTOS SEPTEMBER 10.

Distant thunder rumbles; the cloud bank has grown and advanced. Across the street are cornfields. I never thought I'd be happy to see Ohio crops. So here's another hypothesis: I just wandered too far from home. My leg is bleeding worse than I think, and I blacked out. Did I hit my head when Kandy was chasing me, when I tripped and fell? My chin is sore, and my tongue is cut where I bit into it. I press my fingers along every inch of my scalp. No tender spots. No headache.

"Ruby?"

I spin around to face a guy who's standing way too close. He looks a year or two older than I am, and strangely familiar. Dark eyes, slightly pointed nose, dimple in his chin.

He points at my bloody shin. "What happened?"

I take a step backward.

"Your hair, Ruby," he says with dismay. "And why are you wearing those glasses?"

I turn my back on him and start walking—fast. This guy has screwball written all over him.

He follows. "Where are you going? You're late for French Club. Why are your clothes wet and muddy?" His voice hits a hysterical pitch when he asks, "Is that a tattoo?"

I hold my breath and break into a run. How does he know my name? I can hear him directly behind me. God, I'm sick of getting chased. "Leave me alone!" I scream over my shoulder.

Within seconds, his hands are around my waist. He lifts me off the ground, my legs still moving in midair.

"Do I know you?" I shriek, wriggling out of his grasp.

"Ruby!" he says, planting his hands on my shoulders, looking me squarely in the eye. "Did someone hurt you?"

I stare back. "Could I borrow your cell phone?"

"Why?"

"I'd like to call my father," I say, swatting his hands off my shoulders. "So he can come pick me up."

He cringes, jerks his head back. "*Your* father?"

"Yeah. Is there a phone inside the school I could use?" I gesture toward the stone building.

"What are you talking about?" The crazed look on his face intensifies. He motions to the street that runs in front of the school. "You're five minutes from home."

I narrow my eyes at him. "You know where I live?"

"Since you were born! What happened to you?" He reaches out to touch my head, but I duck away. "You seriously don't know who I am," he says, and a look of angst sweeps across his face. "Forget French Club." He suddenly has my wrist and starts dragging me along.

I twist my arm out of his grasp and take off. He chases me again. The jerk must be a football player, because he easily grabs my legs and pulls me to the ground. I slap at his arms and try to kick him off.

"Patrick? What's going on?" It's a girl's voice, above us. I look up and see Kandy. She's pointing at my leg. "She's bleeding."

"No shit," I snap at her, pulling myself to my feet. "Where are we, Kandy? How do we get back to your house?"

Kandy gives Patrick this perplexed look, like I'm speaking another language. "What's with the hacked-off hair?"

I thrust a thumb toward Patrick. "Who is this guy? Your boyfriend?"

"Boyfriend?" Kandy says with total disgust. "Are you kidding me? Your brother?"

My face burns with anger and confusion. "I don't have a brother!"

"Something's wrong with her," Patrick says. "Amnesia or something."

"Whatever," Kandy says. She glances at her watch. "I'm starving. I need to go pick up the wings."

"Kandy!" I'm ready to punch her. "Where the hell are we? Quit joking around!"

Patrick talks to me like I'm a two-year-old. "Can you walk?"

"Duh," I say. Then I turn to Kandy. She's the only person, place, or thing I recognize. I have no choice but to ask her for help. "Get me to a phone. That's all I ask. And a glass of water."

"Shut up and hurry up." Kandy looks at the looming black clouds. "It's about to rain."

"And don't touch me," I add as we walk off together, me about twenty feet behind them. Patrick keeps turning around to ask if I'm okay. "I'm super," I say. "Fabulous."

Once I got lost walking home from a birthday party. I was eight years old. After about two hours of wandering through backyards, I sat down on a bus stop bench. Dad screeched up to the curb in his car, jumped out, and scooped me into his arms. He'd kissed my face a hundred times. "I love you," he'd said, sobbing. "Thank God."

I keep scanning the road, hoping, half-expecting Dad to show up here too.

Finally, Kandy, Patrick, and I turn onto a residential street named Corrán Tuathail Avenue. Is that English? Seriously, where are we? Soon we're walking up Patrick's driveway, toward a squat brick house. In the center of the lawn, a red wheelbarrow is tipped on its side. White impatiens spill from the wheelbarrow, winding their flowery way down the mulch bed. Something about it bugs me, other than its cloying cuteness. It's giving me déjà vu.

In the driveway are two cars. One is a Toyota hybrid, same as Willow's, but blue instead of cream. The other is a black Jeep, like Dad's, only a newer model. It's disturbing. Like a familiar song, only one key off.

Patrick enters the garage door code, and we weave our way through a maze of stacked moving boxes. In the corner of the garage is a single bed, which looks like it's just been slept in. Patrick leads the way through a narrow laundry room, pausing to kick a linoleum square back into place. Kandy edges next to me, and I step aside to let her go past.

"Personal space, if you don't mind." She's close enough to sink a knife between my ribs.

"Relax," she says, giving me an annoyed look.

The laundry room opens into the kitchen, and I head straight for the phone. I dial Dad's number.

"The number you have dialed is not in service. Please hang up and try again."

I try Dad's cell phone again. And again.

I can't quite remember our home number. It's too new. "Kandy, what's your home phone number?"

"You mean this number? Here?"

I growl with frustration and notice a cell phone plugged into the wall to charge. Without asking permission, I grab it and scroll through the apps. I hit the GPS button. "137 Buck Pass Road," I say into the phone.

The screen blinks and a voice asks, "Which city and state?"

"Ennis, Ohio."

"Did you say Eaton?"

"No." I type in the address and submit the information.

The phone responds with an exclamation point and *No Matches Found*. I scroll through the apps again. "Don't you have Google Earth on this thing?"

"Tell me it's fake." Patrick is behind me, breathing on me. "That's not a real tattoo, is it?"

I slap my hand over the nape of my neck. "Do you have a phone book?" I ask Patrick.

"Seriously, Ruby. What's wrong with you?" His voice is a whispering plea. "You know you can tell your big brother anything."

"Look, you're creeping me out." I step away from him, but he matches my move. "If anyone's got amnesia around here, it's you."

"Come on," he says. "You know me. Think!" He thrusts his face toward me, and I'm forced to concede that he might resemble someone I may have met. Somewhere, briefly. He could be the waiter who served us a few days ago at Ennis's burger joint, or the talkative cashier at the grocery store, or that guy I saw jogging. But wasn't our waiter blond, and the cashier older, and the jogger super-skinny? The dots won't connect.

I run my hands across my head again, checking for a lump or sore spot, and still don't find anything. "Just back off, okay?"

"No, it's not okay," he barks, but he hands me a thin yellow directory and a glass of cold water anyway. The directory's cover says *Ó Direáin and Surrounding Areas.* There's a small list of other towns, but Ennis isn't one of them. Patrick must see the panic on my face, the color vanishing from my cheeks.

"Sit down," he says, pushing a chair underneath me.

Kandy twirls a set of car keys. "What kind of dressing do you want for your salad?"

Dressing? How can she act so nonchalant, like this afternoon's near-homicide never happened? Like this is all normal? I glare at her. "Did you follow me through that tree?"

"Tree?" she asks, twisting her face.

Patrick sighs and rubs his temples, just like Dad does when he's worried. "If you don't start making sense, I'm taking you to the ER. I think you've got a concussion."

"Brain tumor," Kandy adds with a laugh. Outside, thunder cracks.

"Could I use the bathroom?"

"Why are you asking permission?" Patrick sounds angry. "You're in your own house!"

"Right," I say. I down the glass of water, set it on the counter, then wander through the one-story house until I find a bathroom. Whoever decorated this place sure likes ducks. And plaid.

I peel my jeans down, slowly. Talk about a bloody, sticky mess.

After some wincing and swearing, I get my jeans off and take a good look. Yeah, I need stitches. Without them, I'm going to scar, big time. Oh, well. I mean, it's not like I aspire to be a lingerie model.

Under the sink I find a washcloth, antibiotic ointment, and three big Band-Aids. A butterfly bandage would be better, but no such luck.

There's a knock.

"What?"

Patrick's voice. "I'm just setting these inside for you." The door opens a crack. "Your favorite jeans and a polo."

In tumbles a fresh pair of jeans and a pink top. "No thanks," I say.

"What's wrong?" Patrick asks through the door.

"Pink."

Patrick is silent for a beat, then, "You love that shirt."

"Really, I don't," I say. "But thanks for the jeans."

I hear him sigh heavily, then retreat down the hall. After I clean and bandage my leg, I wiggle into the jeans, even though they're tight. Much worse, they've got these fake diamonds along the tops of the pockets. I run my finger across the jewels, wondering if I can pop them off. Maybe they say something in Braille: *I'm mentally vacant. That's why I'm dressed like a poodle.*

I wad up my bloodstained jeans and shove them to the bottom of the trash can, splash cold water on my face, use the toilet, then just sit on the pot. What am I going to do next? Crawl out the bathroom window and make a run for it? I can't. It's storming like mad. I mean, thunder and lightning and a torrential downpour that would make it impossible to see four feet ahead.

I rock back and forth, my stomach twisting with worry. A high-pitched sound fills the room, like a kitten mewing, and with a start I realize that it's me. Whimpering. I put my hand over my mouth and start to pace, from the bathroom door to the toilet.

"The important thing is not to stop questioning." That's what Einstein once said. No problem, Albert. I've got a million questions. Maybe I can answer one or two by snooping around.

I sneak down the hallway toward the bedrooms. The walls are folk-artsy with wooden American flags, corn, cows, and chickens. I've never understood how farm animals and home decor equate. I guess it's better than Willow's black paintings—the ones that look like truck exhaust and tar puddles. The bleak period.

I continue to scan the wall as I tiptoe down the hallway. After a large, polka-dotted pig, there's a framed photo of Patrick in a football uniform (I knew it), then an eight-by-ten family photo.

It's Patrick, Dad, a woman with short black hair, and . . . me? At least it looks like me. All of us wearing matching khakis and white button-down shirts. The photo is maybe five years old. Patrick is wearing glasses, and my hair is in pigtails. My hair? No, that can't be me. Of course it can't.

The woman looks so familiar. Like a cousin or an aunt I've met once, at a wedding or a graduation party. Something about her far-away eyes. And what's Dad doing in this photo?

It's unnerving. Creepy. I have to turn away.

That's when I notice a bedroom door. In dark red letters, it says RUBY. Yeah, it says Ruby. Ruby! I can feel the bile rising in my throat.

I'm overwhelmed by the urge to run, then the urge to open the door. It's a fierce tug-of-war, like positive charge versus negative, proton versus antiproton. The sum equals zero. So I just stand there, statuelike.

Deep breath.

With the tips of my fingers, I push open the door.

Inside, there's a twin bed with a pink patchwork quilt. Above the bed hangs a poster that says PARIS, JE T'AIME. It's a collage of photos of the Champs-Élysées, Eiffel Tower, and the Louvre. On the bookshelf are a few romance paperbacks. Then some yearbooks. I pull down the most recent and go straight for the index. My finger lands on "Wright, Ruby, 11, 27, 32, 54, 96." Page eleven is topped with Ó Direáin High School's Best (or Worst)! Photos of smiling kids are captioned by Most Likely to Succeed, Biggest Flirts, Most Detentions, Biggest Gossips, and Best Dressed.

> **Ruby Wright lands the coveted title of Most Likely to Lead. Class President, President of the Pep Club, and President of the French Club, it's no wonder Ruby's smiling. C'est cheese!**

It's me. Or someone who looks like me, though I've never owned a fuchsia V-neck sweater. And my hair has never been that shade of reddish orange—the color of iron oxide, the color of Mars.

My name, my face, my smile.

Panic pulses through my veins. I can't process this. With trembling hands, I slide the yearbook back into its spot on the bookshelf.

Now my eyes are drawn to a shoe box on the bottom shelf. The box's top is off and I can see that it's loaded with postcards and letters. Yeah, I know. The last time I read someone's personal stuff, I got chased smack into a coffee table. I'll just read one or two things. I need to get my bearings; I need some clues.

A handwritten note on top, dated a couple of days ago.

> Dear Ruby,
>
> I can't remember the last time we talked (really talked, like we used to), and I know that's at least half my fault. So I thought I'd try the old-fashioned way to get a few things aired out. We can't scream at each other in a letter, or storm off angry. For me it's a better way to organize my thoughts and feelings. Maybe if you like this method, you can write me back, and we can work out a few things this way.
>
> So I wanted to say thanks for letting Willow and me escape for a weekend. I wish your mother would have kept her promise to stay with you three at the house, but I don't blame her. I hope that someday we can be on friendly terms again, but that will no doubt be a slow process.
>
> Please spend some time with Kandy while we're gone. Willow is hopeful about the new medications . . . Kandy seems to have found her footing. I think eventually you'll be fast friends. We need to talk again about the two of you sharing your room. We can find a way to divide it fairly. Just keep an open mind.

*I understand that this has been difficult for every-
one. I apologize for the hurt, Ruby, but you know that
your mother and I have been heading in different
directions for some time. I love Willow, and my hope is
that we can all move forward with forgiveness and
acceptance.*

Love,
Dad

*P.S. No parties! And enjoy Patrick's gourmet cooking. I
don't know where he gets his talent.*

I know that handwriting. It's Dad's. I start to read the letter a second time, trying to make sense of it. Kandy is on medication; Mom
was supposed to stay for the weekend.

Mom? Whose mom?

A voice jolts me. "Ruby?" It's Patrick, shouting from the kitchen.

"I'm fine!" I holler back.

The house is starting to smell like food. Kandy must be back with
the wings, and maybe Patrick is baking something too. Smells like
chocolate chip cookies.

If I weren't so completely disturbed and confused, I would be
tempted to eat. But right now I just feel queasy, frazzled.

As I push the box of letters back into its slot, the corner of a photo
catches my eye. I pull it out and hold it in the palm of my hand. It's my
three-year-old self, wearing a red-gingham blouse with denim overalls. I'm sitting on Mom's lap. This is my photo, from my dresser!

Only it's . . . not. In this version, Mom is looking straight at the camera and she's forcing a smile. This photo is in focus.

Oh my God.

I rush back into the hall and hold the snapshot next to the eight-by-ten I saw earlier: Patrick, Dad, a woman, and me. All of us wearing khakis and white button-down shirts.

The woman in both photos is Mom.

But it can't be! My eyes dart back and forth between the old photo I recognize and the eerie eight-by-ten wall photo. Mom is dead, has been for eleven years. She can't be in a photo that's only a few years old.

I put my hand in my mouth and bite down on my knuckles. I'm going to throw up. I gotta get out of here, or scream, or both. I don't care that it's raining.

I lock myself in the bathroom, gag into the toilet, then swish my mouth with water. I open the window, pop out the screen, and ease myself through. In an instant I'm soaked. I wipe rainwater and tears from my eyes. Crouched down, I circle the house. The rain's coming in torrents, which is good. Good because Patrick and Kandy won't be able to see out the windows. They won't be able to see me in the driveway.

The Jeep is unlocked. No keys in the ignition, but there's an Ohio road map in the glove box and an umbrella on the floor. I tuck the map inside the waistband of my jeans, close the car door as quietly as possible, then take off running.

The rain is relentless. I slosh through ankle-deep water at the edge of the road where the storm sewers are backing up. A gust of wind blows the umbrella inside out, bending the metal frame. I keep scanning the horizon for a landmark, but it's too bleak to see.

I'm cold. Every once in a while a searing jab of pain cuts through my shin, and I limp until it subsides. Finally the rain lets up, and I spot something recognizable—the spire on the high school's stone building.

After a little effort, I find the courtyard where the Shakespeare rehearsals were going on earlier. The broken umbrella goes into a trash can, and I duck into a nice, deep doorway. Shelter from the wind and drizzle. I yank my T-shirt off, wring as much water out of it as possible, then put it back on.

Kind of stupid. I just soaked the cement. There's barely enough dry ground for me to smooth out the Ohio road map. I squat down and study the alphabetical listing of cities with grid coordinates. *E. E* is for "Ennis." I read the list once, twice. It goes from Englishville to Eno.

"No Ennis," I mumble.

O. O is for "Ó Direáin." The map coordinates are H-5.

I flip the map over and scan the northeast corner. Exactly where Ennis should be is a black dot and Ó DIREÁIN in bold print.

I don't understand. Cleveland, Columbus, and Cincinnati are where they're supposed to be. It must be a typo, or the map is outdated. Nothing computes.

A bird squawks. Sounds like a blue jay. The sun breaks through a patch of clouds. I look up at the clearing sky, fold the map, and start walking.

Mom could be here, alive. You could go see her.

I press my palms against the top of my head, as if that might slow the barrage of confusion. My vision blurs and the pebble walkway becomes a haze of gauzy brown. Fluid. The sky tips forward. I drop to my knees, breathing deeply, trying to coax away the urge to black out.

You can't go see Mom! This isn't right. You don't belong here, Ruby. You need to get home.

Mom is dead. I don't have a brother. If I'm somewhere with a dead person and a nonexistent person, I don't want to be in that somewhere. I need to get out of this limbo land.

Really, only one thing makes sense. Only one course of action feels like the right choice:

Head back to the tree, and get the hell out of here.

chapter four

"Damn!" I yank my hand away from the copper doorknob. The static shock and lightning spark take me by surprise. With the humidity from the rain, it seems impossible that the metal could've been charged. But it was. Electromagnetic force in action.

I shake the sting from my fingers, and wait while the door swings open. "Here goes," I say, with a feeling of utter dread. I step into the pulsating oak tree, and a vivid memory surprises me.

I'm ten years old, with Dad, in Jewel Cave in South Dakota. The calcite formations—stalactites, stalagmites, flowstone, and frostwork—make my brain fizzle. Fizzle in a good way. The cave's tour guide is an old guy with a mop of yellowish hair. He makes a big deal about a rare formation called a hydromagnesite balloon.

Then he turns out the lights. A complete void. Not a single visible wavelength.

Dad presses my head to his chest. I can hear his steady heart. "They'll leave the lights off just long enough to spook everyone."

Right now, inside this dark oak tree, there's no one to hold me. My own heart beats frenetically, like a maxed-out Geiger counter. I can't turn the wheel. My hand just keeps slipping around the perimeter.

"Please," I moan.

One more try, and the disk rotates. There's a single clank—the out-of-tune bell sound. Fresh air spills through the widening crack, and I grab the edge of the door to hurry it open. Out of the tree and into the blinding sunlight, I cover my eyes with my hands, waiting for my pupils to adjust, wondering what I'm about to see. What if I'm nowhere recognizable again? What if I'm at the edge of our solar system, clinging to an icy rock in the Oort cloud?

Get a grip. You wouldn't be breathing right now. There's no atmosphere on a comet.

Wherever I am, I could use a warm, dry sweater. That rainstorm in Ó Direáin left me drenched and shivering. I pull my hands away from my eyes, and as far as I can tell, I'm back in Ennis. It's got that good, fresh-air smell, and the tree is surrounded by cornfields. I have to admit this feeling of relief, so strong, is a moment of sheer joy. Do I have to call it home? Okay, fine. I'm glad to be home!

Still squinting, I step over the gnarled roots of the tree and walk into the cornfields, looking over my shoulder at the tree, half expecting it to reach out with a limb and grab me, Stephen King–style. So what was that? A passage to another place, a tunnel of some sort. Makes no sense. My scientific brain doesn't like it, not one bit. Kandy's voice—*brain tumor*—resonates through me, and I get a fresh wave of the chills.

There's nothing metastasizing inside your skull, Ruby. What's the speed of light? 186,000 miles per second. Layers of the earth? Lithosphere, asthenosphere, mesosphere, outer core, inner core. Layers of a peanut buster parfait? Hot fudge, peanuts, vanilla soft serve.

See? You're fine.

Fine, but confused and disoriented. Because even though I've made this return trek once before, my confidence dwindles once I'm five minutes into the field. It's like being in a carnival funhouse, in a maze of mirrors. Everything looks the same.

I push the giant leaves aside, burrowing through the cornstalks. With every step my shoes make a sucking noise. I pluck the front of my wet shirt away from my stomach and scrub my head, getting the water out of my hair. All the while I'm eyeing the sky, looking for rooftops.

Finally, a fence. Through the rusting iron, I see a greenish swimming pool littered with inflatable toys. A dog barks. A sprinkler ticks behind me, and I barely escape the arc of water. The next backyard isn't fenced in, so I limp-jog across the patchy lawn and onto the road, passing bent mailboxes and curbside litter.

There's Dad—pacing the driveway.

"Ruby!" he calls when he spots me. He taps his finger to his wristwatch. "Where've you been?"

I jog to him, grinning. "Dad!" I wrap my arms around him and press my face into his chest. "I kinda got lost," I say.

He pushes me back, holding on to my shoulders, looking me in the eye. "I've been worried sick!" The quiver in his voice startles me. "You don't know this town, or anyone in it yet."

"I honestly didn't think you'd notice," I say. "You were so busy with work."

"How could I not notice? Willow and I got back from our walk, and you were gone," he says. "We didn't know what time you left or where you were headed. You should have left a note. Willow thought you might have walked to that shopping plaza bookstore to get some magazine you mentioned, so I drove there to look. I asked everyone I saw if they'd seen you."

I thrust my thumb over my shoulder toward the fields. "There's something I want to show you. I found something."

Dad looks me over. "Why are you wet? Did you fall into a creek or something?"

My hand goes to my shirt. "There was a thunderstorm." The jeans that Patrick gave me are wet, but they hide the bandaged gash in my leg. "I need to tell you what's happened."

"Thunderstorm?" Dad presses his eyebrows together and looks up at the cloud-covered sky. "It hasn't rained since last night."

"That's what I'm trying to explain! I wasn't here. That oak tree that's off in the cornfields—" I stop short. How am I going to recap my afternoon without sounding nuts? "Look, I have to show it to you, otherwise you won't believe it. I was falling asleep under a tree yesterday when I noticed that—" I fumble again for the right words. "It's just about a half mile—"

"You were gone all this time because you fell asleep under a tree?" He sounds exhausted, and I notice the dark circles around his eyes. "Don't scare me like that. Ever again."

He's not listening. Maybe I'll try telling him later, when he's not so worked up. "You never minded when I took BART into San Francisco," I remind him.

"That was different," he says. "You knew your way around, and you were always with me or a friend."

I was always with George.

"Did he call today?" I ask. "George?" It would be so nice to hear his voice.

"How would I know?" Dad says, exasperated. "I was out looking for you!"

"I'm sorry."

"Come on, I'll warm up some food for you." He takes my hand like I'm a little girl and leads me up the driveway and into the house. I let him; I'm happy to. Once we're inside, he nudges me toward the stairs. "Go dry off before you catch pneumonia."

"Pneumonia comes from bacteria, not wet clothes." I hesitate, one foot on the bottom step.

"Kandy upstairs?" I ask, looking over my shoulder at Dad. He nods. "Did she, uh, say anything to you today?"

"About how well you're getting along?"

I'm stunned. How well we're getting along?

"She mentioned that you chatted this afternoon, and then you disappeared." Dad shakes his head. "You took off and didn't tell anyone where you were going."

Yeah, right. Kandy is the reason I disappeared for hours. She's the reason my leg is throbbing. Though I guess, in a manner of speaking, Kandy hasn't seen me all day, or all week. Because she has that endearing way of looking right through me. Like I don't exist.

"She said we chatted?"

"Yes," Dad says, heading for the kitchen. "She said you had a very nice talk, and that you're getting along great. Now go upstairs and change."

A very nice talk. So that's how she's going to play this. What in the world is she up to?

I backpedal to grab my cell phone off the coffee table and then scan my messages as I tiptoe upstairs. There are five missed calls from Dad and three texts from George. Just seeing his name on my phone's little screen makes my chest feel warm. I can't open his messages fast enough.

The first is a photo of a golden-colored brownie centered on a white plate. Our favorite dessert at the East Bay Café, loaded with caramel chips and walnuts. I can practically taste its creamy crunchiness. The next text is another photo of the brownie, only this time it's crookedly cut in two. The subject line reads Bigger half 4 ruby.

The third message shows the brownie again, half-gone. George's piece has been eaten, crumbs on his side of the plate. This time the subject line says Where IS she???

I'm here, George. I'm right here. I sigh and thumb a message back. Crazy day! Will call u.

There's no way to explain the tree in a text message, so I don't even try.

Inside the bathroom, I flip the little dead bolt on the door before peeling off my wet clothes. Gruesome. The Band-Aids are blood-soaked, and the gash stings. I roll the bejeweled, poodle-collar jeans into a ball and shove them to the bottom of the trash can. Good riddance. Under the sink I find a tube of antibacterial cream, which I glob onto my shin before rebandaging it, and then I wrap myself in a towel.

Luckily, Kandy's door is shut, and I silently pad into my room unnoticed, tossing my wet T-shirt and underwear onto the floor. Something peeks out from underneath my clothes; it's the snapshot of me sitting on Mom's lap. Me with my red-gingham blouse and denim overalls. I must've tucked the photo in one of my pockets without thinking, back at that brick house on Corrán Tuathail Avenue. I'm glad I didn't lose it along the way, though now it's bent and damp. I study Mom's forced smile and the sparkle of joy in my toddler eyes.

Are you there, Mom? In that other place?

On my dresser is the faded, out-of-focus photo of Mom and me, the one that I've had for eleven years. She's gazing distractedly off to the side, pensive, wistful. I prop my newly acquired version in front of the old. The new photo is in sharp focus, and Mom is looking straight at the camera. It's jarring.

"Ruby?" Dad calls from downstairs.

I quickly dress in jeans and a gray sweatshirt and silently make my way down the hall, eyeing Kandy's closed door as I ease past. I'm holding my breath, taking one stealthy step at a time, when a sudden *boom-boom!* stuns me. The blood drains from my head and I feel woozy. It's music, pounding.

Now my heart is pounding too. Hammering.

"Your food's ready!" Dad calls, and I bolt downstairs.

As I enter the kitchen, he's pulling a dish out of the microwave, and the smell of Indian spices instantly warms me. Somebody—I'm assuming Willow—made a homemade dish with peas and potatoes. A nice change from the takeout garbage we've had all week. I eat in silence while Dad does the dishes. "Amazing curry sauce," I finally say, mouth full.

Dad nods. "Do you want seconds?"

Before I can answer, he's scooped another ball of basmati rice onto my plate, and more vegetables. He hands me a cup of hot tea. "So you went for a walk?" He raises his eyebrows, waiting for me to fill in the blanks.

"Um, you could say that. I cut through the cornfields, and then . . ." My voice trails off. I'm still struggling with how to tell him. "I'd really love to show you."

"Ruby, those fields go on for miles. You could get disoriented." Dad looks at me wide-eyed. "Completely lost!"

"Yeah, I'm aware."

"They'd have to send out dogs!" He drops a plate into the sink with a crash.

"Would you relax, please? You're hyperventilating." Secretly, I'm starting to smile. It's nice having Dad worry about me. It's like he forgot about writing gnocchi packaging. He's thinking about me instead.

"There have been a record number of lightning strikes the past few days," Dad continues. "The weather people can't get over it. It's dangerous out there."

"Dangerous," I repeat. Yes, I know. I've been to a place with a not-dead mother and a nonexistent brother. To get there, I've been through a tree with a door and a steering wheel. The strange inscription over the door could very well be a dire warning.

Dad slides a piece of mail next to my napkin. It's a postcard. "I don't know if he called," Dad says. "But you got this in today's mail."

My heart leaps. On the front there's a photo of a woman walking down a city street. Her head is a computer monitor. I flip it over and read:

> Rubes—Saw this and thought of you. Because you have a computer brain. Recognize the street?
> Miss you.
>
> George

This is even better than a text message. George's own handwriting, in smudged blue ink. I study the photo on the postcard and make out the red awning of the East Bay Café.

Dad winks at me.

"What?"

"He likes you," Dad says.

"I know." I hold the postcard to my nose, hoping to catch a hint of George's sandalwood soap, but it just smells like printing ink. "We're twenty-five hundred miles apart."

"So what? If you're meant to be, it'll work out. You'll end up at the same college or working in the same city, someday, somewhere."

"Fate?" I say, rolling my eyes. "You know I don't believe in that stuff."

"Call it what you like," Dad says. "Fate, destiny, effort, coincidence. True friendship defies distance."

"That sounds like a headline for an ad," I say, "for an airline. You should write that down in case you ever need it."

"For what?" Dad asks over the clanking of dishes. He pulls a soapy mug from the sink and rinses it.

"A headline." I hand him my dirty plate and grab a clean one from the stack of drying dishes on the counter. I hold my phone over it and take a photo of the empty plate. Then I write George a quick text. **Brownie was 2 die 4. Licked the plate clean. Thanks!**

"Should I ask?" Dad says.

"Nope."

"Didn't think so." He kisses my forehead and drains the sink. "I've got to get back to work. I'm on deadline."

"Gee. What else is new?"

"You wouldn't happen to know how my computer ended up on the floor, would you?" Dad asks.

"Sorry." I can picture it crashing to the floor, the second after my shin collided with the coffee table.

"That's my lifeblood, Ruby." Dad's voice turns preachy. "There are hundreds of important files on that hard drive."

"I said I was sorry." I turn and leave the kitchen, my face flushed with anger. Some things will never change. "Maybe you should back up more often," I mumble to myself, though I know he can hear me.

"Ruby!" His voice is a warning; he's on the edge. "It's been a long day, so spare me the attitude!"

I wince under his lashing tone. Outside, underneath the cloud cover, the sun is making its way toward the horizon. I glance at the wall clock and figure we still have a couple hours of daylight. Enough time to take him to the tree. I can just imagine the slack-jawed expression on his face. I'd have to hold him back from stepping inside the doorway, though, because I'm not interested in taking another gamble tonight, slapping down money on what feels like a dubious carnival game—Step right up, sweetheart! Just slip on this blindfold and spin the wheel.

Still, I feel like I need to tell him something—anything—about where I've been. "Hey, Dad? I . . ."

His back is to me; he's drying dishes. "Let's just call it a day, all right?"

"Um, but . . ." But there's this tree. And I need to show you. "Where's Willow?" I ask. I could take her to the tree. She noticed that there was a strange vibe about it; she would understand if I told her I needed to show her something important.

"She's in Cleveland." Dad clicks the lights off in the kitchen. "She had to meet with a gallery owner and go buy some new brushes and canvases."

He sidesteps me and sits on the couch, firing up his computer. "I need to put in a few hours and then get some sleep."

"Sure. I get it." I take the hint and climb the stairs as quietly as possible, even though Kandy's music is still blaring. I hold George's postcard in my hand and reread it. *Miss you.*

I think about calling him right this second to hear his voice, to find out what's been going on since I left. I'd like to know who he went to the movie with yesterday. I'd thank him for the brownie and tell him about the tree. Er, I guess I'd tell him, but where would I begin?

What would he think? Ruby, you're off your rocker, cuckoo, mentally disordered, buggy, certifiable.

Really, I can't tell anyone. Seeing is believing. Otherwise I'm setting myself up for trouble. Dad will rush me to the nearest therapist to talk about my pent-up issues. I can hear it now: She's been under a lot of stress. She's just trying to get attention. Is this sort of lying normal?

My bones ache for my soft mattress; I can't wait to sink my face into my down-filled pillows. The door to my room won't open, though. A shirt is jammed underneath, strangely. How did that get there? I shove and pull and reach around the door to kick the shirt out of the way.

Paper everywhere. Clothes draped over lamps, cracked DVDs, torn posters. The Hubble book from George is in shreds. My face turns hot. Even the tips of my ears burn with fury. That psychopath trashed my room.

Before I think it through, I storm across the hall to her room. She's on her bed with a pair of scissors, surrounded by *People* magazines.

She aims a remote control at her stereo and turns the music off. "Darn," she says, snapping her manicured fingers. "I thought you were gone for good."

"What did you do to my books?" I say, thrusting my thumb over my shoulder. "To my room?"

"We're even," Kandy says. She fishes through the magazines until she finds her pink journal. She holds it up with one hand, and she brandishes the scissors with the other.

I'm reminded of the fact that she checked the box next to "yes" on her design school app. Yes, she's been convicted of, or has pled guilty to, a crime other than a traffic offense. Vandalism? Assault and battery? Attempted murder?

"We're even?" I spit back at her. "My shin is still bleeding."

Kandy narrows her eyes at me. "Stop talking," she says, waving her hand in the air like I'm a bothersome insect. "Your voice irritates me."

"Your existence irritates me." Maybe I'm being too bold, knowing what she's capable of, but I'm shaking I'm so angry. "I'm going downstairs to tell my dad. You're busted."

Kandy's ears perk up, like this is what she's been waiting for. "I'm going downstairs to tell my dad." She imitates me using a high-pitched, little-kid voice. Then she adds, "Go ahead. They'll never believe you."

"Of course they will. There's evidence all over my room."

"You did it. To yourself. It's so, like, obvious you hate it here, and you didn't want your dad to marry my mom. You're trying to sabotage it." She starts in with the little-kid voice again. "Kandy ripped up my books. We can't live here anymore. We have to go back to California. Boo-hoo."

"You're sick." I take a step backward.

"You know," Kandy says with a creepy smile, "just before you chickened out and ran into the cornfields, I had the chance to finish your sorry ass. Next time I won't hesitate."

"He-si-tate," I say, reaching behind me for the door. She's more psychologically damaged than I realized. "Wow. Three syllables." Can she hear the spooked tone in my voice?

The expression on Kandy's face changes from annoyance to malice. "Just stick to the rules. You stay out of my life, and I'll stay out of yours." She holds up her journal again. "Understood?"

"You suck," I say. I slam her door and hurry back to my room before she decides to leap off the bed and rip my intestines out through my nose. I sure as hell hope Dad is still downstairs, within earshot. Otherwise I could end up a grainy photo on the back of a milk carton. *Have You Seen Me?*

I lock my bedroom door, then shove a few moving boxes against it. At least that'll slow her down, if she tries to get in while I'm sleeping. It wouldn't hurt to put a baseball bat underneath my pillow.

With a heavy sigh, I flop down on my bed. I'm beat. But I can't ignore the mess. It's like someone split an atom in here. All my lovely books, paper corpses everywhere. A pure and penetrating sorrow hits me, same as when I see a dead roadside animal. Little lives. Flesh and blood—an impossible combination of carbon, hydrogen, nitrogen, oxygen, phosphorus, and sulfur. So much like books. The elegant combination of words. Arranged just so, to make a genius work of literature. How could Kandy not respect the life—the brains—that went into those pages?

Moron.

I pick up the pages, one at a time, and sort them into piles. After about an hour, I've got the papers organized into the books they used to be. There were nine victims, including Brian Greene's *The Hidden Reality: Parallel Universes and the Deep Laws of the Cosmos*, and two Michio Kaku books. My Einstein biography is beyond repair. And *String Theory 101* looks like it's been through a shredder. I wonder if Kandy used her teeth. Her fangs. I wouldn't be surprised.

Oh, wait. She used her scissors. The ones she was still holding in her hand, taunting me.

The noise that comes from my chest is half moan, half wail. I stare at the stack of pages that makes up my mangled Hubble book from George. I look to my dresser to take inventory. George's photo is still there, so are the two snapshots of Mom. The dogs are missing. Probably knocked behind the dresser.

I pick up my garbage can and center it in the midst of the unread-able books. Really, there's no use in having piles of paper like this. Pages are missing, ripped too badly. First in the can, the remains of *String Theory 101*. Such a good book. Next is the Einstein biography with its broken spine. A few pieces of paper are hidden under the bed. I reach underneath, ready to angrily crumble them into wads.

Half a page drifts across the floor, and when I pick it up, the words "multiverse" and "parallel worlds" catch my eye. I hold the paper in my hand and read the entire paragraph.

> *One of the quirkier aspects of superstring theory is that it calls for eleven dimensions of space and time. This version of quantum theory also allows for the multiverse, or parallel worlds. In these worlds, alternate possibilities play out.*

Parallel universes. Alternate possibilities. My breath catches in my throat and I keep reading.

> *A unified theory is what Einstein was after for thirty years but never achieved. It would change our understanding of everything, from subatomic particles to immense galaxies.*

It would redefine our concept of space-time and the flexible fabric of the universe.

My hand goes to the back of my neck. I run my fingers over my tattoo. The Einstein tensor, $R\mu\nu -\frac{1}{2}g\mu\nu R = -\kappa T\mu\nu$, which expresses space-time curvature. No, it can't be. I hungrily read more.

Space could be peppered with connections that link distant points; hidden spatial dimensions might be right next to us, and we just can't see them.

The tree. Could it be a wormhole?

I dump the trash can onto the floor and shuffle through the loose pages, looking for Brian Greene's book about hidden realities, but instead finding an index that corresponds to another. "Wormholes, pages 178–181." Now where are those pages? I should march back across the hallway and rip into Kandy's clothes closet. Take her designer shoes and hack off the heels with a kitchen cleaver.

There's page 177. Almost. And under that are the pages I need.

Simply put, wormholes are tunnels, connecting two positions in space-time.

I scan ahead and find this:

In an infinite number of parallel universes, infinite possibilities play out. At every quantum juncture, what could

happen, does. As Yogi Berra once famously said, "If you see a
fork in the road, take it."

I wander around my room, rooting through the moving boxes, pulling stuff out in handfuls. Now it really looks like a bomb went off in my room. I unearth a flashlight, my digital camera, my wallet with twenty-seven dollars cash, and a fresh notebook and pen. I toss it all into my backpack, along with a change of clothes. Into the front zipper pocket, I slide the postcard from George and the new snapshot of Mom.

At daybreak, I'm going back to the tree. If it really is a wormhole, I'm about to prove string theory and make science history.

And maybe, just maybe, I'll bump into Mom.

chapter five

I hit my snooze button again. I feel weak, burned, like I've spent too much time in the sun, electrolytes zapped. About ten percent of me is saying, Get your butt out of bed. But ninety percent of me wants to sleep. It's a simple case of mathematics. I guess traveling through space-time takes its toll. So does a gash to the leg.

By the time I push the moving boxes away from my door, put on some jeans and a T-shirt, and haul myself downstairs, everyone's in the kitchen. Yeah, I'm super-anxious to get back to the tree, but I need to eat, and breakfast smells good.

"Morning, sunshine." Dad stands over a griddle. He flips an enormous golden pancake. Butter, flour, a bowl of batter, and a package of bacon clutter the countertop.

I cock my head, give him a look. "You're cooking?"

Dad grins. "At it again."

"Seriously," I say. "I thought you were strictly toast and cereal."

Now Dad gives me a funny look. "What?"

There's something different about Dad. I guess I didn't notice it last night, but he looks . . . hmm . . . younger? Yes, that's it. It's his hair. It's more black than gray. When did he start coloring it?

"Good morning, Ruby." Willow dabs egg from the corners of her mouth.

I shove a giant cardboard box out of the way and sit down. "'Morning," I say to Willow, not Kandy. Kandy gives me a venomous look, which I return in kind. Then we proceed to ignore each other. A symbiotic relationship, though I can't ignore her perfume. Between that and the hairspray, a mushroom cloud is forming over the kitchen table.

Dad shuffles to the table in his slippers and slides a giant pancake onto my plate. "Spread some lingonberry preserves on it," he says. "Tell me what you think."

"You're wearing a paisley apron," I say, trying to blink the sleep out of my eyes.

"Of course I am. You bought this apron for me, remember?"

I try to remember. A mouse pad, an electric shaver, a jazz CD. Those are the most recent birthday and Christmas gifts.

"Eat your pancake before it gets cold."

I reach for the lingonberry preserves. I've heard of cranberries, blueberries, strawberries, blackberries, even gooseberries. But lingonberries? I search the table for the maple syrup, but there is none.

"The batter is Irish oatmeal, whole wheat flour, buttermilk," Dad says. "It's for *Gourmet* magazine."

"For an advertisement?" I carve out a bite. It's perfect. Light, fluffy, sweet.

Dad hands me a hot cup of coffee. "Drink this. Wake up, space cadet."

Willow pushes her plate away. "I can't eat another morsel," she says. She checks her watch. "We need to push off for Cleveland."

"Have fun, you two," Dad says. "Don't max out the credit cards."

"Weren't you just in Cleveland yesterday?" I ask.

"Yes, but that was a spur-of-the-moment appointment," Willow explains, digging through her purse and finding her keys. "And I guess I should be glad I wasn't home. I would've been worried sick about you."

Dad glances at me with a look of reproach.

"Yeah, I'm really sorry about that."

"Today we're going to a mall." She turns to me, an apology in her eyes. "Ruby, we didn't invite you because we didn't think you'd care for it. It's sort of—"

"High fashion," Kandy finishes. Then she looks at me with total disgust, like I've got the pneumonic plague.

"I told Kandy I'd treat her to one splurge item," Willow clarifies. "For the start of the school year. If you'd like, we can bring you something—"

Kandy snorts. "What would she do with designer heels, Mom?"

"Oh, Kandinsky," Willow says with an admonishing tone.

Kandy's posture turns rigid. "Do. Not. Call. Me. Kandinsky."

"It's your name."

"For another two hundred and eighty-one days. When I turn

eighteen, I'm filing the paperwork for a legal name change. Then I'll be Amy or Jennifer. Something normal."

"Why would you want an ordinary name?" Willow looks wounded. "Well, I know you still like Kandinsky's art."

Kandy rolls her eyes.

I point my fork at my plate. "Good pancakes, Dad," I say, mouth full. "Yum."

"You like?"

"I love."

Kandy stands up, leaving her plate at the table like she's at a restaurant or something. "My opinion? They're too sweet, or big, or, like, I don't know."

Dad's face goes blank. "Too much sugar?"

"I guess," Kandy says. "They need cinnamon."

Dad scribbles on a notepad.

Kandy grabs her purse—a huge thing with a flashy metal logo—and Willow kisses Dad good-bye. As they leave, Willow harangues Kandy about being civil to her, seeing that she's the one with the credit card. The garage door grinds up, and car doors slam shut. A few moments later, the garage door is back down with a satisfying, final jolt.

"Scrambled or over-easy?" Dad asks.

"No thanks."

"You're eating too fast."

"I'm in a hurry," I say. "I've got a lot to do today." I shouldn't have slept so late. I need to get my gear and head for the oak tree.

"Really? What's on the agenda?"

I'm tempted to spill the beans, but now I feel like it's a secret I need to keep to myself, until I have more data and a better grasp of what's really going on. I don't want the word getting out yet. I want the tree to be my discovery—all mine—at least for a while.

"Library," I say, which is true. Because now I need something on string theory since my books are torn too badly. Thank you, Kandy.

"I'll give you a ride," Dad says.

"I can walk," I say, though I wish I could find a pair of crutches to keep the pressure off my leg. After a long night's sleep, it feels okay for now.

"I'd rather drive you," he says.

"Da-ad," I moan. "I'm not a little kid. Besides, you have work to do."

His eyes go to his notepad, and the writing he needs to finalize. "Be back by five," Dad says. "Don't make me panic again."

"Promise." I'm finally a little more awake, and my mind is racing ahead to all the field work that's waiting for me. Taking photos and notes, translating the foreign inscription that's over the tree's door.

I'm about to eat the last bite of pancake when I notice a framed photo sitting on top of a moving box. It's the one of the dogs, Isaac and Galileo, their ears straight up, looking through our sliding-glass door.

"What's this doing down here?" I ask, picking up the photo. "This was on my dresser."

"We haven't unpacked that box yet," Dad says.

"But—"

"What was it you said about that photo?" he asks.

Even though the photo is black and white, I know that Isaac's collar is green, and Galileo's is blue. "It's like they're still waiting for me to open that sliding door," I say. "Like they're still right there." My cheeks burn hot. Man, I miss those dogs.

Isaac and Galileo. Perfect dog names. But wait. I couldn't have been the one who named them. We got the dogs when I was two years old.

"I never thought about it before. Who named the dogs?"

Dad clears his throat. "Mom did."

The thought of Mom hits me hard and morphs into that fresh image of her, that in-focus snapshot of her staring directly into the camera, forcing a smile. Then my mind flashes to that eight-by-ten family photo hanging in that brick house in Ó Direáin.

"You know she loved astronomy," Dad says. He gets this intense, far-off look in his eyes. "You've got her genes, kiddo."

Another reminder of what's missing. All these little pieces of Mom. That she loved emeralds, pineapples on her pizza, and the smell of gasoline. That she hated pantyhose and watching the nightly news. You'd think the pieces would go together to make a whole, not more emptiness. But it's like a black hole. The more matter you feed it, the bigger it gets.

Dad goes on, "She worked at the Leuschner Observatory in Lafayette for about a year. You probably don't remember. You were really little. Anyway, she liked having good tools to see the universe. You can mistake a planet for a star with the naked eye."

"I remember when I was a kid, I thought airplanes were shooting stars," I say. "Meteors."

"Exactly." Dad points his dishwashing wand at me to punctuate the point. "Your mother liked to remind me that sometimes things aren't what they appear." Then Dad shakes his head and starts putting dishes into the dishwasher. "Maybe we can get another dog, Ruby."

I snort. "Kandy would want one of those rodent dogs that you carry around in a purse."

"We'd get a Lab," Dad says. "Or whatever you want."

I push my chair back and hand Dad my dirty plate, shoving another moving box out of the way with my foot. It's half-open and full of books, dozens of the same book.

I reach down and pull the box's cardboard flaps wide open.

Parsley, Parsnips, and Paisley: More Inventive Cooking from Alan Wright.

Alan Wright? That's Dad's name. That's Dad's photo on the front cover! He's wearing a paisley apron and holding a wooden spatula, for crying out loud.

I yank a book from the box and hold it in both hands. I hold it hard, like there's no gravity and it might fly away. My heart pounds as I flip to the back flap. Next to a small, square photo of Dad is this:

ALAN WRIGHT is a regular contributor to *Gourmet* and *Cooking Light* magazines. He is the author of three cookbooks, including the *New York Times* bestseller *Please Pass the Paisley: Artful Cooking with Alan Wright.* He is a graduate of Le Cordon Bleu Program at the California Culinary Academy in San Francisco.

Oh God.

I'm in the wrong universe.

In this universe, Dad doesn't write ad copy. He's a chef. He writes recipes. In this universe, Dad went to culinary school.

Frantic, I look around, like I'm waiting for the house to implode. Now I notice. I notice all the differences. The stove is a stainless steel Viking with eight burners. The refrigerator is enormous, like it belongs in a restaurant. I spot a Julia Child cookbook. Back in the other Ennis, we have basic white appliances and maybe one grease-stained cookbook.

My heart races as I scan the room. What else is different here? Who am I in this universe? What is this Ruby like?

"Uh? Dad?" I'm not even sure what to call this guy. I mean, I guess he's still my father.

"Ruby, you know I'd love to talk more," he says, "but I've got to finalize this pancake recipe."

"Sure," I say, glad to have an excuse to flee. "It doesn't need more cinnamon," I say as I hurry out of the kitchen. My lungs are tight, my blood vessels clamping down. I'm not a candidate for a heart attack. But I might pass out. Do a total face-plant.

Just calm down, Ruby. Take a deep breath. N_2 and O_2 in, carbon dioxide out.

I don't know what else to do, so I run up to my room to grab my backpack. My room? My backpack? I'm not really sure if I can say "my." Is there another Ruby that I've somehow displaced? Has that Ruby switched places with me, and she's as confused as I am? Did I completely vanish from home yesterday, and no one knows where I am? What kinds of ripples in space and time am I causing?

I sit on the edge of the bed and try to think. Try to get a grip. The wound on my leg is throbbing, pounding along with my heart. I stare at my M. C. Escher poster that needs to be hung, one of the few things Kandy didn't rip to shreds. Escher understood symmetry, negative and positive space, and creating dimension. Mathematical art. Nothing like Willow's often haphazard smears of dark paint. In this Escher drawing, water appears to be flowing both up and down at the same time.

It's impossible.

But apparently, sometimes things aren't what they appear.

chapter six

Thousands of shadows are cast by the oak's leaves, making a collective blanket of shade. I stand under the mighty tree, feeling small, kicking nervously at a root that protrudes from the ground. My stomach is heavy with pancakes, lingonberry preserves, and strong coffee. My head is heavy with confusion.

The humming under my feet reminds me that there's a power source. Some sort of mechanism is running. So where's the instruction manual? How does this tree work?

I run my fingers over the weather-worn door—the carved and twisted lines, a grid with warps and ripples. The fabric of space. Of course.

What do I know about space-time? What do I know about string theory? Uh, honestly? Not much. I mean, it's not like I've had a chance to fill my brains at Harvard. No PhD in theoretical physics. Not yet, anyway.

Here's the not much that I do know: We once thought of an atom as the smallest unit, the most basic unit of matter. But look closer and you find that atoms are made of electrons, neutrons, and protons. Keep looking closer. Protons and neutrons are made of quarks. Quarks are made of vibrating loops of string. As strings vibrate, they warp the surrounding fabric of space, producing black holes, tunnels, and other oddities, like U-shaped universes with shortcuts from one stem to the other.

Turns out Sir Isaac Newton was wrong about space and time. He thought they were constant and predictable. That they behaved themselves and stuck to the rules. He wrote something in the *Principia* about space being immovable. I remember that word. Immovable.

But no. Space can be pinched, torn, warped, or rippled. Which means that wormholes—doorways—could exist.

There's nothing immovable about that.

I dump out the contents of my backpack and grab my pen and notebook, suddenly realizing that I've taken clothes, a wallet, digital camera, and flashlight that aren't really mine. I pat my back pocket for my cell phone—which isn't mine either—and realize I left it plugged into the bedroom wall to recharge. That's fine.

My attention goes to the carved sign at the top of the door, and I copy the inscription into my notebook: **Gry kbo iye coousxq?** Is it an Eastern European language? Code? Alien?

"Who knows," I say to no one but myself. It must be important, if it's above the door. It could be user instructions. An equation, an explanation. It might be a warning.

I ponder the jumbled letters a few minutes, until my thoughts stray to another topic. I draw a U shape with a few lines that link the left and right stems. I label the lines wormholes. Finally, I draw a chart:

Universe One	Universe Two	Universe Three
Ennis, Ohio	Ó Díreáin, Ohio	Ennis, Ohio
Normal Me	Not-normal me wears pink and is president of class, Pep Club, French Club	Normal Me
Dad is copywriter	Dad's occupation unknown	Dad is chef
Mom died 11 years ago	Mom ALIVE???	Mom out of picture (assume dead 11 yrs ago)
Dad with Willow	Dad with Willow	Dad with Willow
Kandy insane	Kandy on medication	Kandy insane
No siblings	Older brother, Patrick	No siblings

I tap my pen against the page. A thought creeps into my brain. A crazy possibility. What if I go back to Universe Two? To take scientific notes and, well . . . see if Mom is there.

Please, Ruby.

It's absurd. It's frighteningly irrational.

Let it go.

"She's dead!" I say. I hate the sound of that word, and I wish I hadn't said it out loud. She's gone. Unreachable.

Okay, so what if I stay here in Universe Three? It's almost right. I mean, it's just that Dad's a successful chef and not a stressed-out copywriting fool. I think about his gray hair, and how he has less of it here in Universe Three. He looks younger in other ways too. Fewer wrinkles, smoother skin. Maybe Chef Dad is happier than Copywriting Dad. Maybe he's had an easier life. He's been eating better food, no doubt.

Big questions: Did we ever go to Jewel Cave in South Dakota? Did we camp at Mount Tamalpais last year for my birthday? Did we see that cougar attack a deer? Did we plant tomatoes for my seventh-grade science project? Did we slice them and shower them with salt and call it dinner?

My memories, my experiences are at stake. In this universe, what never happened?

Because, while Dad was in culinary school, he would have met people, frequented different places, and followed paths that wouldn't have presented themselves otherwise. It's not just the kitchen appliances at Willow's that are different here, that much is certain. The more I think about it, the less I like the idea of staying. It seems like a footnote, no big deal—it's just Dad's job—but there's the inevitable ripple effect, the butterfly effect: the seemingly insignificant flapping of a butterfly's wings can effect an atmospheric change, which can alter the path of a tornado. Little alterations, big repercussions.

It's clear—I need to get home. Back to Universe One.

The digital camera is armed with a fresh battery and memory card, so I click away, taking photos of the door, doorknob, and the inscription: ᏩᎡᎩ ᏦᏏᎣ ᎥᎩᎬ ᏣᎣᎣᏳᏚᏔᏈ?

I can't think of anything else to do, as much as I'd like to put off the inevitable. But it's time. Time to go through the portal. My hands turn clammy. My stomach churns. I hate this. I hate not knowing how to control the tree. I hate not knowing where I'll end up.

From the front pocket of my backpack I pull out gardening gloves, the kind with little rubber bumps all over them. I grabbed them on my way past Chef Dad's fledgling backyard herb garden, and I tug them onto my hands now so I won't have to endure the zap of the doorknob.

I place a single finger on the knob, but nothing happens. Wincing, not sure what to expect, I grip it with my entire palm. No spark, no shock, and the door still doesn't open. When I attempt to turn the knob, it won't budge.

"Must you be so difficult?" I groan.

It seems to require a charge exchange, so I have to use my bare skin. I reluctantly pull the gloves off and touch the metal. A lightning-spark leaps.

"Not nice," I say to the tree, flexing my fingers. The door creaks open; a whoosh of air ruffles my shirt. Oh, man. That smell! Decaying bark, stagnant water, mildew. I search through my backpack, find a sock, and cover my nose and mouth. Flashlight on, I wait for the door to seal shut. Slivers of daylight make their way around the doorframe for a final second, and then the darkness is total, and deep-bone creepy.

Even with the beam of the flashlight, I feel consumed by it. Panic begins to kick in, and I have to remind myself to breathe. N_2 and O_2 in, carbon dioxide out, Ruby. The sock smells like it sat in the washer too long before going to the dryer. More mildew.

I aim the flashlight at the steering wheel, which I can now see is positioned in the center of the room.

A thick metal pole extends through it, attaching it to the floor below. The pole also extends above the disk about three feet, and is topped by a metal sculpture the shape of the sun, wild with flares.

"Cool," I say with a surge of excitement.

Etched onto the surface of the disk, around the perimeter, is this:

wkccsfo cyvkb pvkbo 1864 = kdwyczrobsm ovomdbsm cebqo. dboo bodksxon zygob 87 ryebc. ceppsmsoxd cebqo boymmebboxmo sxmkvmevklvo.

And welded onto the top is an ornate arrow, its tip extending out beyond the edge. That's the sharp triangle I felt yesterday when I was feeling my way around in the dark.

The sock I'm holding over my mouth and nose goes into my backpack. It wasn't helping much anyway. After a little digging, I find my notebook and pen, then tuck the flashlight under my armpit so I can have both hands free.

I meticulously copy each word—word?—into my notebook, triple-checking my spelling. I take a digital photo of the etching, the camera flash momentarily blinding me.

The arrow must correspond to something, but where is it pointing? I stand directly behind it, lining myself up with the trajectory of the arrow, then I aim the flashlight along that line. There's nothing on the interior tree wall, other than markings that remind me of DNA maps. Long vertical lines with smaller dotted lines on top. But I decide they're just water stains or fungus or something.

The tree's thrumming noise engines on, and I point the flashlight straight up. The beam isn't strong enough to show much. Looks like the perfect place for bats. The floor, for the most part, resembles a rotted-out tree stump. A couple puddles here and there. Yeah, try not to step in one of those again.

But something shimmers on the floor beneath the disk, like light reflecting off shallow water. Like light reflecting off . . . metal. Excited, I squat down and wipe away the dirt. Yes, it's a ring of metal. I work my way around it, clearing it off, and find that it has ten symbols etched at equal intervals.

They're simple line drawings, nothing I recognize. After I take photos and copy the symbols into my notebook, I stand and press my left hip against the disk, the tip of the arrow slightly pressing into my side. My body draws a straight line down to the ground. I lift my right foot, and sure enough, there's a symbol underneath. This must be some sort of navigational device. This is where I am now—at the position marked with what strikes me as an F topped by an other upside-down F.

$$\models$$

That's enough. One more sweep of the flashlight to make sure I'm not missing anything, but at this point, I'm ready to go regardless. Claustrophobia is setting in. I've been in this coffin too long.

Think, Ruby, calm.

I've turned the wheel twice, clockwise both times. So that means if

I go back one notch, I'll be in Ó Direáin. If I go back two notches to the symbol marked

$$\daleth$$

I'll be home—back in what I'm calling Universe One. Back in Ennis, Ohio. Easy enough.

Even if the gardening gloves didn't save me from the static shock of the doorknob, they should make it easier to turn the cold, slippery disk. Holding the flashlight with one gloved hand, I twist the wheel with the other, counterclockwise, aiming for two notches back.

"Move!" I put my soul into it, but I can't get it to turn. "Come on, come on, come on," I chant, but the wheel stubbornly stays put. Reluctantly, I click off the flashlight and slip it into my backpack so I have both hands free. The darkness is immediately sickening, strangling my senses. I'm shaking, my nervous system amped into overload.

The wheel still won't budge. I keep at it until the tendons in my hands and wrist stiffen.

It's not what I want, but I have no choice. I turn the wheel the other direction—clockwise—and it goes, clanking like an untuned bell, into the next position.

"Fabulous," I announce to the tree. "Thanks for cooperating." Now I'm even farther from home.

The tree hums and the door opens, bringing fresh air and a familiar landscape. There's the stone high school with the slate roof and central spire. I'm in Ó Direáin, though I should assume it's a different version, somehow, some way. The school campus is quiet; it's Saturday. I circle the oak tree, just to make sure it looks the same in this universe, so I can make a note of it in my data journal. There's nothing different about the tree itself, but behind it, the land slides downward gently. Below, maybe a half mile off, there's a town. A full-blown town with sidewalks and shops. This very well may have been here in yesterday's Ó Direáin, and I just didn't notice. I never walked around the tree or looked in this direction.

What to do? I could—I should—hop back into the tree and keep turning the steering disk clockwise, until I go full circle and get back home. That would be the most rational course of action. Step into tree, turn disk, step out. Repeat until safely home. Done. End of story.

Or I can venture into downtown Ó Direáin. Because I'm curious. And because that eight-by-ten family photo keeps flicking through my mind. No matter how hard I try, I can't push it away. I can't hit the delete button. I know my brain's hippocampus has grabbed the image, and is forcing me to keep it as a long-term memory. And I know that photo represents a bottomless heartache, a deep and penetrating itch. Maybe I can satisfy it, if I just catch a glimpse of Mom. What's the big deal if I watch her, for ten minutes, from a distance? Just to see her. Just to touch—no, no—just to talk.

Ten minutes, Ruby. Not a second more. And just watching.

"There's no guarantee she's in this universe anyway," I announce to myself, trying to clear the bickering voices from my head.

Absolutely. She might've only existed in that other version of Ó Direáin.

The hill is easy, and a well-worn footpath leads the way, directly to a sidewalk. A newspaper vending machine advertises the *Ó Direáin Chronicle*. Black lampposts hold the street signs at ninety-degree angles.

I'm on the corner of Arainn Street and Breandan Avenue. Pinch me because I swear I'm in a friggin' Disney park. Coffee shops, toy store, bookstore, banks. The smell of cookies wafts out of a place called Sweet Treats. Shoe store, architect office, Chinese restaurant. There's a guy with a T-shirt that says CITY OF Ó DIREÁIN JANITORIAL SERVICES. He's picking up garbage.

It's perfect. The only thing that's missing is the theme music.

After about five minutes of walking, I catch myself smiling. It's cloudy, but there's a sunshine vibe in the air. Kids with ice cream cones hold their parents' hands. People read books under the canopies of stupendous trees. Couples snuggle on benches, dogs chase Frisbees.

A fountain burbles, and a bronze statue dominates the center of the park. It's a man holding a lightbulb, and at the base of the statue is a plaque.

CITY FOREFATHER PADRAIG Ó DIREÁIN WAS BORN
IN 1841 IN ENNIS, IRELAND. A PROLIFIC INVENTOR,
HOLDING 732 PATENTS, HIS MOST FAMOUS
INVENTION WAS THE LIGHTBULB. HIS OBSESSION
WITH ELECTRICITY LED TO HIS DEATH DURING AN
EXPERIMENT WITH LIGHTNING IN 1922.

This could be an important bit of data, so I copy it into my notebook and snap a digital photo. As I work, my mind whirls. There was a scientist named Ó Direáin. So this city is obviously named after him. He was born in a place called Ennis, in Ireland, which means that Ennis, Ohio, is probably named after his birthplace. So he made his mark in more than one universe.

But hang on. Thomas Edison invented the lightbulb, am I right?

I start walking again, trying to wrap my brain around all of this, when I see the library. Seriously, catch me before I swoon and face-plant. It's majestic! It's a castle, I swear. Gargoyles, towers, stained-glass windows. If I could build my fantasy library, this would be it. Thick wooden doors, quarried stone floor. I'm brimming—no, I'm overflowing—with happiness.

Three things I can accomplish here: 1) get a book or two on string theory, 2) figure out what language the inscriptions are in, and 3) look up Mom's address.

"Hi, Ruby," a librarian says to me as I walk past the information desk.

"Uh," I say. "Hi." I read her name tag. "Carol."

"Good to see you," Carol says softly. "Your hair looks cute short."

I run a hand through my bangs. "Thanks."

My face is burning. The computers are in sight, so I flash Carol my best gotta-go smile, and run for it. Okay, so it's bad when you don't recognize someone who knows your name. But in a parallel universe, it causes anxiety to the tenth power. Maybe my parallel-Ruby comes to the library a lot, maybe Carol is related, maybe she's my neighbor. Who knows, and I can't ask without sounding like a lunatic: Oh, you're my aunt Carol? Sure, of course, sorry. I just didn't recognize you, 'cause in my usual universe I don't have any aunts.

At the computer, I let my hands hover over the keyboard while I think. There's no recognizable icon for an Internet browser, but I try each one anyway. Finally, a spiderweb icon launches a security screen that asks for my library card number and a password. Forget it.

So I try the library catalog instead, typing **Gɾy ʁbo iye coousʁq?** into the subject search field. The most logical way to translate a language? No. But right now I just need to know which language I should be tackling. An hourglass icon appears next to the words "Searching Database." The search engine is having a hard time; it's as confused as I am. Finally it responds with "No Matches Found." Of course not.

I try **Gɾy** alone, then **coousʁq**. Both times, the computer directs me to Keyword Search Tips, telling me to check my spelling, simplify, and make sure I'm entering the info in the correct fields. Basically the library's search system is screaming "Idiot!"

This is a total dead end. Shift gears. I type "string theory" into the subject search field, and there's plenty to choose from, though it's odd that the bestselling books I've read aren't listed. Where are Brian Greene's books? Where are Michio Kaku's? They're the guys I want to call when I get back to Ennis; we'll make history together, proving that string theory is a reality. Wrinkles in space do exist!

I tap my pen against my forehead. It bugs me. Where is *String Theory 101*? Where's Lisa Randall? I haven't read her book on hidden dimensions yet, but it's on my list. Do these people have different names in this universe? Did they decide to become chefs instead of physicists?

Maybe the unfortunate truth is that they don't even exist in this universe. If I have an older brother in Universe Two, then people may or may not exist in parallel dimensions. If Brian Greene's parents decided they weren't in the mood for sex on that fateful night of his

would-be conception, he just wouldn't be. One decision, many repercussions. One nuance, different outcomes.

I scribble down the name of a book by Hugh Everett III called
Fluid Universe, published last year. Wacky that Everett exists here in
Universe Four because—I'm pretty sure—he died young, like twenty
or thirty years ago. Wow. That's a major deviance, a fork in the road of
space-time. Hugh Everett III skipped his heart attack here in Universe
Four and kept on living. Could be. Which means that Mom could've
done the same—dodged death—in multiple universes.

Mom could be alive in more than one universe.

The thought lodges itself smack in the middle of everything.

I close my eyes and try to clear my head, heave my backpack on,
then climb a flight of stairs to the science section of the library. The
wrought-iron handrail is unbearably cold, but I need to steady myself.
Every time I put weight on my bad leg, pain wraps around it and pen-
etrates my shin, nearly forcing me to stop and sit. A man passes me
with a worried look. He glances over his shoulder.

"You okay?"

"Fine, thanks," I manage, though I'm grinding my teeth.

I sit on the top step for a full minute, waiting for the dizziness to
pass. Once I feel steady, I stand up and take in my surroundings. Despite
the nagging pain, my mood lightens. All around me are books about
cosmology, inorganic chemistry, nuclear physics, you name it. Little
wooden benches, painted teal, are placed at the end of each aisle.

It's those benches that remind me of the Golden Gate Bookstore.
The place where everything changed between George and me.

Jamie was browsing the poetry journals, and George had followed me into the science section. A book was lying open underneath a bench, abandoned, as if the reader had given up on the intimidating equations. I picked it up and closed it, ready to slip it back onto a shelf.

"Wait!" George had said, his voice full of interest. "What was that?"

"An explanation of sine and cosine."

"No, no. Flip back. A couple more pages. Those graphs. There."

In that moment, something clicked inside George's consciousness. I could feel it in his body language. In the way he leaned over the book, fidgeting over the pages. He'd made a discovery that day. And I was standing right next to him when it happened. "They're beautiful," he gasped.

"You've never seen calculus functions graphed before?"

He shook his head. "Never."

"Graphs of polar equations make all sorts of cool shapes. Flowers, spirals, butterflies."

"Are you serious?" He was breathless. "This is what I've been waiting for. This is exactly what I need to finish a sketch I've been stuck on. I never thought I'd find it in a math book."

I grin at him. "Did you ever have one of those spirograph toys when you were a kid?"

"Yeah, with the plastic plates that guide your pen."

"To make pretty looping patterns. You probably didn't realize that you were tracing hypotrochoid and epitrochoid curves."

I'd waited for him to give me a look, the kind I normally get when I shift into geek-speak. But he only seemed more interested.

"It's all connected," I went on. "Math, nature, art, physics. People think subjects are separate, but they're not. They're linked. The shape of a spiral galaxy, or the spiral on a snail's shell, gets translated into architecture as a spiral staircase. There are logarithmic spirals in so many things. In hurricanes, in fingerprints. In the cochlea of the ear! And this math equation"—I tapped the book—"creates a spiral when graphed."

He said nothing, processing it all. So I kept going, pointing to the ice that was melting at the bottom of his drink. "You see ice and think what?"

"That it's cold?"

"What else?" I pressed.

"It's translucent with little fracture lines," George said.

"Yeah, but what about the fact that the crystalline structure of ice makes a stunning geometric pattern. It's hexagonal. I'll show you sometime. Remind me and I'll bring some of my books the next time we get coffee at the café."

From that point on, I was more than just Jamie's friend who sometimes tagged along. And George became something to me other than Jamie's cute boyfriend. We had our own connection, our spark.

Now I'm trying to make my own discovery as I browse the Ó Direáin library shelves.

String Theory Basics looks good, as does *Parallel Places & Peculiar Physics*. I sit on a bench and lean back against a shelf. Extending my legs gives me a little relief. After scanning the index of *Parallel Places*, I turn the smooth, thin pages to read a passage about Hugh Everett III's PhD dissertation, which was written in the mid-1950s. His many-worlds theory explained that an observer, simply by observing, can change the outcome of an event. The observer then becomes correlated to the system, and is in turn affected.

I press my fingers to the bridge of my nose, as if this will help me understand.

Observation causes the collapse of wave functions. Wave functions map the possible states of a system. So, if wave functions branch in different directions, independent of each other, then there are countless alternate realities playing out.

Mom could be alive in more than one universe.

The math is completely beyond me, but it sure is pretty. Theorem 4's equations are spectacular; they'd make a great tattoo.

I flip through the other books, scanning some more passages, grumbling with disagreement over this one:

> *Traversable wormholes would require the center of a black hole—a singularity—deep in outer space, at such a distance that it would take millions of lifetimes to get there. If you somehow survived the long journey, you would then learn that black holes are unapproachable. They emit enormous amounts of deadly radiation and are defined by crushing gravity.*

Black holes? The closest one to Earth is in the constellation Sagittarius, thousands of light-years from here. But obviously a wormhole can function without a black hole. The tree isn't relying on one to work.

"Ouch," I mumble. This time it's my neck that hurts, not my leg, from craning over the book too long. My stomach is grumbling too.

I crack my neck and my knuckles and head for the phone books. Perhaps this will be easier than decoding **ᏃᏒᎩ ᏦᏸᎾ ᎥᎽᎬ ᏟᎾᎾᏬᏕᏂᏇ?** and noodling through string theory. I flip to the residential section and look for Wright.

My finger trails down the silky-thin pages until it reaches WRIGHT, SALLY . . . 1104 CIUNIÚINT STREET.

It's like a jolt of electricity. Mom? My Sally Wright? I flatten the phone book across the glass of a nearby copy machine. Sure, I could write down the address by hand, but this is proof. Like the eight-by-ten photo, this is evidence, data, a precious piece of documentation. It's Mom's name and address, for real. I want a photocopy, an ink-on-page, black-and-white artifact.

The copy machine keeps spitting out my dimes. I've only got three, and it doesn't like any of them.

Behind me, a white-haired man sighs impatiently. He reaches around me and inserts a coin. "There you go."

"Thanks," I say. "I guess it wanted a quarter." I flip to the Ó Direáin street map at the back of the phone book and copy that as well. "Sorry to hold you up."

The papers are still warm as I fold them and tuck them into my backpack. 1104 Ciuniúint Street. That's where I'm heading. Ten minutes, Ruby. Not a second more. And just watching.

"Ready to check these out?" Carol asks when I lay the books on the counter.

"Yes, please," I say.

"Card?"

My face goes blank. "Oh, geez. I—uh."

Carol laughs. "Oh, Ruby. Don't worry. We've got all your info in here." She pats the top of her computer. "I'll just pull you up."

"Thanks," I say, tapping my foot nervously.

"I talked to your mom today," Carol says, adjusting her glasses. "Seems like she's doing okay. What a rough breakup. So sad."

"Mm-hmm," I say vaguely.

"Do you like her new apartment?" Carol scans the barcodes on each book and demagnetizes them.

I cough, choke. "Sure, I guess." How old is that phone book? Carol said new apartment. Did Mom just move? Is the address in the phone book right?

"It must be hard on you," Carol says. "My parents got divorced when I was ten. I remember how confused I was."

What am I thinking anyway, trying to find my not-dead mom? It makes me lightheaded. What if she sees me? What if I can't help myself and I run to her? What if I wrap my arms around her, kiss her warm cheek, smell her hair, hear her voice? Then what? How will I ever let go? Will I ever care about getting back to Ennis?

Carol gives me a warm, sympathetic smile. "Enjoy your reading, honey," she says, handing me the physics books.

I should just ask Carol: So what *is* my mom's new apartment address? I keep forgetting it. Can't put my finger on it.

But I don't want to deal with Carol's perplexed and concerned reaction. She might call Mom, tell her I'm here. Then the whole thing is out of my control. I slide the string theory books into my backpack and take a step toward the door.

"Wait, honey," Carol says. "Something's off kilter here."

My heart pounds. "Excuse me?"

"Strange, very strange," she says, staring into the computer.

"What's wrong?" My voice quivers. Did she just figure me out somehow? Does she realize I'm the wrong Ruby for this universe? "I really need to get going. I'm—uh—late for—"

"Looks like you overpaid on a late fee, honey." Carol shakes her head in dismay, like this is the most mysterious thing to happen since the Big Bang. "We owe you two dollars." She opens a desk drawer and hands me two bills. "Sorry about that."

"No problem." I manage a smile before quickly shoving the money into my pocket and heading for the exit sign.

Outside, I take a deep breath and force myself to laugh. It's funny, right? I owe library late fees in a parallel universe. Hilarious.

As I walk down Arainn Street, the smell of fried food hangs in the air, a major temptation. Takeout at the Chinese restaurant. Maybe just a bowl of wonton soup, though I know it's unwise to blow my limited cash supply.

Then I get a whiff of chocolate, and my olfactory receptors go berserk. I'm standing in front of Sweet Treats, and I can't resist. The allure of refined sugar. Besides, I just scored an extra two bucks at the library. Door chimes jingle as I walk in the bakery. Glass display cases showcase scones, muffins, oatmeal raisin cookies, chocolate chip cookies, brownies, and carrot cake cupcakes. Rich, strong coffee adds to the aroma.

"The smallest, cheapest version of coffee you make, and one of those tiny cranberry-walnut mini-scones, please," I tell the girl behind the counter.

"What? You don't even say hello?" The girl gives me wry smile. She twists a blond pigtail around her finger.

"Hello," I say, trying to sound convincing. Crap! Somebody else who knows me, and I have no clue.

"Cool haircut," she says. "So where's Patrick?"

"Huh? Oh—I'm not sure." My poor heart. How many times in the past twenty-four hours have I subjected it to sudden stress? It's pounding hard again.

"I swear this is the very first time I've seen you without him. It's like you're connected at the hip. I wish I were that close with my brother. It's sweet. You know, I forgot you wore glasses."

"Honestly, I'm in a huge hurry," I say. "Could I just get a small coffee and one of those mini-scones?"

The girl laughs and I see that she's wearing braces. She's sixteen, maybe seventeen. Maybe she's in Patrick's year at Ó Direáin High. "I'm still in shock that you're not getting a Diet Coke," she says.

Yuck. Methanol.

"What?" she asks.

I didn't realize I was talking out loud. "Nothing. It's just that methanol is a breakdown product of aspartame. Aspartame's the artificial sweetener."

"I know what aspartame is."

"Well, they use methanol in camping stove fuel and antifreeze and formaldehyde," I say. She gives me a blank stare, and I add a weak, "Forget it."

"Ruby?" the girl says with genuine concern. "Are you okay?"

"Never better," I say.

She hands me my mini-scone wrapped in a thin napkin. "Coffee will be just a sec," she says. "I'm brewing a fresh pot."

I pop the entire scone in my mouth and use it as an excuse for my silence. I shrug and point to my mouth as if to say, *Sorry, can't talk with my mouth full.*

"Five fifty," the girl says.

I hand her the ones I got from Carol at the library. Then I dig through my wallet for more money.

"Here you go."

"What's this?" the girl asks, pressing her eyebrows together. "Who's Washington? Are you trying to give me fake money?" She sounds both amused and offended.

"What do you mean?" I take the money back and examine the bills. The two from Carol have a guy named Henry Lee III framed in the portrait oval. They're a darker shade of green too, but otherwise they look identical to my money from home. No wonder my dimes didn't work in the Xerox machine at the library.

"I think that's illegal, right? Trying to pass off counterfeits."

"I'm sorry, I seriously didn't notice . . ."

The girl's face softens into a smile. "Knowing Patrick, he was probably playing a practical joke on you, putting Monopoly money in your wallet."

"Oh, that Patrick," I say, like I'm admonishing a bad puppy.

"Tell you what," the girl says. "Tell him to come in. He owes me three fifty."

"You sure?" I give her the two Henry Lee III bills and keep my Washingtons.

She nods and hands me my hot coffee.

"Thanks. Gotta go."

Get me out of this coffee shop!

And out of this town? Yeah, I'm second-guessing my impulse to see Mom. It's an impulse, that's all. Totally devoid of logic. I should just get back to the tree. I hurry along the sidewalk, wishing I could run, trying not to slosh coffee all over myself. As people pass by, I'm careful not to make eye contact. What if someone else recognizes me?

What if I recognize . . . George?

It's him. On a park bench, with a sketch pad and a packet of colored pencils. He looks up with those aquamarine eyes; his tank top shows biceps I never knew he had. What is he doing here, thousands of miles from San Francisco?

"Hi, George." My voice fails me. I'm not sure any noise is coming out at all. And I realize that I'm standing like a statue, directly facing him, staring. Absurdly.

Does he know me? What am I to him here? A friend, a fling, a complete stranger? I want to hug him and tell him how happy I am to see him. Tears rush to my eyes. I miss you! I need you!

He cocks his head at me, amused. "You're from French class, right?"

I nod, remembering the yearbook I found at Patrick's house yesterday, in Universe Two. President of the French Club. C'est cheese! So George recognizes me but doesn't know my name.

"I'm Ruby Wright," I say, offering my hand. Touching him delivers a jolt more intense than the doorknob's. Electric. I hold on an extra second.

"George Pierce," he says, sizing me up. "But what's different about you? The hair, the glasses?"

I nod. That's about all I can seem to do. Nod.

"You wanna sit down a minute? You look pale." He pats the bench next to him.

I sit too close and he inches away. "Sorry," I say.

He smells like sandalwood soap, and I'm overcome by the urge to press my nose against his neck. "What are you working on?" I squeak. I clear my throat and try again. "The mountain?"

George taps a gray pencil against his sketch pad. "I don't know. It's weird. Something from a reoccurring dream."

I smile. "It's Mount Diablo. In California."

"Really? You know that for sure?" His face lights up. "I've never been to California."

"Never? I thought you must have moved here—" I stop myself. I shouldn't assume anything. In this universe, maybe George was born here.

"Moved here from California? Yeah, I guess you're right. I was something like two months old. But that hardly counts."

A Ruby and a George, both living in this small Ohio town, both in the same French class. It makes my heart swell, my hands shake. What are the chances? What could it mean? Is my parallel Ruby destined to be with this parallel George, and they just haven't clicked yet? Am I fated to be with my George, back in Universe One? Someday, some-how? The idea of fate and destiny have always made me cringe. If you can't measure it or prove it, you might as well forget it. Coincidence can be explained other ways. I mean, just because there's this uncanny correlation between at least two coexisting states of—

"What did you say?" he asks.

"Huh?"

"You just mumbled something about quantum something or other. Planes?"

"Yikes," I say, my cheeks flaring. "I'm sorry. I have this thing about talking out loud. And I kinda don't realize it." I shrug and smile, attempting to seem amused at my eccentric self.

He gives me a look, like he's trying to decide if that's funny or scary. Or maybe even a little cute?

I clear my throat and point to his sketch of Mount Diablo. "If you hike up to the Juniper Campground, which is at about three thousand two hundred feet, you can see the Golden Gate Bridge."

We've actually been there together, not that long ago, in Universe One.

"So it's in San Francisco," he says.

"Across the bay."

George studies his drawing. "Maybe I was there in a previous life."

I grin. "Or in a parallel universe. If you believe in that sort of thing."

His stomach growls, volume ten. He laughs, embarrassed. "Sorry. I was just about to get Chinese food for lunch. You wanna come?"

"I'd love to, but I'm broke," I say. "And I should get going. I mean, I think I should leave now, though maybe there's no compelling reason after all. To go or to stay. No, no. I take that back. I mean, I need to get home. Plus I have this coffee here." I raise my cup, as if that's my closing argument.

He takes the coffee from my hand and sets it on the edge of the bench. "Coffee's not very filling. Come on. I want to hear more about Mount Diablo."

Suddenly I worry about the butterfly effect. The seemingly insignificant flapping of a butterfly's wings can effect an atmospheric change, which eventually can alter the path of a tornado. Little alterations, big repercussions.

I don't belong here. I need to click my way through the universes and get back.

"Is that a yes or no?" George asks. His lips are parted, half-curled into a smirk, and he's daring me. To say yes. I slide closer and this time he doesn't inch away.

So I lean in and kiss him. It's what I should have done last week on that leather couch at the East Bay Café. It's not the kiss of my dreams, but it's George, and he's not pulling away. In fact, he laces his hands behind my neck and pulls me in closer. I feel dizzy, totally off-center. But in the best possible way.

"Is that a yes or a no?" he asks again, raising one eyebrow. "Girl-I-hardly-know-from-French-class-who's-suddenly-kissing-me?"

"You're buying." I nudge his side with my elbow. "And I'm warning you, I'm hungry."

He laughs, and I feel weightless.

chapter seven

Location: Universe Four, Cloud Nine. Shanghai Restaurant.

George pushes the soy sauce out of the way and hands me a menu across the table. "The steamed pork buns are really good," he says. "Have you had them?"

I realize that he expects that I've eaten here before. It's a small downtown, and this is probably the only Chinese place. No doubt everyone who lives in Ó Direáin has been to every one of the businesses on this street, time and again. I dodge his question by saying, "I love pork buns."

"The Peking duck is awesome, so is the barbeque assortment platter." George studies the lunch specials, and I study him. So far he seems a lot like my George from Universe One. The way he smells, the way he raises one eyebrow when he's teasing, the way he holds his neck in the palm of his hand when he leans on the table.

"You wouldn't happen to know a girl named Jamie, would you?" I try to ask casually, but my voice quivers. I hold my breath, waiting for his answer.

He looks up from his menu. "Jamie?"

I nod, eyes locked on his. Is he taken? Did he and Jamie break up in this universe? Or are they meeting up for ice cream and a walk through the park tonight?

"Nope," he says. "I can't think of a Jamie I know. Why?"

"She's someone from California." My voice trails off.

He looks perplexed. "So how would I—"

"Stupid question, sorry. Never mind." I guess Jamie doesn't even live here. Never moved here. But I couldn't assume anything, because after all, a version of myself lives here alongside George. "You have a little sister named April, right?"

"Yeah. And a dog named—"

"Trigger!" I blurt before I can stop myself.

The look on his face transforms from confusion to suspicion. "How do you know so much about me?"

"I, uh . . ." My eye catches the Facebook logo at the bottom of our menus. *Like us!* "We have a bunch of mutual friends on Facebook? I, um, read some of your posts. You know, just clicking around." I sound like a stalker. Just shut up, Ruby!

"Is this your complicated way of asking if I've got a girlfriend?" He raises an eyebrow, his voice settling on that familiar teasing tone.

I breathe, relieved. "Yep, that's it." It would have been so much easier to just come out and ask.

"Nah. Besides, I just started hanging out with this quirky new girl I kinda dig."

Me? ME?

Our waitress suddenly approaches. A tiny woman with black hair wound into a bun. "Are you ready to order?" she asks. "Drinks first?"

"Green tea," George says.

She looks at me. "That's fine," I say. "Bring a pot."

Once she's gone, George closes his menu and leans across the table. "So what else do you know? From Facebook or whatever."

"You like art. And symmetry."

"Repeating patterns," he says. "Yeah." He flips through his notebook until he finds a pencil drawing of a field of flowers. I've seen this sketch before! George was working on it last week, just before I left Walnut Creek.

"Each flower is like a mini-spirograph," he says.

I know! I was the one who showed him how to do this.

"How did you put math and art together like that?" I ask, knowing it couldn't have been me or my alter Ruby. "Did you go to an exhibit or something?"

"No. It was a fluke thing. This guy at school dropped his homework on the floor one day, and I saw the graph paper and the repeating lines all curled together like some growing, living thing, and inspiration struck," George says, breathless. "But I don't know anyone who can show me more, unless I make an appointment with the math department, I guess."

"You've got room for a butterfly." I point to an empty space above one of the smaller flowers. "Graphs of polar equations can look like butterflies."

"Yeah?" His voice surges with enthusiasm. "What's a polar equation? Can you show me?"

I already have. Back in Universe One. "Sure," I say, my cheeks glowing. "I'd love to."

Oh, he is so George. My George, in dozens of ways. Every way, as far as I can tell.

So why is George so much the same here, and why am I so different? Maybe it's because his forks in the road have been subtle. Little jogs instead of life-altering detours, like losing a parent. If Mom had survived, I could be president of the French Club. Maybe I'd even—against all odds—like the color pink, just because she did, or because she made me a pink dress when I was five that I loved, or because Santa brought me a giant pink teddy bear when I was six. Things that never happened, but could have. I can't deny the possibility that I'd be a very different person if I could subtract tragedy from the equation.

I study George some more, trying to find some hint of difference. The only thing I can say is that I'm pretty sure he never wore tank tops in Universe One.

He suddenly looks up from his menu and catches me blatantly staring, mostly at his biceps, so I blurt, "Rice noodles!"

He grins. "How about I order a few things and we'll just split?"

I clear my throat and try to recover. "What I meant to say was 'the rice noodles stuffed with shrimp sound exquisite.'"

"You're funny, girl-I-hardly-know-from-French-class."

I shrug innocently and look around the restaurant at the paper dragons hanging from the ceiling, the jade pots in the windows, the Chinese characters painted onto the walls. Near the door is a crate of toys for people getting takeout, to keep their kids occupied while they wait for their food.

"LEGOs," I say, pointing to the box. "Loved those when I was little."

"Yeah, the way you can take the same bunch of pieces and make totally different things with them."

"Exactly," I say, thinking of parallel universes. "Identical building blocks, varied configurations."

"I had this pirate set, and my sister kept making puppies out of the black and white blocks. Totally drove me crazy."

I groan. "Oh boy. That reminds me of a childhood incident."

"Childhood incident," George repeats warily. "Do I want to hear this?"

"Scarred for life," I say, nodding solemnly. This is a story I've never told my George, back in Universe One, so now this George will know something personal about me that my George doesn't. Another deviance between universes. "A babysitter ruined my LEGO space shuttle."

He gasps in mock horror. "No!"

"I had this perfect—and I mean flawless—replica of *Discovery*."

George gives me a sarcastic yeah-right look.

"It was! Down to the rocket boosters. So I went to bed, and when I got up the next morning, she'd made it into a house."

"A house?" George laughs. "That sucks. Have you made it through therapy?"

"The boosters were now a chimney."

He leans across the table. "Why did you kiss me?"

"I—" My cheeks flush. I look out the window, and on the other side of the street I can see the library. I'm reminded of the Xeroxed address I have in my pocket, my mother's address. "I've been wanting to, for a long time."

"I don't get it," he says.

"I know you don't. I'm some girl from French class who whacks off her hair, and gets a tattoo, and starts kissing guys on park benches."

"Guys? Plural?"

"No! You know what I mean."

"I don't."

"It's like the LEGOs," I say, looking into his aquamarine eyes. "I took that stupid house and tried to rebuild my space shuttle, but I couldn't do it. No matter how hard I tried, I couldn't get it back to the way it was supposed to go. I wanted it to be perfect again, but I couldn't make the pieces fit together right. It was so frustrating."

Before George can ask another question, our waitress is back with our tea. "Are you ready to order lunch?" She sets a bowl of shrimp chips on the table.

"Number five and seven," George says. "And the pork bun appetizer."

We hand her our menus, and she hurries to another table, scribbling on her notepad as she goes. George looks after her, then back to me. "I like you," he says.

"I like you too."

He snaps his wooden chopsticks apart and arranges them in a V-shape. "Mount Diablo, you say."

"Yes. That's your mountain."

We spend the rest of lunch talking about his sketch, and I give him some details to fill in about the plants that only grow in the Mount Diablo area: fairy lanterns, manzanita, chaparral bellflower, bird's beak, and Mount Diablo sunflower.

When our waitress places the bill on the table, I sigh. "I should get going."

"See you in school tomorrow," George says.

"Right," I say, but I know we won't. Maybe he'll see Other Ruby in school tomorrow. Once I leave, maybe she'll be back. I've got six more universes to click through. If I'm back in my own bed, in Universe One, before nightfall, maybe all will be set to right. No harm done. No one will be permanently displaced from where they belong.

So I need to keep moving, regardless of how tempting it might be to stay here. Besides, I realize now that the "real" George back in Universe One can be mine. All I have to do is make a move like I did here. I mean, if I can spontaneously kiss him on a park bench in a parallel universe, I can do the same in my own universe, where we already have a spark. It's not too late. We're not too far apart.

I replay what Chef Dad said to me yesterday: *Call it what you like. Fate, destiny, effort, coincidence. True friendship defies distance.*

Then I remember telling Dad he could use that as an ad headline. For an airline.

The plan forms itself instantaneously in my mind: I'll get a part-time job, working after school and on the weekends. It won't take long to save enough money for an airline ticket back to California. I can tell Dad I'm going to tour Stanford, which I want to do anyway. I'll make a trip every six months until we graduate, until we can make plans to live in the same city.

George pushes the restaurant's front door open for me, and I brush past him to walk outside. We barely touch. My shoulder connects with his wrist, but it feels electric again. Suddenly, he grabs my hand and pulls me toward him for another kiss. His lips are soft and taste faintly of soy sauce. His tongue brushes across mine, and I'm light-headed, delirious.

I want to remember how this feels.

"Bye," he says, ruffling the hair on the back of my neck.

"Until we meet again," I say, walking away, trying not to limp. My leg is suddenly throbbing mercilessly. I wish I hadn't spent my only useful money on coffee and a mini-scone when what I need is extra-strength ibuprofen and fresh bandages.

"*Au revoir!*" George yells.

I look over my shoulder and wave. I hate saying good-bye to him—again—but this time feels much better than last week's farewell in Walnut Creek. I'm beginning to understand the expression "head over heels," because after kissing George I feel like I'm in zero gravity. Like I'm upside down, floating.

I'm trying to focus enough to cross the street without getting flattened by a truck, when a familiar—and frantic—voice jolts me from behind.

"Ruby!" Before I can react, Patrick has my forearm in a viselike grip.

"Oh, it's you." Not on my agenda.

"Where the hell have you been?"

"Would you let go of my arm? You're kinda hurting me." I try to get around him, but he blocks my way, left then right.

"One minute you're behind me on your bike, the next your bike is lying on its side." Patrick's voice escalates. "You're no longer on it. You're nowhere to be found."

People are stopped on the street, watching us. Patrick's on a roll. "Vanished! Gone!"

I turn around and head back the way I came, toward the downtown shopping district. He follows, screaming, "What's that on the back of your neck?"

Oh boy. Here we go again. "I got a tattoo."

"You did what?" His voice is straining with worry. He puts his hands on my shoulders, forcing me to stop. His breath is fast on my neck as he looks at the tattoo. "What does it mean, and what did you do to your hair?" he demands. "Is that where you've been?"

"Yep, that's what I've been doing these past few hours. I cut my hair and got inked."

"Oh my God." The veins in his neck are popping. I pull away and hurry on, thinking about the Ruby who normally resides here. She disappeared. She was riding her bike one minute and was gone the next. What happened to her? Where did she go? I'm guessing the second I set foot in this universe, she was displaced. I shudder, hoping she's okay. I'm definitely causing ripples, distortions in space-time.

Patrick's suddenly in front of me, walking backward.

"Hey, so what time would you say your Ruby—I mean, what time did I disappear?" I ask, trying to remember when I left Chef Dad's house and entered this universe. "Around ten a.m.?"

He ignores my question. He's got too many of his own. "Where did you get these clothes?" He points to my pant leg. "Is that blood? Are you bleeding?"

I look at the stain on my jeans. A trickle of red has made its way onto my white shoelaces. "It's nothing."

Patrick stops me by the shoulders again. Smoke practically comes out of his ears. He's beyond furious. "Where are you going?"

"None of your business." I adjust my backpack. "I've got data to gather, people to see, things to set straight. Now move."

"No." He forces me to face him. That slightly pointed nose, that dimple in his chin. So much like Dad. Patrick points to the Jeep parked across the street. "Get your ass in the car."

"Why should I?"

"Because I'm your big brother, and I'm in charge, and you've been missing for hours." He's trembling. Tears are welling up in his eyes. "Because the divorce is making us both crazy, and it's my job to take care of you, to get us through all this."

"Oh," I say. "Okay." I feel the urge to wipe the tears from his eyelashes, but he brushes them away first. I guess I shouldn't be so hard on Patrick, considering how things look to him. I'd be pulling my hair out with worry too. "I'm sorry about the way she . . . the way I disappeared on you." I'm just not used to this kind of intense attention. I mean, it's tough getting Dad to detach himself from his computer for ten minutes, let alone ask me how I'm doing.

For a moment Patrick looks exhausted and defeated, but he suddenly gathers his strength and is mad again. "Ass. In. Car."

There's no point in arguing. If I try to run, he'll easily catch up;

I've got a leg injury and a ten-pound backpack slowing me down. If I walk, he'll just continue to follow me like an annoying insect, like a moon in orbit, bound to me.

Besides, maybe I can get him to drive past Mom's place, just so I can see where it is. Just to look. And then it's urgent for me to get home.

"Fine," I say. We cross the street. I toss my backpack in the Jeep's backseat and strap myself in. "Take me to Mom's. Or take me near Mom's. Please."

"We're going to the ER," Patrick says, shifting into drive.

"For what?"

"For what? You're bleeding. You obviously fell off your bike and you probably hit your head. That's why you're acting insane! You have a concussion. Your brain could be swollen. You need an MRI." Patrick stops at a red light and presses his fingers to his temples. "My head is killing me. I need some Tylenol."

"Maybe you're the one with the swollen brain," I say, staring out the window, watching the town go by. Watching the world move. Thinking that the Earth is rotating and orbiting the sun, and the universe is expanding. The universe is expanding 74.2 kilometers per second per megaparsec. Just because we can't feel it doesn't mean it's not happening.

"Doubtful," Patrick says.

"But anything's possible," I say. "You could have encephalitis."

Patrick lets out a colossal sigh. "You're the one who's acting weird. Not me. I'm just stressed."

Remind me—why did I get in the car with this guy? If I'd only stayed in the library another half hour, Patrick probably wouldn't have found me. If I'd skipped Sweet Treats, he'd have missed me, or if I'd had one more cup of tea with George. But then again, I could get something worthwhile out of this ER detour. It wouldn't hurt to have a medical professional take a look at my leg. At this point, I know I need something at the prescription level.

"So what do you think of Mom's new apartment?" I ask. "Her street looks a lot like this one, right?"

Patrick gives me a look.

I slide down in my seat. "Never mind."

"Kandy's been shoplifting again," Patrick says, gripping the steering wheel. "I searched the house for you, and I found a bag of new clothes and makeup. So much for her medication working. Between the two of you I'm going to have a nervous breakdown."

A bag of stolen makeup. I think of that bag of lipstick and eye shadow I found in my room, and suddenly I know that Kandy was busted for shoplifting. Question number twenty-one: Have you ever been convicted of, or pled guilty to, a crime other than a traffic offense? That's why she marked "yes" on her application to design school.

"The clothes weren't cheap, either," Patrick says. "I don't know how she managed to get them through the detectors."

Deviant and clever. That's a dangerous combo. That's the stuff of sociopaths: high IQ, criminal tendencies.

Finally, we turn into the hospital parking lot. Patrick parks and then hurries around the Jeep to my side and opens the door for me.

"How chivalrous," I say.

"I'm not being polite," he says, grabbing my wrist. "I'm making sure you don't disappear again. Come on."

He practically yanks me across the parking lot and through an entrance labeled EMERGENCY ROOM. It's quiet, other than a young mother with a baby pressed to her breast.

At the front desk, a woman in scrubs eats the last of a doughnut. "Sign in." She taps a fingernail to a sheet of pink paper on a clipboard. Powdered sugar cascades across the sheet. "I'll need your driver's license and insurance card."

I wipe the paper clean and sign *Ruby Wright*. All I have is a student ID with my old California address, which is tucked into the pocket of a wallet I took from Universe Three. So it's not even my ID, technically. And does Walnut Creek exist here, in this universe? Does it have a different name? Maybe the western edge of the state has cracked off and fallen into the Pacific. In another universe, there could have been a massive earthquake.

Patrick presses his cell phone to his ear. "Come on, Mom," he breathes. "Pick up." He shakes his head and tucks the phone in his back pocket.

"Look," he says to the woman. "Let me cut to the chase. We're both minors. She's fifteen and I'm seventeen. Our dad's on his honeymoon and our mom's phone is probably buried at the bottom of her purse. Can someone help us?"

The woman sweeps her long hair over her shoulder, revealing a name tag. Amanda. She looks unfazed. "No one gets turned away," she says, taking the pink sheet of paper away and replacing it with a blue one. "We prefer to get parental consent before we administer treatment. Fill in your address, your parents' addresses and phone numbers, your parents' employers, insurance carriers, if you know them. Sign at the bottom. It's slow at the moment. It'll only be a minute before Maria calls you back."

I take the clipboard and sit down. Patrick sits next to me. I blink at the questions I can't answer. This is what it must feel like to take a test you haven't studied for. Not sure of my address here in Ó Direáin, no idea where either parent works, couldn't even tell you the area code or zip code.

I hand the clipboard to Patrick. "You're right. I don't feel so hot. Could you fill this out for me and I'll just sign it?" I put the back of my hand to my forehead.

Patrick gives me a look. Worried? Annoyed? "Sure," he says.

I sneak sideways glances as he pens in the information. Patrick writes *548 Corrán Tuathail Avenue* as the home address, and journalist as Dad's profession. He works for the *Ó Direáin Chronicle*. Mom is a high school math teacher. I'm painfully reminded of all the times I've written *deceased* next to *mother's name*.

"Ruby Wright," a woman in scrubs calls into the waiting room. She's propping open the door to the emergency patient rooms.

"Me," I say, standing up. Patrick jumps to his feet like he's springloaded.

"Right this way." We follow Maria into room four. She motions to a stretcher. "Have a seat." She takes my blood pressure, pulse, listens to my heart, and sticks a thermometer in my ear. Patrick keeps sitting down, then standing up. "Any allergies or preexisting medical conditions?" Maria asks.

I shake my head.

"Are you currently on any medications?"

"No."

Maria keys my information into a computer. "And what are your concerns today?"

"She might have a head injury," Patrick says.

I roll my eyes. "I have a nasty gash on my right leg. That's all."

"Blood loss," Patrick says with this eureka! look on his face. "Maybe that's why she's acting strange."

"Are you up to date on all your immunizations, including tetanus?" Maria asks.

"Yes," I say. "I think so."

Maria nods and gives me a warm smile. "Doctor Leonard will be with you shortly." She gently closes the door behind her.

A wall clock ticks audibly as I sit in silence. I watch the second hand sweep. After five long minutes of Patrick pacing and peppering me with questions I can't answer, there's a knock, then the door opens.

"I'm Doctor Leonard." He extends a hand. His ash-white beard hides a young face underneath.

"Ruby Wright," I say.

"I'm her brother, Patrick." He grabs the doctor's hand and shakes it vigorously. "She's not doing well," Patrick says, pointing at me. "Head injury, amnesia, something."

Dr. Leonard pries himself from Patrick's grip and reads the information on the computer screen. "Let's take a look at the laceration on your leg, okay, Ruby?"

"She's just not herself. She's acting really weird." Patrick's talking a mile a minute. "First off, she disappeared. Poof." He snaps his fingers. "Gone. I was about to call the police, but then I found her walking around downtown. I hardly recognized her in those glasses." He waves his hand toward my face. "She doesn't need glasses! She's had LASIK surgery. She's not dressing like she normally does, and she whacked off her hair."

When Patrick finally comes up for air he must sense that he's operating in hysterical rapid-fire mode. He visibly regroups, straightening his posture and making eye contact with Dr. Leonard. He even drops his voice to a deep, authoritative tone. "Look, Doctor Leonard. The thing is, our parents don't exactly have their heads in the game these days. I'm the one in charge."

The doctor gives Patrick a curt nod, then looks at me with concern. "What did you do to your leg?"

I roll up my jeans to my knee and peel the bandages off. "Ran into a coffee table."

"How long ago?" Dr. Leonard asks.

"Yesterday," I say.

The door opens a crack, and Amanda peeks in. "Sorry to interrupt. I spoke with Sally Wright, Ruby's mother, and she gave verbal consent over the phone." She looks at Patrick and me. "Your mom was shopping in Cleveland. She's on her way." Amanda retreats and the door clicks shut.

"You should have come in sooner," Dr. Leonard says to me. He snaps on rubber gloves and pinches the wound together. "Sorry. I know that hurts. It's too late to stitch it. It will heal by secondary intention, which means you'll have a nice scar. You can take Motrin for pain."

"Could I get something a little stronger?" I ask. "It really jabs at me. I'd like to be able to sleep."

"Is that why she's been acting weird?" Patrick asks. "Pain? Not enough sleep?"

"The pain is likely coming from an underlying bone bruise. It's not uncommon. Unfortunately there's nothing we can do for it, other than give it time to heal. I'll write you a prescription for pain medicine."

"Doesn't she need an antibiotic?" Patrick asks, sounding somewhat panicked. "That's got to be infected. Look at it!"

Dr. Leonard checks the computer. "You're not running a fever," he says, but then he raises his eyebrows at me. "However, Ruby, if you see redness around the cut, pus coming from the wound, or a red streak up your leg, you must return for reevaluation. Understand?"

"Yes," Patrick answers for me.

"Anything else going on, Ruby?" the doctor asks.

"Nothing," I say, looking directly at Patrick. "I didn't fall off a bike and hit my head."

"Anything at home?"

"Things are a little complicated," I admit.

"A little?" Patrick laughs. "Divorce, remarriage within weeks, a stepsister who's been in jail, and our stepmom painting all day long . . . these dark globby things called *Beneath* and *The Obsolete Desire*."

"Bad titles," I agree.

"A lot of stress," Dr. Leonard says. He peels his gloves off and runs his fingers through his beard. "Have you had any headaches, dizziness, blurred vision, or slurred speech?"

"No."

Patrick slaps his hands together. "I know! Why didn't I think of this sooner? It's the tattoo she just got. Maybe the needles were dirty."

I turn my head so Dr. Leonard can look at the Einstein tensor. "What does it mean?" he asks.

"It's one of Einstein's general relativity equations. It has to do with space-time, which has been on my mind a lot lately. More than when I got the tattoo, actually."

Dr. Leonard looks interested, so I continue. "Did you know that two uncharged parallel plates, metal ones, put really close together, create negative energy? Negative energy is what you need to make a wormhole."

"What?" Patrick slumps back into his chair, covering his eyes, as if I've just dropped my drawers and totally embarrassed him.

"It's called the Casimir effect," I say. "I'm not making this stuff up!"

Dr. Leonard runs a finger over the nape of my neck. "It's not a new tattoo."

"Not new?" Patrick leaps up and cranes to see. "Ruby! You've been hiding that under your hair? For how long?"

Dr. Leonard holds his hands out, like he's trying to push some space between himself and Patrick. "Ruby," he says. "Is it possible you need someone to talk to? A family counselor, perhaps."

"Not at all," I say. What I need is someone to translate the inscriptions carved into the tree. I need to get back to the tree, I need to get home, I need to figure out string theory.

Dr. Leonard hands me a business card. "It's up to you. Linda Bell is excellent. I highly recommend her."

The business card is purple and in the shape of a bell, or maybe it's supposed to be a hat.

"I'll call her first thing tomorrow," Patrick says, snatching the card out of my hand. God, his overly worried voice is so like Dad's. It's irritating and confusing to hear it coming out of Patrick's mouth. I still can't fathom that I have a big brother.

"We have some work to do here," Dr. Leonard says to me. "We need to irrigate this wound, get it thoroughly cleaned out, and dress it." He turns to Patrick. "You can go back to the waiting room."

Patrick nods. "Thank you, Doctor." He has his hand on the door, then pauses. He pulls his vibrating cell phone from his pocket. "Text message from Mom. Stuck in construction. Be there asap."

I nod, and even though they say I don't have a fever, I'm burning hot. Burning with an anticipation so intense it hurts. This cannot be happening, but it is.

My not-dead mother is on her way.

chapter eight

Patrick and I sit on a bench outside the ER entrance. I chug a bottle of water that Patrick bought for me from a vending machine. Turns out the quarters also have the face of Henry Lee III on them.

I start reciting the periodic table in my head. It's the only thing I can think of to keep my mind occupied. Hydrogen, helium, lithium.

Patrick checks his watch and scans the parking lot. "Mom should be here any minute." He's fielded at least three calls from her so far, and now his cell phone rings again. I catch a few words here and there: head injury, gash on leg, just not right, and really worried.

Every time Patrick thrusts the phone to my ear and tells me to say something to Mom, I turn away. "I can't," I choke out.

Have I ever felt this particular emotion before? Amped up to the point of short-circuiting? No, not the time I gave a speech to a thousand people at a science fair, and not when I first pressed my eye to a high-powered telescope and saw Jupiter's atmosphere. But maybe when I was ten and climbed too high, into the weak upper branches of a tree. Because once again it feels like I'm teetering on something spindly that can't support my weight.

"I'm driving Dad's Jeep home, and you're going with Mom back to her apartment for the night," Patrick says.

Mom. Ghost Mom. Resurrected Mom. Alive-and-Breathing Mom is coming to pick me up. How can it be? How can this be true?

I remind myself that sometimes complicated phenomena unfold backward. We discover a truth in nature, in the universe, and then we figure out the science and the math much, much later. Or a seemingly zany theory comes first, and then we find data to prove that it's possible. Like when Hugh Everett III, back in the fifties, wrote about his many-worlds interpretation. He wasn't nuts. He was a PhD candidate at Princeton. He was brilliant and ahead of his time.

Science can explain all of this. Somehow.

Mom is coming. To pick you up. She's not dead.

"Stop that," Patrick says.

"What?"

"You just said oxygen, fluorine, neon. You're making me nervous."

"I have the feeling you were born nervous," I say.

You were born.

Born.

The words resonate through my brain, my chest, my gut. "You're my big brother."

Why didn't I think of this earlier? Why didn't I make the connection?

A few years ago—and only once—Dad had mentioned that there

was a baby before me. But something went wrong during childbirth; he didn't get enough oxygen. Now, in my mind, I see a blue baby, tiny but with Patrick's face, his legs pulled to his chest. Stillborn.

Mom got pregnant with me about a year later. When Dad told me this story, I remember thinking: I wonder what they were going to name him.

I look at Patrick and I feel a rush of warmth. Are you my big brother, who died at birth in Universe One?

"Yes, I'm your big brother." Patrick sits up straight, a proud look on his face. "I take that job seriously."

Suddenly, Patrick isn't a stranger anymore. He's the brother I should have had all along. He would have taught me to throw a ball, make paper airplanes, swim underwater. We would've fought over the TV remote and the phone and who got the bigger bedroom. I reach out and squeeze his hand. He squeezes back. "I'm glad you're here."

"It's like Coach Brown always says. Family above all else. Even football."

Too bad Dad doesn't have a similar motto. Family above work. "I like your priorities."

We sit in silence for a long while. "By the way," Patrick finally says, "I didn't tell Mom about Kandy's shoplifting relapse. So don't bring it up."

"No problem." Kandy is the last thing on my mind. I finish the water and realize how dehydrated—how weak—I am. "Could you get me a Gatorade?"

"What's a Gatorade?" Patrick looks at me, weary.

"You of all people should know. It's a sports drink."

He disappears into the ER lobby again, then returns with an

orange drink called TriAthlete. Within seconds, I've drained half the bottle.

"Patrick?" I need to know. "Was Mom ever in a car accident?"

"Ever? I don't know. When?"

"When I was four, and we still lived in California."

Patrick shakes his head. "Seriously, Ruby. Here we go again. We never lived in California. Mom and Dad moved to Ó Direáin before either of us was born."

"I see," I say quietly.

I thought it might be something as simple as Mom forgetting her coffee mug. She went back into the kitchen, and in that three minutes, she changed her fate. Or maybe she decided to stop at the ATM, or fill up the gas tank, or she just kept getting every light red. Anything that would delay her a few crucial minutes. Anything that would make her late for her appointed spot on the freeway.

So that explains it. We weren't living in California eleven years ago, so Mom wasn't on I-580 two cars behind the semi that jackknifed and caused a fifteen-car demolition derby. She was living in Ó Direáin, unaware of her parallel life coming to an abrupt end, unaware of the windshield wiper that sliced her neck and made her vanish from at least one universe.

And now, within minutes, I'll have to process seeing Mom. The urge to get up and run—just run—wells up inside me.

Pull it together, Ruby.

"Rhodium, palladium, silver, cadmium."

"What are you talking about?" Patrick asks, wide-eyed and cringing. Yeah, he thinks I'm off my rocker. At this point there's nothing I can do to make him think otherwise.

"Trying to distract myself."

He exhales, shakes his head. "The whole world is falling apart."

"True. And I need to get my backpack out of the Jeep."

He stands up and pulls the keys from his pocket. "I'll get it for you."

I watch Patrick cross the parking lot, the way he leans into his stride, just like Dad.

And then a car pulls into the parking lot—a red Honda—and I know, just know, it's Mom.

I press my palms against my temples, trying to counter the feeling that my skull is too small, that my nerves are trying to escape my skin. I'm forced to put my head between my legs so I don't pass out. N_2 and O_2 in, carbon dioxide out.

I can hear her footsteps, feel the slight vibration of the earth as she nears. I can sense that she's standing in front of me, blocking the sun.

"Sweetheart?" Mom's voice is gentle and real. It consists of actual sound waves, as opposed to the imagined voice I've only heard inside my head these past eleven years. She puts her hand on my back. "Are you okay?"

"Mom," I whisper, still unable to look up.

How can it be? How can this be true? I slide to the ground, onto my knees. I clutch her legs, the rough seam of her jeans against my cheek.

"Ruby. Oh."

Mom sinks to the ground next to me. She takes my face in her hands. "Look at me."

I shake my head. "I can't."

"Sweetheart. Look at me. Open your eyes."

chapter nine

"I'm just tired," I say, my ears ringing. I wince at a surge of pain that yanks at the back of my eyeballs. "And hungry."

Lunch with George was hours ago. And those pancakes with lingonberry preserves—breakfast in Universe Three with Chef Dad—was eons ago, dreamlike.

"A hot shower, that's all I need."

Mom cradles me. "Come on. Get up." I smell her perfume or shampoo—grape scented, familiar.

"You smell—" I search for the word. "You smell right," I say.

Patrick sprints across the parking lot. "Ruby? Mom, is she okay? Should we go back into the ER?"

"No!" I say. "I'm fine."

Mom helps me to my feet. I brush the dirt off my jeans, and my eyes meet Mom's.

Blue with flecks of amber, just like my own. She's thirty-nine years old, hair short and dyed mahogany, clumpy mascara, high cheekbones, a small chip in her front tooth. I can't bear it; I look up at the sky, at the billowing dark clouds, masses of frozen water vapor drifting in the atmosphere. One is the shape of a boat, another a barking dog.

Mom gives me a gentle shake. "Let's go, sweetheart."

"Oh, but Mom," I say again, trembling. I lay my head on her shoulder.

Patrick reaches out and pats my back. "Bye, sis. I'll call the apartment later tonight."

"Drive safely, Patrick," Mom says, taking my backpack from him.

"Yep," Patrick says. "I'm going straight home."

Mom puts her arm around my waist and leads me across the parking lot. Her car, like her grape shampoo, seems right too. A paradoxical feeling tears at me—comfortable and uneasy. I could slide into this life, this universe. I could stay here. Forever.

The drive is short, and we don't say much. My skin tingles with excitement, disbelief. I keep looking over at Mom, trying to make sense of her, the fact that she is alive. I study her hands, wrapped around the steering wheel. Her small wrist bones; her thin metacarpal bones articulating as she strums her fingers; her purple veins returning blood to her heart. She's alive.

When we stop at a red light, she reaches over and strokes my head. "Was the pixie cut Jack's idea?"

"Yep," I say, no clue who Jack is. Maybe he's Ruby's hairstylist here.

She lets her hand drift to the nape of my neck. "And what's this all about?"

"It's just a temporary tattoo," I say, tired of explaining it. "I wanted pink roses, but this was what came out of the vending machine."

She looks at me sideways, but is more interested in my injury. She wants to know why I couldn't get stitches, if it hurt when the doctor cleaned it, and how long it will take for the wound to heal. I press my head against the window and watch the clouds, some of them turning gray. Dim lightning runs horizontal veins through the bottom of the darker clouds.

Mom turns into the Ó Direáin Pharmacy lot and parks under a sign that advertises a sale on toilet paper. I hand her my prescription slip. "Back in two minutes," she says. Her purse bumps against her hip as she hurries, and the moment she disappears behind the automatic doors, a gripping sense of loss and panic sets in. I want her back in my sight. I want to watch her chest rise and fall as she breathes. Above the pharmacy's signage hangs a large clock. I watch the second hand sweep around once, twice, five times, ten.

She finally reemerges from the doorway, and I let out a long breath. "That was more than two minutes," I say, trying not to sound overly relieved.

Mom slides back into the driver's seat. "It'll be an hour for the medication," she says. "They're understaffed." She puts the Honda in drive, clicks on the radio.

"All eighties, all the time," the DJ says in a voice that's impossibly deep.

Mom pats her hand on her thigh in time to the music, cranes her neck into the words. "I'm for you," she sings. "And you're for me. Every road sign points your way, every guiding star tells me I should stay."

She knows all the words, including the backup vocals. I turn up the volume to egg her on, and she goes for it. "Just know I'm here for you the rest of your life! I'm talking 'bout true love, yeah baby, you know!"

She's lit up like a kid who's tasted cotton candy for the first time. Then she suddenly turns the radio off and looks at me apologetically. "All that noise can't be good for you."

"It was worth it," I say.

"Really?" She runs her tongue along her chipped tooth, narrows her eyes like she's trying to bring my sincerity into focus. "You usually make an assortment of faces when I sing."

"You ooze cheese," I admit, "but it's quality. Like brie."

"Wow. I've finally been promoted from Cheez Whiz." We laugh as she cuts the engine outside a three-story, redbrick building. Its tall windows are framed in white wooden trim. Maybe it was formerly a private home, Victorian era, back in the days when you'd lead your horse to the stables behind the main house, rather than park your car.

"Sorry about the stairs," Mom says. She's on the second floor, no elevator. "Can you make it up?"

"I'm okay, but how about you?"

Mom struggles with my hefty backpack, dragging it up the last two steps. "What do you have in here?"

"Books. I can carry it now. You get the door."

Mom slides the key into the lock and turns the knob. "Home sweet home."

Mom's apartment is tiny and—well—cute. Hardwood floors, denim couch, and some of the Americana art that's hanging back at the squat brick house on Corrán Tuathail Avenue. A large wooden cow, painted in red, white, and blue stripes, with white stars on its head, hangs over the TV.

"Take your shoes off, and relax on the couch." Mom tosses me a blanket. "I'll brew up some hot chocolate with marshmallows."

"Okay." I shouldn't even be here! I promised myself ten minutes of looking, and not a second more. Watching from a safe distance. I never intended to be curled up on Mom's couch with a steamy drink. But now that I'm with her, the idea of leaving fills me with desperation.

Mom opens the refrigerator door, making bottles clink together. "I'll call Frankie's for delivery." She pauses, then laughs. "Hot chocolate and pineapple-bacon pizza. That sounds horrible."

"A little, yeah."

"I've got lemonade, milk. I can make coffee instead."

"Soda?"

"Perfect," Mom says. "You could probably use a good dose of sugar."

I take a deep breath and lean back against an overstuffed couch pillow. My body is aching for rest, my brain needs REM sleep.

Mom dials the pizza place. She orders "the Hawaiian," a Caesar salad, and Italian wedding soup. Too much for two people, but I guess that's what moms do—try to make everything better with food. George's mom, without fail, made brownies whenever there was a crisis. Sometimes he faked some drama just to get the brownies.

"Now," Mom says, settling into the recliner. "We can talk."

"Do I have to?" I'm happy to just quietly absorb. There's so much. I'd like to silently look at photos from the past eleven years and hear stories about Mom's life. I don't want to talk. I don't want to say the wrong thing, dodge questions, or try to explain why I'm acting weird. "You talk, and I'll listen," I say.

"Patrick filled me in," Mom says, searching my face. "I'm worried about you."

I sigh, close my eyes, burrow under the blanket.

"Ruby, you look so . . . different," she says. "Edgy. I feel like you're wearing a Halloween costume. It's a little bizarre."

"Speaking of bizarre, did you know there were once eight-foot scorpions?"

Mom studies me for a long, silent moment. "And?" She raises her eyebrows, begging for me to make my point.

"They lived four hundred million years ago, in swamps. But think about how unbelievable. I mean, can you imagine an eight-foot scorpion? It would be longer than this couch. The point is, the unbelievable is true."

"Like the divorce," Mom says.

"Like a lot of things," I say, twirling the fringe of the blanket around my fingers. "More things than you know."

"That's what this is all about, I know. I'm not stupid. I hate to use a cliché, but this sudden change in your appearance . . . it's obvious you're acting out. You're reacting to a change in circumstances."

"Okay."

"I'm not going to get angry about it. Your hair will grow back. What we need to talk about is your happiness, and how we're going to get that back." Mom turns away, striking the same pose as she did in the old snapshot. Looking wistful. She presses the tip of her thumb against her chipped tooth, biting down on her fingernail, maybe a hangnail. Finally she says, "Sweetheart, you can change your mind. You don't have to live with Dad. He'll understand. You've been through a lot of changes. It's no wonder you wanted to change yourself. I understand."

"Mom," I say, relishing the word "Mom." I don't want to talk, but I could say "Mom" a thousand times. "I can't explain myself. I just can't. All I can say is, I'm happy to be here with you, now, in this moment."

Mom leans forward. "Is there a boyfriend I need to know about? Or is there a girlfriend? Ruby, you know I'd understand, whatever it is. Drugs? Are you smoking that stuff, what's it called? Crust?"

"For real, Mom? Come on."

"We need to get our Ruby back, don't we?" Mom asks. "You're drifting out to sea."

I look into Mom's eyes and see the confusion, the concern. I smile at her weakly. "I admit I'm not the same Ruby you're used to seeing."

"You know I would go to the ends of the earth for you."

"Ditto," I say.

She tries to subdue a yawn. "I don't know where it went wrong. My life, my marriage. I try to figure out the turning point. Maybe our ten-year anniversary. Terrible meal, and we fought over where to park the car."

"Turning point?"

"You know—the point of no return. An event that thrust us over the edge, toward divorce."

"So if you could change that one event, you'd be living in a different world right now?"

"Of course." Mom leans over, pulls her socks off, then starts plucking at an imaginary guitar. "Can't you rewind our days?" she sings, closing her eyes and tilting her head toward the ceiling. "Don't say there's not a way." She motions for me to join in.

I shrug. No clue what the lyrics are.

"Top of the charts for sixteen consecutive weeks in the year 1987?" she prompts. "Have I taught you nothing?"

"I wasn't even born yet."

"No excuse!" She throws her hands up in mock disgust. "I need my slippers. Are you cold?"

She gets up and adjusts the thermostat, then disappears into the bedroom.

"The butterfly effect," I mumble to myself. Guess it's time to revisit my logic; a ripple effect might actually be a good thing. If the flapping of a butterfly's wings can alter the path of a tornado, then a happy event could alter the path of a marriage. Little alterations, big repercussions.

I'm stung with a burrowing, twisting thought. If there was a turning point in this universe, maybe there wasn't in another. Maybe in, say Universe Five or Seven, Mom and Dad are still happily married. They spent their tenth anniversary on a beach in Mexico, renewing their vows. Willow and Kandy never entered the picture.

Suddenly another path reveals itself. What if I don't hurry back to Universe One as planned? What if I explore each universe? What if there's a perfect world out there, where Mom and Dad are blissfully together and Patrick is my brother? And, of course, George would be there too. My heart swells at the possibility.

The doorbell rings and Mom emerges from the bedroom. She puts an eye to the peephole. "Pizza," she announces.

She pays the delivery guy and carries a plastic bag and a large pizza box into the kitchen. I get up and follow, helping her clear the table. "What's this?" I ask, glancing at the papers as I set them on the counter.

Mom grabs two plates from a cabinet. "Lesson plans for this week," she says.

"Fractal geometry?"

"Just the basic concepts, like the Mandelbrot set, making a computer-generated image, talking about some practical applications. Do you think you can handle it?"

"Me?"

"Yes, you. My star student." Mom hands me two forks, spoons, and napkins. "I know you prefer to bury your head in French, but like it or not, deep down you're a math nerd, like me. I thought we'd start with some basic definitions—hyperbolic components, the main cardioid and period bulbs, self-similarity."

Mom is my math teacher? I grin at her, thrilled.

"I wonder if fractal geometry and string theory are connected," I say, excitedly tripping over my words. "You know, space appears to be smooth, but maybe with enormous magnification it's rough—it's fractal. Maybe that accounts for rifts in space-time."

Mom closes the refrigerator door and sets the hot pepper flakes on the table. Then she gives me this look. This amazed, shocked, perplexed look.

"What?" I ask, feeling my face turn hot.

"I've never heard you talk like that, Ruby. How do you already know about fractals? How do you know about string theory?"

Idiot! The Ruby who normally resides here wouldn't be talking about rifts in space-time! "I've been reading a little," I say weakly. I've got to remember to fly under the radar. I already look like an impostor, and now I'm acting like one too.

Mom doesn't seem convinced. "Reading a little?" She pours two sodas. "Sit down and eat."

"Gladly." I dig into the Caesar salad and serve myself a bowl of the wedding soup. The steam bathes my face, and I breathe in the tangy smell. "You have no idea how good this tastes," I say with my mouth half-full.

I've got to remember to tell George about the shapes that a Mandelbrot set produces. Paisley swirls, antenna spires, lightning fingers. He'll run straight for his sketch pad.

Mom says, "Funny you should mention string theory. I just read an article about it in *Scientific American*. It's fascinating, but the math is so complex. They said that it may be beyond human comprehension."

"Our best mathematicians are stumped." I clear my throat. "I mean, can't anyone figure it out? How hard can it be?" There. That sounded sufficiently ignorant.

Mom slides a huge piece of pizza onto my plate. "It's a wild-goose chase," she says. "People have been researching string theory for decades. Maybe they should admit they're wrong, or that they've reached a dead end. Sometimes you just need to quit and move on." The way she says it, with such a resigned sigh, makes me wonder if she's talking about string theory or something personal. Like maybe her marriage.

She stares at me intently, and I get the feeling she's testing me, baiting me. I can't tell if she's unnerved by my out-of-character behavior, or if she's pleased that I'm talking about math. "Which books have you read?"

"Oh, well. Really, I just saw a show on the Discovery Channel, so that's why it sounds like I know more than I actually do." I shift in my seat and pay extra attention to my food.

"And your tattoo just happened to be the one to drop out of the vending machine?"

"Yeah. I have no idea what it means. Does it have something to do with string theory?" I force a "what are the chances?" laugh to come out of my mouth. "Like you said, I prefer to bury my head in French."

Mom waves a hand dramatically in the air. *"Voici mon secret. Il est très simple: on ne voit bien qu'avec le cœur. L'essentiel est invisible pour les yeux."*

"Huh?" I need a distraction, and as if on cue, I accidentally bump my shin against the metal leg of the kitchen table. A searing pain radiates from the wound and reaches into my stomach and chest, taking my breath away.

Mom jumps to her feet. "Are you okay? Go lie down on the couch. Are you supposed to keep that leg elevated?"

"Painkiller would be good," I say, my face wrenched into a knot. "Can you go pick up my prescription?"

"Sure. Don't worry about the food. I'll put it away when I get back. Did you get enough to eat? Go lie down. You need to rest. Do you want the TV on? Of course not. You need peace and quiet." Mom's eyes are brimming with worry.

"I'm okay, Mom," I say. "Calm down."

Mom waits until I'm situated on the couch again. She drapes the blanket over me and puts her hand to my forehead. "You're warm."

"They checked my temperature at the hospital. It was normal." The surge of pain has subsided, enough for me to unclench my fists.

"Back in a jiffy." Mom swings her purse over her shoulder. She puts the cordless phone on the coffee table within my reach. "In case you need to call my cell."

As Mom steps through the door, I call after her. "Wait!"

She turns, and I take in her mahogany hair, high cheekbones, and the chip in her front tooth. I want to memorize her.

"Be careful driving," I say.

"Oh, sweetheart," Mom says. And then she closes the door.

chapter ten

Mom's apartment is hollow without her. Every sound I make echoes.

Someone—Aristotle? Galileo?—said that nature abhors a vacuum. *Horror vacui:* the fear of empty spaces. Yeah, I abhor Mom's absence. I hate the emptiness. After being with her for just a couple hours, I can see how vacant and silent my life has been for the past eleven years.

In this universe, Ruby has never felt that void, and she's a different person than I am because of it. But now I realize that this Ruby is also experiencing a loss, and she will be changed too. Her parents are divorced. She's suffering in her own way.

What else can I do? Somewhere, in some parallel universe, all could be right—no car accident, no windshield wiper through Mom's throat. Happy birthdays, happy anniversaries. A safe and smooth ride through space-time.

If that universe is out there, I've got to keep moving. I've got to find it. I mean, I'd be an idiot to just jump in and out of the tree until I reach Universe One, when my own personal utopia could be waiting for me.

I lace my sneakers and hobble to the kitchen, my shoes squeaking on the hardwood floor. My Caesar salad sits mostly untouched at the table. I finish it, slurp down the rest of my soup, then nuke my pizza in the microwave. If I take off right now, I'm not sure when my next meal might be. I need to eat while I can, so I'm stuffing myself.

My dish clinks as I rinse it and put it in the dishwasher. I gather my things into my backpack and go into Mom's room to snoop. I take one of her sweaters, pressing it to my nose before stuffing it into my backpack. Her messy dresser is littered with receipts, snapshots of Patrick in a football uniform, an iPod, and some coins and a few dollars. I help myself to the cash. Really, she would want me to have it. Before I stuff the bills into my pocket, I give Abraham Lincoln a nod. It's somehow comforting to see that he's still the face on the fives.

Her nightstand holds a thick brown Bible, a few business cards, and some clothes catalogs. A small electronic device sits inside the drawer, and I realize it's a GPS. An ancient one with hardly any features, but it could come in handy, for sure.

After using the bathroom, I grab a bottled water from the fridge and put my hand on the doorknob—ready to go. Although . . .

It would be nice to have my pain meds first. I look down at my leg and notice that my jeans are tight around my right shin. Swollen.

What's the rush? It's getting dark, my body is craving sleep, and I'm about to lock myself out of Mom's comfortable, warm apartment.

I take my hand off the doorknob and pull the copied map of

Ó Direáin from my backpack. The length of my pinkie finger is about three miles on the scale, which means the high school is about five miles from here. That's a long way. Probably a two-hour walk. I look down at my wounded shin as if it can give me some input. Hey, leg, you wanna walk that far? Nah?

But I know I shouldn't be here. I'm displacing my parallel self somehow, at this very moment. Is she desperately lost in some sort of cosmic limbo land?

Mental confusion plus physical pain plus a very full stomach equals inertia. I look for the phone, as if I can call Dad for advice, to tell him to come get me. Dad. What have I done to him? He must be wondering where I am, where I'm hiding. I rub my fingers across the phone's number pad, knowing what will happen if I dial his cell phone. *This number is not in service. This number does not exist here.*

Does he think I've been kidnapped? Does he think I ran away? The last time I hid from Dad, I was six years old and raging mad because I wanted to draw on my bedroom walls. Millipedes and lizards. Or, better yet, lizards eating millipedes. Dad confiscated the Crayolas, and I made myself disappear. I can still see him, standing below me as I clung to a tree limb, leaning against the rough trunk. "Climb down, you little squirrel," he'd said, shaking a bag of M&M'S, trying to lure me to the ground.

I look around Mom's quiet little apartment. Dad can't find me here. Can he? Is he wishing he could lure me home with chocolate? Has he missed his copywriting deadlines because he's been frantic, searching for me?

I almost laugh out loud. No way. I mean, sure, Chef Dad was

waiting for me in the driveway in Universe Three. He was worried, practically ready to call the police. But he's not my real dad. Real Dad never misses deadlines. Real Dad doesn't notice when I'm gone for hours on end.

But I miss him.

I don't know how to weigh the choices. I don't know how to balance the equation. On one side: Click through the universes—simply turn the wheel, full circle—until I get back home. Back to Willow and Kandy and their decrepit house. Back to smelly Ennis High, Home of the Bears. Back to Dad.

On the other side: Take my time in each universe, looking for the ideal. Mom and Dad could be in love in Universe Five or Seven or Ten. And it's not like I'm ditching Dad. Not at all. Because Dad will be there. He'll just be a better version of Dad, one who isn't glued to a computer screen 24/7. We'll be together. Everything will be okay. I step away from the door, let my backpack slide to the floor, deciding.

Ruby, the perfect universe might be one spin of the wheel away, and you have to find out.

Okay, I'm going, but . . . Universe Five can wait until tomorrow at daybreak. That way I get a little more time with this mom, a good night's sleep, and my medicine. All things I desperately need. It's a good compromise; it's a plan.

A half-open closet to my right reveals a tiny stacked washer-dryer, and a bag with the name RUBY embroidered across it. Mine, but not mine. Ruby's bag is full of clothes—a pink T-shirt, a lime-green polo with purple jeweled buttons, and more sparkle-pocket jeans. At the bottom of the bag are flannel pajamas. They're pink—yippee—but they're clean and soft. I take off my smelly clothes, toss them in the washer with some of Mom's darks, then start the shower. I'm careful not to get my freshly bandaged wound wet, but otherwise scrub myself from top to bottom. Yeah, my leg looks nasty. It's puffy and tender, but I convince myself it'll be better in the morning. I breathe in the steam and the grape-scented shampoo, trying to let my nerves unfurl. The moment I'm toweled off and wearing the pink pj's, the phone rings. The Caller ID says Sally Wright—Mom.

"Hi, Mommy."

"How's the pain, sweetheart?"

"It's throbbing but not terrible. I'm wondering if I chipped a bone."

"I've got your medicine. I'm going as fast as I can, but—oh . . ."

"What, Mom?"

"There's this gorgeous buck standing near the entrance to Dublin Estates. I hope he stays away from the road. Okay, I'll see you in five minutes. Should I stop at the grocery store? I thought I'd make you a big breakfast tomorrow. Can you wait fifteen minutes instead of five? Are you miserable?"

"I can wait fifteen minutes."

"We should take you back to the hospital for X-rays," Mom says.

"I'll be okay tomorrow," I say, dreading the idea of negotiating parallel universes with my leg in a cast.

"If it's a fracture, it's not going to feel better tomorrow."

Mom hangs up, and anger wells up inside me. I could kill Kandy for chasing me into that table. Though I suppose she could kill me for reading her diary. Whatever. A sequence of events, starting long ago, eventually led to my leg connecting violently with a glass-top coffee table. I mean, going way back, Willow could've bought a soft leather ottoman instead of the table. Or she could've arranged the furniture differently.

If it weren't for a million decisions and variables, I wouldn't have fled into the cornfields and discovered the door in the tree. I wouldn't be sitting on Mom's denim couch, waiting for her to come home to me. It's like it was meant to be. Maybe I should be thanking Kandy for chasing me? Yeah, right.

I settle back onto the couch, unzip my backpack and open my notebook. I've gotta force my eyes to stay open, to focus on the words inscribed above the oak tree's door:

Gɾy ᴋʰᴏ iɥe ᴄᴏᴏᴜsχɋ?

And on the surface of the steering disk:

ᴡᴋᴄᴄsᴛᴏ ᴄɥvᴋb ρvᴋʰᴏ 1864 = ᴋᴅɯɥᴄzɾᴏʰsm ᴏvᴏmᴅ-ʰsm ᴄeʰɋᴏ. ᴆʰᴏᴏ ʰᴏᴅᴋsχᴏn zɥɋᴏʰ 87 ɾɥeʰᴄ. ᴄeρρsmsᴏχᴅ ᴄeʰɋᴏ ʰᴏɥmmeʰʰᴏχmᴏ sχmᴋvmevᴋᴛvᴏ.

Complex math equations written in abbreviated, encoded form? Several words end in the letter *o*, and there are two identical words: "cebqo." Before I can make any headway, I hear Mom in the hallway, her key in the lock.

"I'm home," Mom says, opening the door. "Don't get up."

"I won't."

She puts down a grocery bag, then pulls a small orange bottle out of her purse. "You're supposed to take one every four hours, with food."

"I finished my dinner while you were gone," I say. "I'm stuffed."

Mom hands me a sizable pill and a glass of water. "Bottoms up."

I gulp it down, then motion to my notebook. "I've got some home-work, then I'm calling it a night, okay?"

Mom ruffles my hair. "You need your rest. The homework can wait." She peers at my notebook before I can close it. "What was that? Code?"

"Yeah," I say, fumbling for an explanation. "Just messing around. It's for, uh, English class."

"English? I thought it was Mr. McBride who made his classes decode Ó Direáin's journal. Did you already start the local history unit? I thought he saved that for second semester."

Ó Direáin's journal? My mind flashes to his bronze statue in the park, near the fountain. The plaque said he was one of the town's fore-fathers. He was the inventor of the lightbulb.

"We, uh, yes," I stutter. "We started the journal. Already."

"I have to admit," she says, smiling, "I love flipping through it at night, right before I fall asleep. I have this fantasy that my subcon-scious will figure out how to crack those uncrackable codes."

There are codes in Ó Direáin's journal? It can't be a coincidence; Ó Direáin must have had some connection with the portal. He was a scientist! He might have discovered the wormhole and then invented a way to navigate it. Or maybe he created the wormhole himself. I need to get back to the library before I leave this universe, to see if I can get my hands on a copy of that journal.

Mom retreats to the kitchen to put the groceries away. Cabinets open and close. I'm lulled by the sound of water filling the sink, and I start thinking about tomorrow, on the move again. I remember my jeans.

"I washed my clothes, Mom. Can you put them in the dryer?"

"No problem," she says, heading to the laundry closet.

It's such a simple, normal thing—Mom doing my laundry—and I feel an unexpected craving, wanting more of it, the sweetness of routine life.

She holds up my wet jeans and T-shirt before tossing them in the dryer. "Where did you get these, by the way?"

"Target."

She shakes her head. "They look like boys' clothes."

I take my glasses off and rub my eyes. Mom is now a fuzzy shape; she's color and movement in the other room, barely discernible. I think of distant galaxies, hidden worlds, black holes, dark matter. There's so much of the universe we simply can't see.

"You okay?" Mom asks. She's in her pajamas.

"I'm hanging in."

"I'm going to have a talk with your father," she says, sitting on the couch next to me. She pats my knee and looks me in the eye. "We should have talked this through better. What do you want, Ruby? Do you want to live with me?"

"What do I want?" I want a universe with you and Dad, and without Willow and Kandy. I want us to be together again. "You, me, Dad. Together."

Mom gives me a wry smile, her chipped tooth showing. "What about Patrick?"

"He's fine too. I like Patrick."

She laughs. "You and your brother are inseparable. You couldn't live without him."

But I have lived without him. Just as I've lived without you.

Mom starts humming and playing the air drums, apparently once again reminded of an eighties song. "No, you couldn't survive," she sings, poking her finger into the air, punctuating the notes she's trying to hit. "It's my time, I'll be fine. There's a crossroads ahead—"

I hold up my hands, palms forward. "Could we give your inner rock star a breather? What are you trying to say?"

"Look at me, Ruby." She gestures to her face. Her Cherokee cheekbones. "I'm at a crossroads. My marriage is over. Patrick is leaving for college in less than a year, and then you're on his heels. No one needs me." She closes her eyes and shakes her head, as if she's trying to rid herself of a bad dream.

"I do!" I blurt.

"Since when?" She laughs, but it's riddled with hurt. "Not since you were about eleven."

The room suddenly feels colder. "I will always need you," I say, wanting to sound earnest, but it comes out a little angry. How could she think that? Does Other Ruby ignore her? Or take her for granted?

"Sweetheart, I'm not dropping off the face of the earth," she says. "But I've decided to rent an RV next summer and drive out west for a month. I want to see some of the national parks and monuments in Arizona and New Mexico. I want to look for a new place to live."

"You're leaving?"

The word "crossroads" rings on—a choice, a splitting of paths. She's about to make a break for it, from the old road. She's looking for a better version of reality. Just like I am.

"Not for a year or two, but yes. I'm craving a fresh beginning," she says. "I don't think anyone can blame me for that. Besides, what am I going to do after you kids are gone? End up a regular at karaoke night? Because I can honestly see that happening."

I imagine Mom with a microphone in her hand, standing on a beer-sticky stage, with tanked, balding guys leering at her. Ugh. No way. That's not what I want for her.

"But if you and Dad were still in love, you wouldn't be leaving, right?"

"Of course not," Mom says. "Everything would be different."

Exactly.

"That pain pill's kicking in," I say. "I'm fading."

"We'll talk more tomorrow," Mom says. "We'll get this worked out. We'll get the old Ruby back." She cups my chin in her hand. "My happy-go-lucky, pretty, smiling Ruby. You'll be okay."

Happy-go-lucky. I've never thought of myself that way. Is that how people see me? Or is the Ruby who's normally here that much different than I am? Is she pretty and smiling because Mom didn't die when she was four? Or because she has Patrick dutifully looking out for her?

Mom hands me a down-filled pillow and a fluffy comforter.

"Thanks. Good night," I say through a tremendous yawn.

Mom kisses my forehead, and I relish the feel of her skin against mine. "Good night, my little girl." She stands and turns to leave the room.

"Mom? Can you see any stars tonight?"

She walks across the room and parts the curtains. She shakes her head. "Total cloud cover. They're forecasting another storm."

Not a second later, a crisp crack of thunder shakes the dishes in the kitchen cabinets. I suddenly remember something else from Ó Direáin's plaque. He was killed while experimenting with electricity and lightning.

"I hope that doesn't keep you up," Mom says. She pulls the curtains closed and clicks off the lamp. A night-light dimly illuminates the room, making Mom look otherworldly.

"Do you think you could crack that code in my notebook, Mom?"

Mom shrugs. "Probably. Is it a simple cipher? Some of Ó Direáin's codes were much more complex. But don't get any smart ideas, because I'm not doing your homework for you."

What's a simple cipher? "I don't know where to start."

"Mr. McBride probably gave you one of the less impossible passages. So if it's an alphabetic shift, you can crack it by process of elimination. That could take a long time, though. It's a lot easier if you have the key. *D* is for 'decryption.'"

"The key," I say, suddenly feeling unable to focus or hold a thought. Sleep is settling in like a fast and thick fog.

"*Dors bien, ma douce*," she says.

"No more French," I mumble. "I can't understand it."

"Sleep well, my sweet." Mom's lips brush my forehead again.

I close my eyes and imagine a clear, starry night. There's Betelgeuse, Bellatrix, and Rigel: the three brightest stars in the Orion constellation. They ground me, make me feel like there's something reliable and constant in the universe. They're impossible to miss, no telescope required. You just need to stop what you're doing and look up.

chapter eleven

"Ruby, sweetheart. Wake up."

I groan.

"It's after seven," Mom says. "Are you moaning because you're sleepy, or because you're in pain?"

I blink the dryness out of my eyes and look at Mom. Mom! I touch her arm: proof that she's alive, that all of this—the denim couch, the sunlight streaming through the window, the multiverse—is real.

"How's your leg?" She lifts the comforter to look underneath, but Other Ruby's baggy pajama bottoms hide the truth. I pull away before she can get a better look.

"Super." I smile to convince her.

"Here's the plan," she says. "You're coming with me to school, where you'll stay in the nurse's office. I need to give a calculus test first period and attend a staff meeting second period. Then I'll take you to the hospital for an X-ray."

Problem: I already have a plan, and it doesn't involve going to school or the hospital. "Why don't I stay here?"

"I'm not letting you out of my sight." She pats my hand.

"Isn't it Sunday?" I ask. "Why is there school?"

Mom's face turns serious. "What do you mean?"

I've said something stupid. There's something I should know about school and Sundays. "Never mind."

She searches my face, and my stomach sinks. At any moment she's going to realize I'm not the right Ruby. I concoct a chipper grin and change the subject. "Are you making breakfast?" The smell of bacon fills the apartment.

Mom nods. "One or two pieces of rye toast?"

"Three. With lots of butter."

I follow her to the kitchen, limping a little. She flips the bacon over in a skillet on the stove and slides the bread into the toaster.

While Mom's busy cooking, I use the bathroom, clean my glasses, splash cold water on my puffy face, and gargle mouthwash. Other Ruby's pink pajamas go into the dirty laundry basket, triple-antibiotic cream and a fresh bandage go onto my wound. There's something filmy that looks like pus around the raw, red edges. No sign of a scab forming, but maybe it's too soon for that. Does it matter? I mean, taking a week off to stay here and recover is out of the question. I put on my clean clothes and rejoin Mom in the kitchen.

She hands me a glass of orange juice and my prescription medicine. "Down the hatch."

We eat quickly and in silence. I can feel Mom's concern lingering in the air between us. Even though she's not voicing them, I can hear all her questions. She pushes her empty plate away and bites her lower lip, which gives me serious déjá vu. Has she always done that when she's worried? Do I remember that gesture from when I was four years old? Yes. I'm sure of it. Dad rubs his temples, Mom bites her lower lip.

The wall clock—a red rooster with a round belly—squawks, "Cock-a-doodle-doo," letting us know that it's seven thirty.

"We need to get going." Mom clears the table, gathers her briefcase and purse. I push my chair back and set my empty juice glass in the sink. It's perfect, actually. Mom's giving me a ride to school—and essentially the tree—because I only have a short hike once we're on school grounds.

I slip the vial of medicine into my pocket while Mom pauses at a small mirror next to the door. She twists a tube of lipstick and glides the color over her lips. I'm having trouble watching. Her breath fogs the glass. She breathes, she lives. Leaving this version of Mom behind would feel like a colossal mistake if I weren't confident about saying hello again soon in another universe. Where everything will be flaw-less and complete, like a balanced chemistry equation.

"Ruby?" She's waiting for me to snap out of my thoughts. "You ready?"

"Sorry. Let me get my backpack," I say. I'm dreading the idea of lugging it around with me. All those books, my notebook, the code . . .

Suddenly I make a mental connection I should have made last night. But I'd been too exhausted, my mind too cluttered.

Ó Direáin's journal!

A vibrating noise startles us, and Mom grabs her cell phone. "It's a text message from Patrick," she says, stepping out into the hallway. "He wants to know how you're doing."

She starts typing a response.

"Just give me a second," I say, ducking back inside and into the bathroom. I close the door and pull the shower curtain and find what I want—the bottle of grape shampoo. I dry it off and tuck it into my backpack. If I can't take Mom with me, it's better than nothing.

Then I slip into her bedroom and visually search her nightstand. The big brown book I assumed was the Bible is there, and now I know it has to be Ó Direáin's journal. Mom said she loves to read it at night before falling asleep.

I flip it open and read:

> *Ó Direáin, an eccentric genius, spent hours at the end of each day encrypting his scientific journal to protect his ideas. At least forty pages of code continue to elude even the best cryptologists' efforts.*

My heartbeat accelerates. This is major.

I shove the book into my backpack, making it a few pounds heavier. I have to strain to zipper it shut. For a moment, I consider ditching one of the string theory books, but I'm not ready to let my science go. Mom is tucking her phone into her back pocket when I rejoin her in the hallway. She locks the apartment door behind us and slips her hand into mine. "Okay?"

"Yep," I say. "Let's go."

I'm jealous. I think of Ennis High and its narrow hallways, its buzzing and yellowed fluorescent lights, and the pitted football field. To go to Ó Direáin High every day instead? A dream. I run my hand along the massive stones as I enter the front doors. It's a castle.

Mom guides me into the main office and explains the situation to the secretary, who keeps sneaking glances at me, trying not to stare. Then Mom takes me by the arm and leads me into a room with a leather couch, an exam table, a sink, cabinets, and a TV.

"You probably should keep your leg elevated," she says, steering me toward the couch. She hands me the remote. "I'll see you in less than two hours, okay?"

It hits me that the time has come to say good-bye, because a few minutes after she leaves the room, I'm taking off.

"Mom?"

"The nurse will be in later to check on you," she says.

"But Mom," I say, grabbing her arm, feeling that same disorienting vertigo I felt yesterday when I first laid eyes on her. As if the Earth is reversing its rotation, the ground shifting beneath us.

I pull her onto the couch next to me.

"What is it?" She takes my face in her hands, searching.

"I—" I choke on a sudden heaving in my chest and concentrate on not crying. "I—"

"Is it your leg?"

"No, not at all."

We sit in silence, and I start to fidget. Will these be the last words we say to each other? What was the last thing she said to me that day eleven years ago before she left for work, for her accident on the interstate? *Be careful on the monkey bars. Don't suck your thumb. Have a great day.*

"What did you pack for me? For lunch when I was four years old?"

Mom bites her lower lip. "In Pre-K? Why?"

"Just wishing I could remember." I try to visualize opening a brown paper bag and finding a peanut butter sandwich, chips, an apple, and a note in my mother's handwriting.

"I don't remember what I put in your lunch, but I do remember what you took for show-and-tell." A mischievous grin spreads across her face. "You had to bring something every Monday, for the letter of the week."

"Like *C* is for 'cat'? I took my favorite stuffed animal?"

Mom shakes her head. "For *C* we took a live cockroach in a jar."

"Really?" I grin. "I bet that went over big. Whose idea was that?"

"Both of ours. We used to make lists of ideas. For *P* you took the potty from your dollhouse, which sent the entire class into giggles that your teacher couldn't contain for fifteen minutes. By the time we got to *W*, we were in big trouble. Whoopee cushion."

"I love that," I whisper. I feel like I've been given a few pieces of an incomplete puzzle, one that I'd given up on a long time ago because I'd lost the box top and didn't even know what picture it was supposed to make.

She pulls my face to hers so we're touching foreheads. "I love you."

She glances at her watch, pops to her feet, and forces a smile. "I'll check on you between classes."

Just like that she's out the door. The room buzzes, the lights seem to flicker. She's gone. I force myself to count to sixty, to take ten deep breaths—*H* is for "heartache"—and then I'm gone too.

The secretary's back is turned; she's busy dealing with two guys arguing about who hit whose car in the parking lot. So I sneak out of the office unnoticed.

The hallway is crowded with students, and I'm going the wrong way, a fish swimming upstream. Finally, I make it to the front door and squeeze my way through, muttering apologies as I go.

Just outside the door a girl thrusts her chin at me. "Check out Ruby Wright," she says.

Another girl claps me on the back. "Your hair rocks. I wish I had the balls to do that."

"Um. Thanks."

I scan the crowd, looking for George, when I catch Patrick's stare from across the throng. He elbows his way toward me, wearing a purple-and-gold football jersey, and I get the feeling that I've become the end zone he's determined to reach. Cut left, roll right. There's no way to dodge him. "Ruby," he says, reaching across three people to grab my arm. Touchdown!

"Hey, big brother," I say. More like Big Brother, because he seems to be everywhere, watching my every move.

"Here. I found this on the Internet last night."

He hands me a piece of paper. It's an article entitled "Long-Forgotten Head Injuries Linked to Mental Oddities and Illnesses."

I roll my eyes.

"Seriously!" Patrick says. "Remember that time you fell out of that tree and cracked your head and broke your collarbone?"

"Yeah?" No. I climbed a lot of trees, but I never fell. I guess the Ruby in this universe didn't have the same luck.

"Old head injuries can cause weird things to happen in the brain. Your personality and memory can be affected. Depression, stuff like that. There's one lady who started talking with a Swedish accent twenty years after she fractured her skull."

Patrick's overbearing worry is annoying to the tenth power, but it's oddly endearing at the same time. No one's ever treated me like this before. "Why do you care so much?" I ask.

"Are you kidding?" He pulls me into a headlock and gives me a gentle noogie. "Remind me to buy you some Rogaine."

I wrap my arms around his waist and press my head to his chest. For a moment, I feel a rush of love. But then my heart suddenly turns cold when I think of the injustices I've endured. Robbed of both a brother and a mother in Universe One. Why did the roads have to fork in those directions? It's too much tragedy for one person. It's not fair. No way I'm going back to that place.

Just then a burly guy wearing a football jersey punches Patrick's arm. "Dude," he says, casting me an up-and-down look. "Got a minute?" A girl in a cheerleading uniform trails behind him. She stares longingly at Patrick. I wonder if she practices that look in the mirror.

I try to hand the Internet article back to Patrick, but he pushes it toward me. "Read it," he says. "Please." Then he walks off with Mr. Muscles and Ms. Vixen.

Good-bye, Patrick. I watch him until he's absorbed by the crowd.

When I turn back toward the parking lot, I'm worried that I've missed George, but there he is. He must have been waiting patiently for me to finish my conversation with Patrick.

"You okay?" he asks. "You're heading the wrong direction, you know. The school's that way."

"I—uh," I fumble. "I forgot something in my mom's car."

"That guy you were hugging . . ." He frowns, and I can see where he's going with his train of thought.

"Patrick's my brother," I say, liking the way those words sound. Patrick Wright is my brother, Sally Wright is my mother. *Is*, not *was*.

"That's what I thought. I wasn't sure."

His aquamarine eyes are hypnotic, and the lines start to blur. I could be George's girlfriend here. I step away from him, shaking the thought. "I wish I could stay, George. I really gotta get going."

"Hang on." For a moment I think he's going to kiss me, but instead he slides off his backpack and unzips it. He reaches in and pulls out a box.

"For you," he says.

"A gift?" I open the box and inside there's a white LEGO space shuttle. It's exactly right, the way I remember it as a child. "Even the rocket boosters are perfect!"

George nods proudly. "But wait!" he says in an infomercial voice. "There's more!" He hands me a sheet of paper. It's grid paper, and he's neatly drawn assembly instructions in ten numbered steps. "If anyone ever takes it apart again and makes it into a fugly house, you can fix it."

"Do me a favor, okay?" I tell him, our faces close.

"What is it?"

I take a deep breath, not sure how to explain. "Later today, soon, I think—I really hope—the old Ruby is going to be back. I'm not sure where she is at this moment, but I'm wishing and expecting that she's okay, and she'll be home when I leave."

George narrows his eyes at me, half smiling, probably not sure if I'm joking.

"I'm dead serious," I say. "She's not going to remember our Chinese lunch yesterday. She's not going to know we kissed."

"Ruby—" He inches backward.

"Just promise me you'll ask her out," I say. "Because I think there's a reason you're both here, in this town, taking French together. I think you're, well, I think you're—I mean we're—meant to be."

"You're making no sense."

"I know it sounds insane. I don't really believe in fate, but there's this undeniable and uncanny correlation between at least two coexisting planes—"

George holds up his hand to stop me from talking. "You sound completely bonkers, Ruby. Daffy, lunatic."

I nod. "Demented, I know." Unreal. We're replaying the conversation we had last week at the café, on the leather couch, when he took out his iPhone and hit the thesaurus app. Only then we were talking about my dad, not me.

Before George speaks, I can already hear the words in my head. "Cracked, brainsick, *non compos mentis*," he says.

"Please!"

He looks alarmed. "I was just trying to lighten the mood."

I look up at the sky and its converging rain clouds. If only I could make this work somehow. Take George by the hand, walk into the fresh air, and just keep going. Through downtown Ó Direáin, past the library and the park. Away. Away from all this tangled-up confusion. I can see us walking through fields of wildflowers. Add a rainbow.

"Ruby?" George touches my arm and jolts me back.

"You're amazing," I say to him, cradling the LEGO spacecraft. "Thank you for this."

The bell rings, and we're the only two left standing outside. George doesn't seem to mind that I'm making him late.

"Could you do me a favor?" From my backpack, I pull a piece of paper and a pen. I quickly scribble a note, fold it in half and write "For Sally Wright" on the outside of it. "Could you give this to the secretary in the office?"

"Sure." Another bell rings and George inches toward the door. "See you in class," he says.

I give him a quick kiss on the cheek and turn away, pretending to head toward Mom's car.

"Unbalanced, unhinged, nutso!" he calls out after me. Then I hear him laugh with that teasing tone in his voice. And I know I haven't ruined it for George and Ruby in this parallel world with my perplexing behavior. He still likes her/me.

Besides, it's hard not to notice the thread. Call it what you want, there seems to be something bigger at work, and I'm beginning to believe that no matter where I look, we'll be together.

The universes are aligned in our favor.

chapter twelve

I'm going back to the tree, but not quite yet.

At the edge of the parking lot is a bike rack. A black Trek isn't locked onto the rack, so now it's mine. I push my glasses back up my nose, straighten my backpack, and attempt to pedal with mostly one leg.

When I get to the brick house on Corrán Tuathail Avenue minutes later, Kandy is watching television, feet up on the ottoman, drinking a diet soda. "Welcome home," she says like she sincerely doesn't mean it. Her pink lip gloss glistens in the flicker of the TV. Some reality show about rich housewives in LA. Lots of boob jobs.

"Home," I say. "Right." As far as I can tell, this house is identical to its parallel-self in Universe Two—the house where I gagged in the toilet and climbed out the window into the pouring rain. "Aren't you supposed to be in school?"

"Ditched. Because your mom was gonna do some heinous thing about period bulbs."

"Period what?"

"The Mantlebrain set."

"The Mandelbrot set," I correct. "You're in my mom's math class?"

"Are you brain-dead?" Kandy looks me up and down with disgust. "Patrick wasn't kidding when he said you turned goth. So pretty!"

She aims the remote at the TV and turns the volume way up. A woman with injected lips leans toward the camera, raising a blue cocktail. "This girl loves her martinis!"

Fine by me. It's not like I want to sit and chat. I'm just here for two minutes, to get one thing.

I head down the hallway toward the bedrooms, glad to see the wooden American flags and farm animals. Yes—there's the large polka-dotted pig, and yes!—there's the eight-by-ten framed photo of Dad, Mom, Patrick, and me. Well, it's not really me, or the family I've known. But it's proof I've had Mom all along, if only here. I press my hand against the photo, run my fingers along Mom's cheekbones.

"I'm gonna find you again," I say. "In another universe. It's going to be perfect. You'll see."

I lift the photo from its nail, take it out of the frame, and roll it up, the four of us in our khakis and white button-down shirts, Patrick wearing glasses, and my hair in pigtails. The four of us—no fatal car crash, no stepmother or stepsister.

I'm ready to leave now, but as I tuck the photo into my backpack, my eye is drawn to Other Ruby's half-open bedroom door. Call it intuition—something's awry. Is the door off its hinge? It looks askew.

I push the door open and trip over a bright-pink shirt, tangled on the floor.

"Oh no." I groan.

It's a shockingly complete job. Other Ruby's room is trashed. The Paris poster is ripped down the middle and dangling from the wall; the mattress is tipped on its side; books, papers, clothes, photos, magazines are scattered everywhere. It's like someone split an atom. Kaboom.

"Not again." I could kill Kandy. Yeah, technically, this isn't my room, or my stuff, but it's the principle. Kandy's committing acts of malice in too many universes. Ruby's room back in Universe Three— and probably my room in One—is no doubt still a mess, my science books shredded. And now she's done it again.

I grit my teeth, remembering how Kandy jumped on me and pummeled my sides, how she chased me through the house. It's like it's happening again. The edge of the coffee table slices into my leg. Rage pulses through me.

I march back into the other room. On the TV, a tiny dog pokes its head out of a purse as its owner browses in a jewelry store. "Do you have any diamond-studded dog leashes?" the woman asks.

"You're insane," I say matter-of-factly, standing directly in front of the television, facing Kandy.

"Me? Take a look in the mirror. Patrick thinks you have multiple personality disorder."

"Please." What I have is multiple universe disorder.

She strains her neck to see around me. "Move!"

I snap my fingers. "I know! A manicure went wrong. You gained half a pound. Your Hollywood crush got married. Something tragic, right? That's what made you go berserk and trash Ruby's room."

"Ruby's room?" Kandy says. "See? You are nuts, talking about yourself in the second person."

"Third."

"Move!" She throws her soda can at my head. I duck and it explodes against the TV.

"No," I say, trying to keep my voice steady. "I'm not moving." I realize I might get tackled and smacked again, or worse. But I'm not backing down. I'm not running away, apologizing, or taking her crap. "Why are you such a sadistic witch?"

Kandy leans forward, narrows her eyes. "What did you say to me?"

"What's. Your. Damage?" I cross my arms over my chest.

She sizes me up. "Just because you mowed your hair off and got a tattoo doesn't mean you're tough."

"Were you just being an angry shithead, or were you looking for something? Maybe a bag of stolen clothes and makeup?"

"What do you know about that?" Kandy's eyes widen.

I shrug.

"Yeah, so what if that's what I was looking for? I should've known I'd find it in Patrick's room. It was on his desk chair. He was gonna narc on me." Kandy leans back, studies her fingernails. "If you tell my mom, I'll deny it. You can't prove anything. Besides, I went off my meds, so I can't be blamed for anything I do."

"Perfect," I say. "You've got it all worked out."

Kandy's voice quiets. "I hate this house. I hate your dad and your brother. And I hate you."

I give Kandy a look of revulsion, then step away from the TV, clearing her line of vision. She can go back to watching the fake boobs. But Kandy clicks the television off, and a menacing silence fills the room.

"My mom lied to your dad," Kandy says. "This isn't her second marriage. It's her fifth."

"What?"

"Yeah, fifth."

"Shut up."

"Seriously. She changes husbands like she changes her painting periods. You know, the bright period, the bleak period, the far period, the near period."

Dad is just a number, a notch, the next ex? He and Willow seem so in love, though, at least in Universe One. Maybe he won't get hurt there. Maybe he will . . .

And if the marriage to Willow crashes and burns, we could move back to California. Back to our apartment in Walnut Creek with the blue carpet and the too-cold swimming pool. Back to George.

"I liked the third husband, Bruce," Kandy says. "He helped me with my homework, drove me around. He actually asked about my life. Anyway. I can't wait to graduate and get out of here. Live where I want to live."

I find it hard to believe that Kandy is sharing secrets with me, but then again, nothing she says or does would surprise me at this point. I blink, watching Kandy, her entire face defeated, pulled into a frown. "Yeah," I say. "I know the feeling."

Words from Kandy's diary come back to me. How many days she'd been stuck in Ennis, how she was applying to fashion school in

Miami. All over the margins of her journal, she'd written the name Maddy.

She digs her fingernails into the couch pillow, and smiles her evil, creepy smile.

"What?" I say, watching her eyes.

"Run," she whispers.

"No. No way." I widen my stance, bracing myself for an attack. This is what I should have done two days ago, back in Universe One. I should have shown some backbone.

"I said RUN!"

"Who's Maddy?" I ask.

Kandy gasps. "Maddy."

"Yeah, who is she?" I think of Patrick and how he exists in some universes and not in others. How anything can happen. "Did you have a sister? A biological sister, and that's why you hate having a stepsister so much? That's why you hate me?"

"No one knows about Maddy." Her voice turns brittle. "How do you know that name? I was talking in my sleep, wasn't I? Or talking to myself."

"I do that too," I say. "I don't realize I'm talking out loud."

"There is no Maddy," she says. "There is no Maddy."

"Got it."

"And do you seriously have to ask me why I hate you? Like, really? I'm sleeping in your garage," Kandy says, punching a couch pillow. "Like a dog."

The word "dog" seems to trigger it. The snuffling, panting noises that come from the kitchen. A blue collar and a green collar. Muzzles gray and hazy old eyes.

"Galileo!" I drop to my knees. "Isaac!" My long-dead dogs waddle into my arms. I press my nose into their necks, breathing in their musty fur. Galileo's tongue sweeps across my cheek.

"Oh," I sob. "That was even better than a kiss from George!" I scratch and rub and nuzzle, using the top of Isaac's head to dry my tears.

I'm in a dreamlike state, time slipping by unnoticed, until Dad's voice—"Hello!"—is the unwelcome alarm. The dogs shuffle away from me, toward the front door. "We're home," he announces.

Dad and Willow are back from their honeymoon! I don't want to see either of them. I need to get back to the tree. I'm finding it hard to breathe through the panic, to move through the kitchen toward the laundry room, toward the garage.

"Ruby? Is that you?"

"Uh."

Dad drops his suitcases and pounds across the room. "What did you do to yourself?" He slides his hands across my head. "Your hair!"

"Your weight!" I say.

Dad is a good fifty pounds heavier. His shirt stretches across his belly. The worn holes in his belt mark the progression of his weight gain.

"Turn around," he commands.

Before I can comply, he twists my body by my shoulders. "Easy!" I protest.

He rubs his thumb into my neck. "It's real?" He goes to the sink and wets a paper towel.

"It's not coming off," I say, ducking out of the way.

Dad throws his hands into the air. "I hardly recognize you!"

"The feeling is mutual," I say. Behind him, Willow watches, wordless. She's still holding her suitcase. Kandy stares at the television.

"Why aren't the two of you in school?" Dad asks.

"I was just heading there now," I say, angling for an opening, a way past his hulking body. "Welcome home."

"Welcome home?" Dad puffs. "Outside. Right now. We're taking a walk." He grabs my forearm (Patrick-style) and leads me through the living room, out the front door. We walk down the driveway, then stop. Dad looks up and down the street, trying to decide which way to go. He's already out of breath. "Ruby."

"Dad."

"What's going on?"

"I could ask the same," I say. Dad's eyes are practically lost in his fleshy face. "You're a cheeseburger away from a heart attack."

Dad thinks for a moment. "Is that what this is about? You're sending me a message about how I look?"

"Sure. Why not?" I glance over my shoulder, in the direction of the school and the tree. On the lawn, not twenty feet away, is the bike I borrowed, lying in the grass.

"My divorce attorney warned me that this could happen. Teen rebellion. I never imagined this." He waves his hands at me, like I'm the dictionary definition of stark raving mad. Unglued, crackers, bats in the belfry.

"It's just a haircut."

"Next thing you know you'll be dyeing it pink."

"Not likely."

Dad's eyebrows are pressed together into a solid line of furrowed anger. "What does all that scribble on your neck mean? It looks Satanic."

"It's a math equation."

He rubs his temples. "How could you have changed so much while I was away? I should've never left town. Let's walk. I need to clear my head."

I start toward the bike but pause. "How long have you been doing that?" I ask, pointing to the wheelbarrow in the front yard's landscaping bed.

"What?"

"The white impatiens spilling from the tipped wheelbarrow."

"I don't know. As long as I can remember." He huffs through his nose. "Why are we talking about flowers?"

Because they remind me of Mom. Because they're a reflection of love, one of those touches that makes a place feel like home. Because you wrenched me away from my home in California.

"Those flowers are important," I say. "They mean something. To me. A lot of things mean something to me, and you don't know how much. And then you take them away."

There's so much anger inside me—more than I realized—and now it's rising like hot air, pushing its way up. Suddenly, I feel like hurting Dad as much as he's hurt me. I want to take everything out on him, for falling stupidly in love with Willow, the stupid move to Ohio, his stupid job, and even things that weren't his stupid fault, like Mom's death.

I blurt at him, "You're just stupid selfishness, everywhere I go! Look at yourself!"

"Come on, Ruby," Dad says wearily. "Aren't you sick of fighting? Could we please stop this never-ending screaming match?"

Screaming match? I never once let Dad have it back in Universe One. I've kept it nearly vacuum-sealed, a snide comment here and there.

"You never think about how your decisions affect other people." It feels so good to unload. "How they affect me!"

"That's not true!" he says, but then he seems at a loss for words. He has no defense.

"Obviously you have no trouble feeding your own needs," I say, motioning to his belly.

Dad grabs his gut with both hands, gives it a squeeze. "This is what a failed marriage does, okay? I ate my way through the unhappiness."

I cringe at the word "failed." "Things could be different," I say. "If you'd worked on it harder, we could be together. Right here. I wouldn't have to go searching."

"We're all searching, hon. That's life." Dad leans in, cups my cheek in his hand. "I'm sorry, Ruby. I'm sorry for everything."

I yank my face away from his fingers. "I mean, this could be the right place! The high school is amazing. Downtown is amazing. Even George Pierce lives in this universe! How perfect is that?"

"Hey, my little girl," Dad says. "You're confusing me. What are you talking about?"

"And the dogs!" The thought of leaving Galileo and Isaac behind shatters me. Why are they alive here and not in Universe One? Did they really die of cancer? Or did Dad give them away? I was only ten. Still easy enough to lie to. "You ruin everything!"

"I don't know what else to do but say I'm sorry." His face collapses into defeat, sorrow. "I'm sorry, Ruby."

Forget the extra pounds, Dad's eyes are the same, and I'm reeled in by a force that feels magnetic, irrepressible. He said he was sorry, and he sounded like he meant it, and I wish I could accept his apology and tell him that I'm okay with the entire broken, divorced/widowed, complicated mess. But I'm not okay. I take a deep breath and step back. "I'd like to be alone, if you don't mind."

Dad extends his hand, but I'm beyond his reach. "Where are you going?" he calls after me as I trot toward the bike. I bite my lip, ignoring the jab of pain my leg inflicts with each stride.

"Ruby!" Dad shouts as I ride off, a hint of panic in his voice. "Come back! It's starting to rain."

I glance over my shoulder at him, still standing at the end of the driveway, his arms outstretched like he's expecting me to return to him, to simply fold into his embrace.

chapter thirteen

I can see them from the high school parking lot. Two boys stand in front of the giant oak tree, their bikes on the ground.

"Get away from there!" I scream, limp-hopping toward them.

They look at me, panic on their faces. Like they've been caught. One glances at his bike, then his friend. I'm feeling my fair share of panic, too.

"Whatever you do, don't touch the knob," I say. "It electrocutes the hell out of you. Heck. It electrocutes the heck out of me."

They stare at me, mouths open.

"It's worse than putting a fork in an outlet, trust me."

"Who are you?" the bigger boy asks. He's wearing a SpongeBob T-shirt.

"Police," I say. "Go home and forget about it. It's under investigation. We've got the whole area under surveillance."

The smaller boy looks up, searching the sky for a helicopter, for hidden cameras. His hair is still that baby shade of white-blond.

"That's right. We're recording this," I say. "It's top secret. If you speak a word to anyone, we'll know. They're processing the video footage now. In ten minutes I'll know your names and where you live."

"But—"

"I'll be in touch," I say, patting SpongeBob's back. "Just keep quiet and everything will be okay."

I scan the sky, looking for a helicopter, for hidden cameras. Gray cloud banks gather, a light drizzle becomes steady rain. Under the tree's umbrellalike canopy of leaves, we stay dry.

"Hurry home." I twist an imaginary key over my lips.

The smaller boy is first to his bike. In his rush, he has a hard time finding his balance. He finally gets his feet firmly on the pedals, then zooms madly down the hill, toward downtown Ó Direáin.

"Wait up!" the bigger kid calls. He glances over his shoulder at me then disappears, mud flicking behind his bike tires.

I sink to the ground, wasted. My hands tremble. My leg throbs, hot. What can I do? Will they come back? For the next half hour, I stand sentinel at the top of the hill. No sign of them. And I can't wait any longer; it's time to go.

I brace myself for the static sting, and it's fiercer than I remember. My teeth still vibrating, I step inside the oak and wiggle my fingers into the gardening gloves, ready to turn the cold and slick steering disk. The sunlight of Universe Four trickles around the edges of the door until it seals shut, and I'm once again alone. In the dark.

chapter fourteen

This time, when the door opens and I step out of the tree, I'm in the middle of the woods. Here in Universe Five, I'm surrounded by trees— elm, oak, hickory, and maple. Other than the twittering of birds, it's quiet. No sign of Ó Direáin's high school, no sign of Ennis's cornfields. No sign of human existence.

Maybe this is it. This could be the happy-family universe. I'm thinking it's good to be in unrecognizable territory. That's what I need. A totally different world. Maybe our house is on the edge of a national park. Or maybe Ó Direáin or Ennis was developed a few miles away, and I'll find civilization if I walk a while. Mom, George, Patrick, the dogs.

And Dad.

My nerves are still firing after our knock-down. In a good way. I feel plugged in, energized. And it's a relief to get some of that heavy-as-lead anger off my chest. It makes me wonder . . . if I'd gone to war with him back in Universe One, I might've created a different quantum junction and in turn, an alternative path. Maybe I could've talked him out of moving to Ohio if I'd spoken up for myself.

If only.

I attempt to mark my position on Mom's GPS, but it can't find a satellite signal. Shaking it and calling it a piece of crap doesn't seem to help. If I walk a very short distance I might not get lost, and maybe I'll be able to see the purple glow of the tree if I get disoriented. Even better, I pull a few sheets of blank paper from my notebook knowing I can poke them onto low, skinny branches as I go.

A male cardinal flits nearby. Fungus-covered logs litter the ground. After a few minutes, the burbling of running water leads me to a stream. A walkway of stones dots the water, so I could cross here and continue on. I study the stream and notice that a few of the stones are small, some spaced far apart. The Basic Coordination Skills of Ruby Wright—let's take a moment to review, class. Yeah, it's highly probable that I'll lose my balance, drop my backpack, and soak everything. Including my change of clothes, Mom's sweater, my postcard from George, my eight-by-ten family photo, and the little snapshot of Mom and me in my red-gingham blouse.

Makes more sense to check the other directions first. I retrace my steps to the portal tree, following the markers I created with my notebook paper. Then I try the opposite direction. This time I'm stopped by an enormous fallen oak, covered in moss, too big to climb over. I start back toward the portal tree when a rustling noise startles me, and I see movement behind a cluster of skinny saplings.

"Hello?" My voice cuts through the air, a strange resonance in this world of wildlife sounds. An acid taste rises in my throat. The singeing rush of adrenaline feels like poison, making my chest contract.

It might be those two boys. They followed me.

More rustling, then a sudden flutter of wings and a sharp *cluck-cluck*; not more than ten feet away is a startled wild turkey. I leap back, lose my balance, and sit hard on the ground. He's enormous, a dark-brown mass of brown feathers, probably four feet tall. *Cluck-cluck-cluck!* Within seconds he's disappeared into the woods, only his red throat visible for a moment after he's otherwise vanished. An afterimage.

I hold my hand to my chest. Calm down, heart. It was just a bird. A really huge bird, but that's all.

As I put my hands down to push myself back to my feet, I feel something hard. I look down and pull a narrow shaft of wood from the debris of fallen leaves and twigs. It's an arrow.

But it's not a modern, bought-it-at-Walmart arrow. It looks handmade, like it was whittled, and the arrowhead is flint. It's in perfect condition. It's new.

I stand up and find myself eye-to-eye with another arrow, this one stuck into the trunk of a tree. Someone's been hunting in these woods recently. Maybe today. Maybe right now.

My heart picks up the pace, beating the living daylight out of my chest. Blood rushes through my head in dizzying quantities. I've got to get out of here.

What's going on in this universe? The land hasn't been developed. Did a major historic event take place, or not take place? No wonder the GPS isn't working. Satellites were never invented! Is this area still inhabited by Native Americans?

I try to remember which tribes lived in Ohio. Shawnee? Iroquois? What would they do if they found me out here, unable to speak their language, in clothes that would seem foreign to them, with electronic gadgets? I mean, what would they think of my digital camera? Would they murder and scalp me?

I do my best to move noiselessly back toward the tree, but I'm stupidly loud. Every branch that cracks underfoot makes me a target. Why did I have to call out "hello" earlier? Duh!

My tongue turns dry. All I can imagine is that I'm being hunted. I feel light-headed and realize I'm not breathing.

N_2 and O_2 in, carbon dioxide out. Breathe, Ruby, breathe.

Four notebook sheets to go. I look over my shoulder. I'm hearing things that aren't there, seeing things that may or may not exist. Was that another wild turkey? A snake? When a falling leaf hits my head, I swing wildly at air.

And to make matters worse, an undercurrent of disappointment gains volume, crescendos. I have to cross this universe off the list. It's not perfect, not even close.

The last sheet of paper, then the tree.

My hand on the doorknob, I'm zapped, once again, with a surge of static electricity. It's strong, the strongest current of electricity so far, but it doesn't faze me. I'm too focused, putting my shoulder into the door and pushing to hurry it open.

I squeeze through the door and into the tree. My back against the inner wall of the trunk, I slide down to the ground and hold my head in my hands, blanching with panic. The door closes too slowly. Please, hurry up, before someone else slips into the tree. Finally, the last rays of sunlight are choked out. I exhale with relief.

The tree's engine purrs rhythmically. And for the first time, I feel safe inside this dark, rotten chamber.

chapter fifteen

The tree door opens, and I stumble out into Universe Six, onto a pebble walkway, which leads to an iron gate. Beyond that is a cemetery, shrouded in the shade of giant trees. Stupendous. My nerves are still jangling from the last universe. A stroll through Creepyville is the last thing I need.

Relax, Ruby.

I take a breath, clearing my sinuses of the rotten tree smell, trying to calm the chemical and neurological havoc in my body. There's no deerskin-clad Native American armed with a hatchet tailing me. So stop the rapidly firing neurons, please.

With trembling hands I unzip my backpack and find Mom's GPS to mark my position before I get too far from the tree. Just in case this universe is a bust and I need to find my way back to the portal. I doubt that will happen. Honestly. Because Universe Five sucked, this one should compensate and correct. Probability theory, law of averages. Something should be on my side.

The cemetery gate creaks as I push it open, and flecks of black paint stick to the palms of my hands. I wipe them off on my jeans as I take in the tombstones and mausoleums. Actually there's nothing horror movie about this cemetery. It's peaceful. The grass is green and mowed, flowers bloom around the newer graves, the walkway is free of weeds.

I wipe my glasses clean and strain to see beyond the confines of the graveyard. I don't see the school, or any other signs of Ennis or Ó Direáin. The air is crisp, tinged with the smell of apples. A blue jay flits from tree to tree, and I realize that fruit hangs from the branches. I reach up and twist an apple off, taking a bite. It's sour, not ripe. I spit it out and continue along the pebble path through the cemetery, reading the tombstones and doing the math. Samuel Black was thirty-three years old. He died in 1907. A miniature stone marks the grave of a baby. James Cross was fifty-nine. One loss after another. Beloved mother. Father of eleven. An angel on earth. Forever remembered.

I make my way through the obelisks and cherubs, the statues of saints and the Virgin Mary, speculating on the causes of each death. Cholera, dysentery for the older graves. Cancer, heart disease for the recent. And, of course, car accidents. How many of the dead people I'm standing over were rear-ended, sideswiped? How many flipped, rolled, caught fire? How many would have been okay, if a windshield wiper hadn't struck with arrow-accuracy?

Oh, please—don't let me stumble across Mom's grave in this cemetery.

Stop reading inscriptions, Ruby.

My leg throbs. My head hurts. And I realize I never visited Mom's grave in California. Never. Not once. We should have gone to plant flowers, to scrub the headstone, to tape photos or something. Anything. I stop walking and consider this revelation. Regret and guilt bubble and combine to form a toxic thundercloud in my chest.

That's when I see a tombstone, crooked and cracked from age, for a man named Edward Percival Smith. *Perished Whilst Trying to Down the Oak Tree.* Under his name is a picture of an ax etched into the stone.

Willow's story. It was true? Was this the man who tried to cut the tree down and burst into flames? That means he was killed by the tree in at least two universes. Just a few days ago, I tried to convince myself that the tree was just a tree. A bunch of xylem cells and phloem tissue. Not a serial killer. Now I'm wondering otherwise.

I shake the thought, turning my attention back to the pebble path. Ahead, a large mausoleum dominates, the name Ó DIREÁIN carved into the gray granite above the iron door. Ó Direáin!

The mausoleum is the size of a one-car garage. I approach it cautiously, but my curiosity is raging. I need to get inside and look around. The door is ajar, but it's stiff, reluctant to open. I push and pull, working it back and forth until it loosens enough for me to shoulder through, into the cold room.

There's no coffin, so I'm guessing the deceased inhabitant is buried under the floor. Natural light filters in through the open door, but I can't see much. I dig through my backpack until my fingers find the cold metal cylinder of my flashlight. I click it on. The beam of light reveals nothing until I shine it on the wall to my left. Ten oak trees stand shoulder-to-shoulder—drawings carved into the granite, each no less than four feet tall.

Under the trees, there's an equation:

$$\partial(x) = x - n \quad (\mathrm{mod}\ 26)$$

Goose bumps spring up along my arms. Modulus 26. What significance does the number twenty-six have? In what system is that number crucial? I can think of nothing else but the twenty-six letters of the alphabet. My brain starts to whir, and I can hear Mom's voice: D *is for "decryption."* This has to be it!

I pace back and forth, thinking it through.

In order to get the decrypted value of *x*, you take *x* and subtract *n* positions. A math equation I can understand! If I'm right, all I have to do is shift the letters. For instance, if the encoded letter is an *R*, then I count backward through the alphabet for a set number of letters, and whatever I land on is the decoded value. But it would be nice to know the numeric value of *n*, which is how many positions to shift. Is this what Mom was talking about, what she called a simple cipher?

I look around the mausoleum, scanning the walls. The flashlight helps, especially in the corners. Finally, I shine the beam on the ceiling.

"What's that?" The writing is so small it's practically invisible. You could mistake it for a spiderweb. I aim my digital camera, then zoom in and capture the image. Now I can see it, on my camera's screen.

 = 10

I fumble excitedly for my notebook and pen, and write the letters of the alphabet, and then directly below that, the alphabet with a ten-letter shift. I should've guessed the key would be ten; after all, I've been navigating a ten-universe system with similar elements, rearranged. Decoding the cryptic message that's carved above the portal door should be a breeze now.

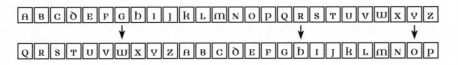

A	B	C	D	E	F	G	H	I	J	K	L	M	N	O	P	Q	R	S	T	U	V	W	X	Y	Z
						↓											↓							↓	
Q	R	S	T	U	V	W	X	Y	Z	A	B	C	D	E	F	G	H	I	J	K	L	M	N	O	P

gry kbo iye coousxq? = who are you seeking?

I slump with disappointment. It's just a philosophical statement, nothing about how the tree works. Nothing scientific. A waste of time.

I leave the mausoleum and circle it to investigate the exterior walls, just in case there's a clue. A plaque hangs on the rear wall, and etched into it is this:

PADRAIG Ó DIREÁIN WAS BORN IN ENNIS,
IRELAND, IN 1841. HIS FAMILY DIED AS A
RESULT OF THE POTATO FAMINE, AND Ó DIREÁIN
IMMIGRATED, ALONE, TO THE UNITED STATES AT THE
AGE OF TEN. AFTER Ó DIREÁIN PULLED A
TWO-YEAR-OLD FROM THE PATH OF AN ONCOMING
TRAIN, THE TODDLER'S GRATEFUL FATHER TOOK
Ó DIREÁIN UNDER HIS WING AND TRAINED HIM
AS A CARPENTER. Ó DIREÁIN WAS WIDELY KNOWN

FOR HIS MATHEMATICALLY PRECISE WOODWORKING,
AND HE EVENTUALLY EXPANDED HIS WORK INTO THE
FIELDS OF ARCHITECTURE AND CITY PLANNING.

Mathematically precise woodworking. Like the intricately etched design on the tree door, the gridlike pattern.

I dig into my backpack and retrieve Ó Direáin's thick brown journal. It's broken into three sections: Biography, Codes for the Uses of Electricity, and Unbreakable Codes. In the biography section, there's this:

> *His obsession with electricity ultimately led to his death, a result of his work on what he called a "travel tunnel." Few records remain in regards to what he described as this "supreme and powerful machine" because Ó Direáin encoded his lab notes, or because he burned the pages at the end of each day. He also noted that his invention was "well-hidden, encased in an everyday object." Historians suspect that this mysterious and ambitious project was an attempt to build an aircraft powered by jet engines.*

Um, no. He wasn't attempting to build a jet airplane. He was inventing something more like an elevator. A door opens and people casually stroll out of a wall. Others go in and disappear, transported to an unseen place. The portal isn't so different. It's an Einstein-Rosen bridge—a connection between parallel universes, a traversable wormhole. It's a quantum elevator.

We may never know, since the world's most renowned cryptologists have been able to decode little of the section of his journal that Ó Direáin himself labeled "Unbreakable Codes." Part of what makes his codes inscrutable is that he mixed English letters and numbers, as well as the Celtic ogham, a runic alphabet. Regarding encryption, he wrote: "I am obsessed with rearranging. I sort things out after attempting various combinations. This is how scientific revelations occur."

It all fits! The travel tunnel, encased in an everyday object. That would be the oak. The runic alphabet might explain the symbols on the floor of the tree, around the metal ring. And attempting various combinations means so much, on so many levels. Whether attempting various math formulae, or chemical compounds, or codes. It's all about rearranging letters, numbers, and ideas, until you get it just right.

It's all about trying various parallel worlds, until you find the right one. The perfect world.

Instead of hand-copying Ó Direáin's biography into my notebook, I snap a few digital photos of it. The graveyard fence runs just behind the Ó Direáin mausoleum, and there's another gate, half-open. Now I can see the spire of the stone high school in the distance. Nice to spot a familiar landmark, even if it's at least half a mile from its usual location. If Ó Direáin High School exists in this universe, then beyond that might be a neighborhood. And—maybe—in that neighborhood there's a house where Mom lives.

I trip over a low tombstone, and a stabbing pain hits me so deeply

I actually groan. I need medical help. I need another night's rest on Mom's denim couch. Maybe I'll happen upon a walk-in clinic and make a pit stop. If they could just drain the wound, that might do the trick.

I head toward the school, my backpack bouncing against my spine, my prescription pills rattling in their orange vial. A water fountain in the shape of a shamrock hugs the side of the stone building; its organic shape blends with the manicured hedges. Take one pill every four hours. Breakfast at Mom's was about that, give or take. I pop one pain pill, then another for good measure, and gulp down water.

A crack of thunder. Lightning darts horizontally through cloud-bottoms. Instinctually, I crouch down, shielding my head. "Major voltage," I whisper, eyeing the sky. Pillars of vertical clouds line the horizon like chemistry beakers on a shelf, dark and roiling.

Even though it can't be noon yet, it feels like dusk. Across the street, a field of corn bends with the wind. It's a collective reaction, like a flock of birds suddenly shifting, averting. I shiver and dig into my backpack to find Mom's sweater, the one I swiped from her apartment bedroom. It feels good, and smells right.

My injured leg is getting stiffer by the minute. I have to swing it out alongside me as I hurry in the direction of Corrán Tuathail Avenue, toward the squat brick house, the place where our fractured family lives. But the scene will be different in this universe. I'll peer in the windows and find Mom and Dad sitting together at the kitchen table, playing cards, sipping hot chocolate. There will be no sign of Kandy or Willow. The dogs will be sleeping, curled up on their beds. Patrick might be there too. And later on I'll get a call from George, who's been hanging out at Sweet Treats or Shanghai, waiting for me. I'll apologize for being late.

The asphalt road gives way to cobblestone, and I know I'm not going to find the brick house. Not here. There's been a variation, a fork in the road of space-time. In this universe, this section of town was built at a different time, by people with a different vision. The houses are straight out of a fairy tale—green with purple trim, blue with pink trim, topped with gabled roofs and ornate cornices. They practically look edible; if only they had licorice shutters and gumdrop chimneys.

My heart leaps with hope. Different is good. This could be the place.

The sidewalk winds through towering oaks, not quite as big as the portal tree. Roots have sent fracture lines through the sidewalk, producing piles of chipped stones, sections entirely popped out of place.

Ahead, I see a wheelbarrow tipped on its side, overflowing with white impatiens.

Mom! Home!

I stand at the cusp of the slate walkway, fighting back the urge to march through the front door and into Mom's arms. The house is yellow with white trim, subtle shades compared to the rest of the neighborhood. I follow the walkway through a thick patch of ivy, which has been trimmed to the edge of each stepping stone. A plump robin flits into an overfilled bird bath, then darts into the trees. Potted geraniums line the porch's three steps. A porch swing rocks, pushed by the wind. There is no doorbell, so I knock. I can't see into the house through the door's stained-glass window, but I see a shadow, a shape, moving toward the door.

A lock clicks, the door swings open, and there's Mom. My hands go to my head, as if pressing my skull will help me from blowing a circuit, from totally losing it. "Hi" is all I can manage. I want to kiss those cheekbones, press my nose against her neck and inhale. That grape smell.

"Can I help you?" Mom's face is friendly but blank. "Are you selling something?" She looks me up and down, shifts uncomfortably.

She doesn't recognize me. "No, I'm here to—" I can't finish the sentence.

Suddenly her face softens. "You must be here to see Ruby." She turns and calls over her shoulder. "Ruby! Someone from your class."

I start to protest, but Mom takes my arm and leads me in. "I noticed the backpack. Do you have an English study group?" she asks.

The living room is decorated like Mom's apartment. Denim couches, Americana artwork. A redheaded girl pops up from the couch. "Hello," she says, cocking her head at me. Freckles dot her cheeks like constellations. "Do I know you?"

They're both staring at me, waiting for me to say something. My face burns, my entire body feels hot. I think of my leg and infection and fever. "I'm, well, I'm just new here, and I, uh . . ."

Ruby claps her hands. "You moved into the salmon house at the end of the street. I saw the vans yesterday."

Mom holds out a hand. "Nice to meet you. Welcome to the neighborhood."

I shake her hand, holding on too long. I don't want to let go of those fingers, that soft skin. My eyes drift to the living room and the fireplace mantel. Above it hangs an enormous family photo. Mom's arm is wrapped around the waist of a man I've never seen before. He's got red hair, and a red beard. Sitting on the floor in front of them is this redheaded girl named Ruby. They're wearing khakis and white shirts. I'm not in the picture.

"I'm Sally." Mom presses her hand to her heart. "What's your name?"

"It's Ruby too."

"Really? What a coincidence. Our Ruby was named after her great-grandmother. What about you?"

"Look," I say, stepping backward. "I'm not . . . I should get going."

"But what about your study group?"

"There's no study group today," Ruby says.

"Well, it's about to rain," Mom says. "There's lightning. You should stay and have some hot chocolate. We're ordering pizza for lunch."

"Yuck, Mom," Ruby says. "Hot chocolate with pizza?"

I stare at redheaded Ruby, then Mom. "You've got the same eyes," I say vacantly. "Blue with flecks of amber."

An awkward silence hangs over us.

"Do you mind if I take your photo?" I ask, digging for my digital camera. Why didn't I take some photos of Mom in Universe Four? I can picture her at the kitchen table, eating her Hawaiian pizza. I can see her in her pajamas, covering me for the night.

When I look up, I see that Ruby's face is twisted into a wince.

"You'd better hurry home before the storm hits." Her voice is loud and authoritative; she's taking charge of a situation gone awry. "You'll be fine if you leave now." She returns to the couch and picks up a book, glancing at me sideways.

Alternate Ruby. In a sense, she's my half sister. Mom's DNA, but not Dad's.

"At least you can take this." Mom hands me an umbrella. "You don't want to get that nice sweater wet. You know, I have one just like it. Isn't that a coincidence?"

"Who would believe it?" My voice quivers.

Mom holds the door open for me, and I can't take my eyes off her. What if she's not in any of the other worlds? What if this is the layout of the remaining universes—Mom with the redheaded husband—and the parallel worlds that include Dad and me are few and far between?

"You look so familiar to me," she says. "I can't put my finger on it, but you remind me of someone."

Oh, Mom. My eyes are blue with flecks of amber too.

"I've got that kind of face." I turn and hobble down the porch steps, eager to get away before the tears spill down my cheeks.

The sky is a sickly shade of green. A bruised color. I look over my shoulder and see Mom standing in the window, her fingertips pressed against the glass. She raises a hand and waves.

Bye, Mom. Again.

I press my nose into the crook of my elbow and inhale, trying to find the smell of hope. Mom's sweater is her apartment, her perfume, her laundry detergent, her sweat, her grape shampoo. But it's not her.

When I look back at the window again to blow her a kiss, she's gone. The curtain's still swaying.

Above, clouds promise to unleash gallons of rain. It's time to motor. I watch my feet, dodging the tree roots and upended chunks of sidewalk. That's all I need. Another injury.

"Watch it!" A girl pushing a stroller nearly flattens me.

"Sorry." I barely glance up, but from the corner of my eye, I catch a glimpse of the manicured nails, the shiny purse shoved into the stroller basket, the lip liner, the impractical heels. It's Kandy. Kandinsky.

"I go by Jennifer now. Do I know you?"

Great. I didn't realize I said her name out loud.

The little girl in the stroller pops a strawberry into her mouth, pink juice sliding down her chin. She points a finger at me. "Who that?"

"I don't know, bug," Kandy says.

"Excuse me," I say, trying to maneuver around them.

"But you know my name," Kandy says.

"Just from school," I say. "You're a senior, I'm a sophomore." It's the only true statement that comes to mind. *You're my psycho stepsister in alternate realities* doesn't seem to be the appropriate response here.

Kandy shakes her head. She ruffles the toddler's hair. "I dropped out of school three years ago. You've probably seen me waiting tables at Shanghai."

"She's . . . yours?"

As soon as I ask, I realize the absurdity of the question. The little girl's got the same almond-shaped eyes, the same fine hair.

"Mommy! Go!" The girl leans forward and rocks.

"Stop it, Maddy," Kandy says. "You're splashing my soda everywhere, bug."

Maddy. Maddy. Maddy from the journal? Wait. So what happened back in Universe One, in Ennis? Why is there a Maddy here but not there? Was Maddy a miscarriage, an abortion, a stillbirth? Is that why Kandy's so bitter?

"Hurry up, you two!" A man's voice comes from a nearby porch. "I don't want to lose my wife and kid to a lightning strike. Get inside!"

Kandy presses her eyebrows together with concern. "You'd better get going too. Are you close to home?"

"Not exactly."

The man on the purple porch is a good ten years older than Kandy, maybe more. He's holding a sippy cup.

"Do you need a ride somewhere?" Kandy asks. "You're limping, and you've got that huge backpack."

"Nah."

"I didn't catch your name," she says.

"Ruby Wright."

Not a single flicker of recognition crosses her face. She pushes the stroller toward the house but seems reluctant to leave me out in the weather. She eyes the sky, the black clouds that flicker, backlit by pulses of lightning.

I hold up my umbrella and smile. "I'm fine."

chapter sixteen

Orientation at Ennis High with Mr. Burton—the tour of the antiseptic-smelling cafeteria, the pockmarked football field that reminded me of Hyperion—was Thursday afternoon. Now it's Sunday, which means it's been three days since I first walked through the cornfield to the tree, and found it humming, motor on.

That's all? It seems like a year has passed! Einstein was right. Time is relative. And I'm supposed to be starting school tomorrow, at 7:15 a.m. at Ennis High. Yeah, don't think so.

My stomach makes a gurgling, eruptive noise. It's in knots—with worry, with emptiness. Where will I sleep tonight? Is my leg hopelessly infected? When will I eat again? The bacon and toast I downed at Mom's apartment this morning, back in Universe Four, are long digested. But I can't seem to digest the dynamics of Universe Six. Mom and Dad never met? Does Dad exist here at all? Is he a chef in

California? Or maybe he was the one who died? I stop walking and watch the trees move in the wind. Their branches bouncing up and down, leafy hands waving. Good-bye, good-bye.

I don't exist here.

I need to get back to the tree.

Redheaded Ruby's take-charge voice echoes through me: *You'd better hurry home.* Home? I don't even know what that word means anymore.

I limp along the sidewalk. The gingerbread houses look less colorful by the minute. The roiling sky casts a muddy, greenish film across everything, making the houses seem menacing, haunted. Inside, lights flicker, then go off. A buzzing noise permeates the air, and the air sizzles with electrical energy.

A blinding lightning flash. Instinctively I duck, throwing my arms over my head. *Bam!* Thunder, packing powerful acoustic waves. Yeah, it's too close, which means I need to get somewhere safe. This universe has me disoriented, with the cemetery and these Victorian houses that seem to go on and on. Did I walk in a circle? Why didn't I draw myself a map?

The rain comes. In buckets.

The sidewalk curves around the roots of an enormous oak, and I find myself looking for a door in it, even though I know it's not my tree. Where is the high school?

Suddenly I remember Mom's GPS device, and I fish it out of my backpack. Did I mark my coordinates for this universe? I can't remember. I was so paranoid about getting attacked by a Native American when I first arrived, I wasn't thinking straight. Then I took two pain pills. Or did I take three?

Low battery. I shake the GPS. "Come on," I tell it, but the screen goes dark. I take the batteries out, then put them back in. Nothing.

Rain streams off the tip of my nose. Mom's sweater clings to me, soaked. My core body temp seems to have suddenly plummeted, and I'm shivering, teeth chattering. Dark sky and driving rain make it impossible to see. Zero visibility.

I should find a garage and huddle under the awning until this blows over. A porch would be better. Kandy wouldn't mind. I turn back. Her house was purple, right? I wipe rain from my glasses, but it's like someone's holding a garden hose over my head. I take my glasses off and squint. A brick driveway. It must lead to a house, though I can't make it out through the haze of my myopic vision.

Crack!

My knees tear across the ground, shredding my jeans, the skin underneath. I'm thrown face-first onto the driveway. My glasses crunch against bricks. A tree is on fire. A smoldering odor.

My body is heavy, uncooperative. I pull myself to my feet, stumble, limp, fall. Up again. Stumble. Kandy must've hit me. Evil Kandy from home, not the nicer one I just met. She followed me through the tree, she's been stalking me from universe to universe, and now she clobbered me with an aluminum baseball bat. I look around, shield my head against another blow, but there's no one. Just me, and the rain.

What's that smell? That burning smell?

I walk for minutes, maybe hours.

A sign for Arainn Street, then an amazing castle with gargoyles, towers, stained-glass windows. Thick wooden doors, quarried stone floor. Not a castle. This must be the library.

Cold, cold air. I wring my shirt out in a sink. I drink from a faucet. Water, more water. I grip a cold iron handrail, climbing upstairs. I'll live here. I remember thinking this was heaven, the science section. Yes, I'm in heaven. This can be home.

Science books. Books for pillows. Pillows for sleep.

chapter seventeen

I'm dreaming of Dad, kneeling on the ground, his jeans streaked with dirt. "That's some tomato," he says, pride in his voice. He places his hand gently underneath it, ready to twist it off the vine.

"Don't!" I say, pulling his arm back. "We need to take photos first. It's part of the assignment." I'm in seventh grade, making a report for science class.

Then loud voices interrupt. Doctors and nurses are talking over me, like I'm not here. They speak in disconnected words: *She mumbles nonsense . . . picking tomatoes . . . her California ID . . . called the social worker . . . Ruby is a runaway . . . name is Ruby . . . fifteen years old . . . tattoo . . . some cult thing . . . did she say Mom?*

I push their voices away and keep dreaming. "Hurry up with the photos," Dad teases, pretending to take a huge, noisy bite of the tomato. "I'm ready to eat your science project."

The light is perfect. California sunshine, cloudless skies. I take close-ups and wide-angle photos of the entire garden. There are five little green tomatoes, sprouting, plus the huge red one. "Take some photos of me," I say, handing Dad the camera.

"Squat down next to it," Dad says, snapping several shots. "So you're on the same level."

The doctors interrupt again. *It's a good sign she's mumbling . . . if she wakes up . . . neurological damage, post-traumatic amnesia, aphasia . . .*

Dad hands the camera back to me. I scroll through the photos, deleting several and keeping ten good ones. "That should do it." I grin.

Dad doesn't hesitate. He plucks the ripe tomato off the vine. "Remember when you made volcanoes with vinegar and baking soda in fifth grade?" he asks.

"Third grade."

"Well, this is a hundred times better. Remind me to thank your teacher."

Entry point chest, exit point right foot . . . burned hair . . . minimal second-degree burns . . .

We wash our hands in the kitchen sink, and then Dad slices the tomato into thick pieces. "I like mine with salt," he says. "Just salt, nothing else."

"Okay," I agree.

We bite into the salty-sweet tomato, rosy-red and perfect.

Blood work, electrolytes, and glucose . . . CAT scan . . . infected leg injury . . . IV course of antibiotics . . . heart and brain . . . fresh coffee . . . want some?

"We got it made, kiddo," Dad says, ruffling my hair. "Don't we?"

"No doubt."

chapter eighteen

A steady beeping reaches through my sleep, pulls me awake. Why did I set my alarm clock? Where's the snooze button? No, no. It's not an alarm—it's Dad's cell phone ringing. I was finally able to get a call through to him. Good. I need to hear his voice.

No. It's that digital monitor—that's what's beeping. An IV is taped to the back of my left forearm; on my right index finger is a big white clip. I'm in a hospital room. Kandy must've slit my throat or pushed me in front of a moving car.

My mouth is sticky and dry. "Ice cube?"

I don't think anyone's in the room to hear me.

"Could I get some Gatorade?" I try louder. "I mean, TriAthlete?"

I stare at the ceiling, hoping to gather my thoughts. Then it comes to me—quite literally—in a flash. I remember the storm, and the lightning bolt. I can see it leaping off the speed limit sign, bouncing off a tree, then slamming me in the chest. Not a bullet to the chest fired by Kandy, but an electrical power punch courtesy of Mother Nature.

I want to sit up. Where are the controls for the bed? I pat around in the crisp, thin sheets. Where are my glasses? The wall clock is a fuzzy circle, dotted with red shapes that must be numbers.

Give yourself a minute, Ruby. Don't make yourself lightheaded.

Even though I can't see it, I mentally watch the second hand sweep around, making a 360-degree turn. Carefully, I pivot and sit on the edge of the bed. I pull my shoulders back, straighten my spine.

Slow down. Count to thirty.

I squint at the clock, but the second hand remains invisible to me. I know it's there, making another lap. I don't need to see it in order to know it exists. Ultraviolet light is invisible; gamma rays are invisible; electrons, neutrons, and protons are too small to see. Quarks are even smaller.

Now I put my feet on the floor, my gray hospital socks with rubber treads. I cannot put weight on my right leg. Or on my right foot. The whole thing feels dead. Why doesn't it hurt more? I know I'm on pain medication; I remember the orange vial. I remember Mom and her apartment. I remember my last trip to the ER, and now I remember Dr. Leonard with his ash-white beard and young face. Did they give me more pain medication here, just now? Maybe I've had too much, or maybe it's nerve damage, and that's why I can't feel my leg anymore.

I'm going to have to hop.

On a vinyl chair next to the bed, there are clear plastic bags. One contains my damp, burned-smelling clothes. The other holds my backpack. Carefully, I wheel the IV stand, and though the tubes are straining, I can reach my backpack. I root through until I find the spare clothes I packed two days ago. Three days? Four? I'm not sure. How long have I been in this hospital room? The shirt is damp, and the jeans smell like a campfire.

And then I find my glasses. What's left of them. One lens is crushed beyond repair, so I pop it out. The frames sit crookedly on my nose, but through the remaining lens I can see the beeping digital screen where blue, purple, and green lines chart my vitals. My blood pressure is 150 over 60, and I can't remember if that's good or bad. I look at the clock again. It's eight and getting dark outside, so that means p.m. Below the clock is a dry erase board. In blue ink it says TODAY IS SUN-DAY, AUGUST 23.

Can I climb out the window? What floor am I on?

I have a hunch about these EKG leads that are taped to my chest. If I pull them off, an alarm will sound, and a nurse will come. But I'm pretty sure I can pull out the IV without anyone knowing, and then I can get my jeans on, and my shoes. Carefully, I pull the tape away, then slide the thin plastic tubing out. It stings.

It's not easy with the big clip on my finger—I think it's for measuring my blood-oxygen—but I manage to get my jeans on without passing out or throwing up, steadying myself on the bed. Bending over to put on my socks gives me a massive head rush.

N_2 and O_2 in, carbon dioxide out. Breathe, Ruby.

A nurse walks past my open door but doesn't enter. The IV left a little, achy hole in my arm that's leaking fluid and blood. I press the bedsheet hard against it, waiting for it to stop.

Now I'm able to wiggle my feet into my wet shoes, which truly need to be thrown away. I can put a finger clean through my right shoe. Where did that melted-looking hole come from, anyway? Did someone sink a giant cigarette through my shoe? Did the lightning do that? Yeah, of course. It must've been the lightning.

I dump out the remaining contents of my backpack. The two science books are soaked, so I throw them in the trash. They were heavy anyway, adding most of the weight to my load. I guess Ruby in Universe Four is going to have more late fees at the library.

The eight-by-ten photo is wrinkled, but otherwise unscathed, and so is my little snapshot of Mom and me when I was a toddler; they were protected by my change of clothes. I keep Mom's sweater, the grape shampoo, Ó Direáin's journal, and the gardening gloves. The flashlight still works, but my digital camera won't turn on. I toss it into my backpack anyway; it might just be the battery. My postcard from George is warped, but I can probably revitalize it with a clothes iron. The LEGO shuttle is in pieces, but I have George's diagram to rebuild it later.

What seems to have taken the brunt of the water damage is my notebook. The ink has bled, and it's all but unreadable. My chart of the universes, the codes, the runic line symbols, a few notes about Padraig Ó Direáin. Everything smudged into a blur. With a sigh, I throw the notebook into the trash. The umbrella is gone. I probably dropped it when I got struck. The copied pages from the library—the Ó Direáin street map and Mom's address from the phone book—are missing too. So is my wallet, my prescription pain pills, the Internet article Patrick gave me, and Mom's GPS. Maybe the hospital kept them, trying to figure out who I am and where I belong.

Good luck with that.

Ready, set, go! I yank the three EKG leads off my skin. Ow! The whine of the alarm startles me, but it's the rip of skin that makes me shriek. I pull on my shirt, grab my backpack, and hop.

At first I think it's because of me. All the commotion. Someone yells, "The trauma is here!" A nurse smacks a button on the wall and giant glass doors part. An ambulance beeps as it backs up to the opening bay. The smell of exhaust fills the hallway. Dr. Leonard and another nurse rush past me like I'm invisible.

The rear doors of the ambulance open with a metallic moan, and a paramedic wheels a stretcher out. As soon as he makes eye contact with Dr. Leonard, he starts talking. "Car accident. The patient is approximately forty years old. Female, unconscious when we arrived." He rattles off her blood pressure, other vitals.

The ambulance driver joins the other paramedic. "She hit a deer," he adds.

Right now, all I'm interested in is the wide-open ambulance bay. The perfect escape route. While everyone hovers over the accident victim, I inch toward the door. But as I ease past, the shocked expression on Dr. Leonard's face makes me pause.

"Windshield wiper," a nurse says, trying not to sound alarmed, but she is. She snaps latex gloves onto her hands.

Windshield wiper?

My ears fill with a pounding that comes from within. Blood rushes. My heart pumps too much, too fast.

Before I even know what to think or do, I'm pressing my way through the paramedics.

"Mom!" An oxygen mask is strapped across her face, bolsters surround her head, EKG leads connect to a monitor, an IV feeds her saline while blood drizzles out of her neck. "You can't let her die!"

"What are you doing out here?" Dr. Leonard locks eyes with me. "Get back in your room." He sounds like an impatient parent scolding a three-year-old.

Mom's shirt is splattered with red, her pale forehead streaked with it. I want to yank the windshield wiper from her neck, but it would surely cause a flood of bleeding. Like taking the cork off a foaming, angry chemistry vial.

I lunge at Dr. Leonard, grabbing his scrubs, knowing I've got fistfuls of his chest hair underneath. "Save her!"

"Security!" He pushes me away and barks at a nurse. "Get her out of here!"

I watch Mom's chest, hoping to see it rise and fall. But it's still. She's dying. They wheel her down the hallway into a room labeled TRAUMA. "You have to think of something!" My words are full of spit and tears. No one pays attention.

Parallel universes are quasi-similar. There's a repeating pattern, with almost identical subpatterns. What happens in one universe, might, could, or will happen in another.

"She has kids!" I call after them.

Patrick.

What if Mom in Universe Two or Four is dying right now as well? Patrick would be leveled. Now I wish I'd explained everything to him. Maybe he would've believed me, would have made it his mission to keep Mom safe. Mr. Overprotective would've been the perfect bodyguard.

Dazed, I grab a set of abandoned crutches and walk straight out into the parking lot. I'm propelled by sheer adrenaline. I tuck the crutches under my armpits and thrust myself forward.

I hear someone yelling behind me, "Hey kid! Get back here! You can't leave!" Then I hear her yell at someone else, "The patient from room one has fled!"

In the distance, a bolt of lightning connects with the top of a building—the central spire on the high school. For a moment, the glow illuminates the entire sky, which gives me a chance to orient myself. With each flash, the dark clouds turn luminous, and I adjust my direction, keeping my bearings straight. I feel dizzy and nauseated. Hospital drugs, one-eyed glasses, lightning holes in my body.

Mom. Dying. Again.

Should I turn back, hold her hand until her heart goes silent?

Another crooked finger of lightning touches the school's spire. Sparks leap off the slate roof like a meteor shower. Ahead, a fence that appears to be black wrought iron blocks my way. Though everything looks dark in this drizzly dusk. Another lightning strike, and I can see tombstones slick with rain. I'm at the rear gate of the cemetery, not far from Ó Direáin's mausoleum. Navigating with dwindling sunlight and on crutches means I keep tripping over roots and gravestones. I squint, looking for the giant tree, hoping its purple glow will provide a beacon.

"Come on, come on, come on," I chant, waiting for another vein of lightning to give me a chance at reorienting myself.

Finally, a flash. And there's a shape. A towering, massive presence that can only be the portal tree. I hurry toward it and the refuge it offers, even though I know it could easily be a target for the lightning too. Somehow it seems invincible in its size and power. The moment I'm under its canopy, I feel relief. Its massive limbs and thousands of leaves shield me from the rain. Instantly I feel warmer.

"I'm back," I tell the oak, pressing my face against the weather-worn door, the etched and twisted lines—grid patterns depicting the fabric of space.

My fingertips connect with the metal doorknob, but I hardly care about the static shock. The door swings open and a deafening noise spills from the tree. The flapping of wings, dark bodies swooping and darting. Bats! Hundreds of them pour out of the doorway, sending me to the ground. I can feel them all around me, landing on me, hissing, making an insectlike chirping sound.

"Go away," I moan, waiting until the tree is empty of them.

Finally, when all I can hear is my own hard breathing, and after my hands stop shaking, I convince myself that it's safe to continue on.

chapter nineteen

The portal door opens, and the smell of the air—earthy and sweet—tells me that I'm behind Willow's house, and that I'll need to walk through cornfields. My heart sinks, since this also means that Willow is probably in the picture in this universe. And if there's Willow, there's Kandy too. But anything is possible. A single variable might have caused events to unfold differently. Perfectly. Though right now, I can't get the image of Mom on that stretcher out of my mind. Blood-streaked forehead, ghostly white skin. I should've stayed with her, stroked the back of her hand until she left me. Until she was gone, again.

I pull a long breath in, trying to keep it together. She's fine here, Ruby. You'll see.

My flashlight guides me through the towering cornstalks, hundreds of them standing shoulder to shoulder, their stalks like arms pointing me in all the wrong directions. The rain has subsided, though the lightning and thunder take their turns, a flash followed by a wave of rumbling. My crutches sink into the wet ground, but I'm afraid to abandon them. With my leg in such bad shape, I wouldn't make it more than a few feet without them. After struggling for what seems like an hour, my arms are sore, my backpack weighs a ton, and I'm worried. Maybe this universe is different all right, and I'm in the middle of an agricultural empire. Maybe the cornfields go on and on and on. There might be no way out, and like Dad said, I'd be completely lost. I look behind me, but of course the tree is no longer in sight. Why am I doing this? Will I keep finding alternate variations of tragedy, no matter where I go? I feel panic closing in on me, but I shut my eyes and push it away.

That's when I hear dogs barking. They're nearby.

I follow the sound, hoping that their owner leaves them outside a while longer. If the night falls silent again, I'll be left without any sort of guide. A clear night would've given me constellations to follow, to use as a compass. But the sky above is a dark canvas. Moonless and blank. The dogs keep barking, and I come to realize that maybe they're barking at me as I rustle through the field.

Finally, when I reach a grassy backyard, I start to see flickers of light all around me. Am I passing out? How many universes have I been in today, how many miles have I walked? Limped? I must be hallucinating because of the lightning strike. As I reach out in front of me for the dots of light, I realize they're fireflies. A hypnotic light show, a mini-planetarium. They're everywhere, glowing on-off-on with yellow bioluminescence.

I'm mesmerized until, in the distance, I hear the whine of a siren, maybe a police car, possibly an ambulance. I hope it's not for Mom.

I shake the idea and turn my attention away from the lightning bugs. And when I look across the lawn, I can't help but gasp. This is not Willow's three-story dilapidated house. It's the squat brick house from Corrán Tuathail Avenue. I shouldn't be surprised by this divergence, but it makes my expectations flip. And my stomach.

The dogs continue barking, urging me on, so I follow the fenceline until they're right next to me, snorting and snuffling through the metal. There's something about the way they sound. Familiar.

"Galileo!" I shout, realizing who they are. "Isaac!"

I weave my fingers through the fence and they lick me, seeming to know me. Maybe they sense that I'm injured, because they're whining and straining to get to me.

"Hang tight, guys," I say.

Not sure what else to do, I go around to the front of the house, looking for the telltale white impatiens, but not seeing them. When I ring the doorbell, I wonder who might answer. Patrick? Dad and Mom together? The house has a stillness about it, no murmurs of conversation, no sign of a TV on. I glance next door, thinking that if the neighbors see me, they might wonder why Ruby is knocking on her own front door. Like a dinner guest, an out-of-town visitor, a complete stranger.

I try the doorknob, but it's locked. I use my crutches to flip the welcome mat over, but there's no key hiding there. Finally, remembering how easy it was for me to pop the screen out of the bathroom window in Universe Two, I figure it's just as simple in reverse.

I'm right. The screen practically falls out with one nudge, and the hard part is getting my damaged leg over the metal window frame. I toss my backpack in first, then crutches, then I crash into the room, shoulder first, bumping against the toilet on my way down.

"Ouch," I groan, but I'm thankful I didn't hit my head or the gash on my shin. I pull myself to my feet and open the door, only to find that the hallway is disconcertingly different. There is no family photo, no painted pigs or cows or other Americana decor. I call out toward the family room and kitchen. "Hello?" There can't be anyone home, after all the racket I just made, breaking and entering.

I find a sliding-glass door that leads outside, so I open it and the dogs come spilling in, tails pounding, panting like crazy, soaking my cheeks with kisses.

"You smell awful," I say into Galileo's ear. "Your Ruby needs to give you a bath." Though I guess I still can't be sure that there's a Ruby at all here.

They follow me through the kitchen, almost tripping me as I try to avoid catching a paw under the crutches. When I find the doorway out to the garage, I hesitate, take a breath, wince. Then I open the door. No cars. Also, no moving boxes and no makeshift bed in the corner. Kandy doesn't appear to be sleeping out here.

"Two dogs, zero Kandys?" I ask the dogs as they follow me back into the house and toward the bedrooms. "So far the math seems good."

There's Patrick's bedroom, with all his football trophies and an unmade bed. The next bedroom is perplexing. A floral quilt is neatly smoothed across a twin bed, and the air smells like cigarettes. I open a drawer and find a tube of lipstick, cinnamon-scented hand lotion, a pair of socks, and a bunch of bras. Is this Mom's stuff? I check the nightstand for her book of Ó Direáin's codes, but there's a stack of John Grisham novels instead. It doesn't seem like Willow's stuff either—no paintbrushes, no canvases. Generic, framed floral prints line the walls. Maybe Dad has a different girlfriend in this universe. As I open and close every drawer and look through the closet, all I find are polyester dresses and vinyl purses.

Where is Dad's stuff? Is Dad here at all?

My throat tightens, thinking about what this could mean. But I don't have enough to go on yet. I don't want to jump to conclusions. Maybe I'll find some clues in Other Ruby's room.

Just like in Universe Two, her name, my name, is on the door. I immediately look for the PARIS, JE T'AIME poster. Not there. No romance novels or yearbooks on her bookshelf, either. This version of myself has latched on to the ruby-red slipper motif. She's got an entire collection of Oz stuff. It makes me cringe, but I get it. When you've got a name like Ruby, people tend to get cute with gifts. I have more than one pair of ruby earrings from Dad, and I don't even have my ears pierced. He says I'll appreciate them when I'm older. And somewhere in my moving boxes, I've got a stash of Ruby Tuesday gift certificates.

At least she has decent clothes, no bejeweled items in sight. I help myself to a clean pair of jeans and a gray sweatshirt, and I sit down on her bed to take my dirty clothes off. My leg was bandaged so nicely at the hospital, I don't want to unwrap it to take a look, though I can tell from the swelling it's not good. There's also a small bandage on my chest from the lightning. I'm guessing it's a compact burn wound.

I continue to search the room, looking under the bed and up at the ceiling, which catches my attention. In an instant I know why. There are flecks of glow-in-the-dark paint all over. It's a star chart, made with a stencil.

"Nice," I murmur, smiling. I can't help but close the door and turn off the lights. The bed is piled high with pillows, and the painted stars above me are a comfort. Even though I know I shouldn't, I allow myself to close my eyes. Just for a second . . . and then I'm going to check that other bedroom again. There must be a photo album, a passport, a diploma. Something that reveals a name or face.

I'm startled awake. Someone is tapping on the window. Where am I? The clock says 1:16 a.m. The tapping continues, and now a voice. "Rubes?"

Rubes. There's only one person in this whole wide world, in all these worlds, who calls me Rubes. I jump out of bed and pull the window shade aside, my leg angry that I moved so suddenly.

"All clear?" George asks softly from the dark outside. I can only see the outline of his hair and his torso, which seems more muscular here, even more so than the George with the nice biceps in Universe Four. "You okay, babe?"

Babe? I laugh, despite my throbbing shin. "I'm beyond glad that you're here," I say.

He climbs easily through the window, like he's done it a hundred times before. The bedroom lights are still off and before I know it, he's kissing me. On the lips, deeply. He loops an arm tight around my waist, and his other hand goes to my hair. I almost pull away, anticipating a comment about how short it is. But he says nothing.

No reaction. I smile in the dark; this Ruby is more like me than I gave her credit for.

"Are they home yet?" he whispers.

Who is they? Patrick and who else?

"I don't think so," I say, listening for sounds in the house.

"Good," he says, pushing me gently onto the bed. He doesn't smell like sandalwood soap here. It's more like spiced oranges. I press my nose into his shirt, surprised by his solid chest underneath. "Did you get your dress today?" he asks in between kisses, his hips pressed against mine.

"Um . . ." My entire body is tense, not knowing what he's about to do. What if this Ruby and George have sex? All the time? "Dress?" I squeak.

"I trust that you got something extra poofy with a giant bow on your butt." He lowers his voice and pretends to be an announcer. "Ladies and gentlemen, I give you Ruby Wright. Homecoming queen."

Homecoming? He's my homecoming date? Sheer happiness over-takes me as I imagine the two of us. Dancing! Me, dancing? I wonder if the Ruby in this universe wears sparkly red shoes whenever she dresses up. And then I wonder . . . if I should stay here. No sign of Willow or Kandy. I'd have the dogs, Patrick. And not just George, but George the way I want him. As my boyfriend.

"You're wearing your powder-blue tux," I say, trying to keep up with the conversation, like I know what's going on. He's not serious about me being queen, though, is he? "With a ruffled shirt underneath."

"Shiny white shoes," he says into my neck, kissing me up to my ear and back down to my collarbone. I can't help but tremble.

"Are you cold?" George asks. He flips on his side and guides me into the same position, so we're spooning. He pulls the blanket over us, his knees bent into mine. I think of the shape we're making in the bed. An *S*. Just like the *S* on his Superman costume, the one he wore when he was six years old. When I sent him that text from orientation at Ennis High, I'd asked him to come rescue me. And here he is.

"My hero," I say.

He laughs and slides his hand under my sweatshirt, onto my bare stomach. "If Patrick catches me here, he'll murder me."

"I do believe that's a true statement," I say.

"I should go." He sighs, his hand moving up my shirt, closer to my bra.

"Okay," I say, wriggling free. I'm partly disappointed that he's leaving so soon, partly relieved that I won't have to decide about losing my virginity tonight.

"Did he say if their flight is canceled?" he asks, getting out of bed. "I bet Granny is ready to clobber some airline official with her cane."

Granny? Granny Frankie? Is it Dad's mother who's living here? She smokes, and that bedroom smells like cigarettes. I sit up, suddenly feeling ill. I can think of no good reason that we're living with our grandmother. There's usually only one scenario, one situation that forces kids to live with grandparents. Because their own parents are dead.

"I was just thinking about my . . . um . . . dad and mom," I try.

George clears his throat and shifts uncomfortably. Even in the dark, I know what his awkward body language means. "Yeah," he says sadly.

Now I want George to leave. Immediately. Because if there's a granny here, I need to get going. I've spent too much time here already. I glance at the clock.

George squeezes my hand and climbs back out through the window. "Call me when you wake up," he says. I nod, thinking that all of this certainly does feel like a dream, that I desperately need to wake up. Any minute I'll find myself back in our apartment in Walnut Creek.

"George?" I call out into the night, the fireflies still flickering.

"I love you," he calls back, and the dogs start barking again, this time in the hallway. Their nails scrape against the bedroom door, pawing to get in.

I wish I had George's iPhone thesaurus app. I love, adore, idolize, treasure, worship you. There aren't enough ways to say it. I count to sixty until I'm sure he's gone, and then I tumble out of the window, heave my backpack on, and head toward the tree. About halfway back, the rain starts again, heavy, punishing. I don't want to know what happened here. I don't want to know how long ago, or where.

All I want to know is why. Why is this fair? Why?

Finally, I break free from the cornfield and find the oak glowing purple in the dreary rainfall.

"Let's try again," I say, knowing I only have three more universes to check, calculating the odds, trying to stay hopeful. I think of Mom and the Mandelbrot set. Repeating patterns, quasi-similar formations. Do I want to put myself through excruciating disappointment and grief, over and over again, in Universes Eight, Nine, and Ten? What are the chances now of finding my utopia? If I see another Mom with the windshield wiper . . .

"Stop!" I tell myself, stifling a sob. It only takes one good universe, Ruby. And yes, all the pain would be worth it in the end.

I reach for the doorknob but before my fingertips make contact with the copper, the door swings open.

Someone is coming out of the tree.

chapter twenty

I stumble backward, landing hard. I scramble to right myself, thrust my crutches under my armpits, then turn to run.

"Ruby!"

My heart jolts. It's Mom.

She rushes toward me, hysterical. "What is this?" Her mascara is smudged down her cheeks. She's been crying. "Where are we?"

"But you were . . . I saw you . . ." I fumble for words. The image of her in the ER, blood streaming down her neck, is still fresh in my mind.

Then I realize what's happened. This is Mom from Universe Four.

"Did you follow me?" I ask.

"Of course I did!" she responds. She pulls me into her arms and crushes me against her body. She dots my face with quick kisses. "You weren't in the nurse's office." Her voice breaks off into sobs. "I checked your French class, and then I thought you'd taken my car. That's when I saw you way off behind the school. But I still couldn't find you. I looked all around, calling your name, trying to figure out how you were there one minute and gone the next, and that's when I realized that the tree had a door."

Her emotion is contagious. I press my face into her hair. "There was another one of you, d-d-dying at the hospital."

"Who was dying?" Mom asks.

I can barely get the word out. "You."

"Me?"

A feeling of nausea sweeps through me, and I break into a cold sweat; saliva floods my mouth. I pull away from Mom's embrace and convulse with dry heaves.

"Ruby! Are you okay?"

I nod, spitting the foul taste from my mouth and wiping my face on the back of my shirt sleeve.

She gives me a few seconds to recover, pacing, wringing her hands. "Please explain this to me!" She motions to the tree, frantic. "What on earth is going on? I feel like I'm losing my mind!"

"We're in a parallel universe," I say, bracing myself for her reaction of disbelief.

"What?"

"Just try to calm down, okay? Do you remember at your apartment, when we were talking about string theory?" I put my hands on the trunk of the tree and take a deep breath. "This oak contains a portal to the multiverse."

"No." Mom's eyes are wide. "That's impossible!"

"You're familiar with the way the sun—any huge object—causes the fabric of space to bend around it?"

"Yes, of course," she says.

"The bent fabric then causes orbiting planets to act differently— they have to navigate a distorted spatial road." I can see that she's getting impatient, but I continue explaining. "The more massive the sun, the more gravity it brings to bear, which means the warping of both space and time. It can work on smaller scales as well. Subatomic particles can also cause warps—"

Mom holds up a hand to stop me. "Ruby, please!"

"String theory allows the possibility of parallel universes."

"That's what you think this is?"

"The tree is a wormhole of some kind."

"That's impossible," she says again, but not as emphatically. She bites her lower lip. "I thought I'd found you back in that one place. I walked through the woods for what seemed like hours and found this little town. Everyone was dressed so strangely, like Native Americans in animal skins. I saw you, but your hair was so long! Tied back in a braided ponytail. It just didn't make sense. It was you, but it wasn't. And when I tried to talk to you, you were scared. You ran."

"You met my parallel self!" I say, feeling a flood of relief. This is good! If Other Ruby in Universe Five was displaced while I wandered around the woods this morning, that means she was back by the time Mom arrived there. She's okay.

"What does that mean?" Mom asks. "Parallel self?"

"She's me," I say. "In a parallel universe."

The thought seems to settle in. Mom gently turns me around and runs her fingers across the nape of my neck, across my tattoo. "You're not my Ruby," she says, "are you?"

"No," I whisper. "And you're not my mom. My mom died in a car accident eleven years ago."

"I'm so sorry for your loss," she says sincerely, and then a look of panicked confusion crosses her face. "But she was me?"

"No, not you, not exactly," I say haltingly. "That was in another universe, a long time ago."

"But you just said I was dying at the hospital." Her voice fails her; she takes a slow, deep breath before she can speak again. "Tonight?"

A few raindrops make their way through the tree's umbrella-like leaves. Mom shivers and pulls her arms around herself.

"You're fine," I say.

"I'm fine," she repeats with a curt laugh, looking at the tree and then me. "So where's my Ruby? What did you do with her?"

"I didn't do anything," I say, not sure if I'm speaking the truth.

"You made her disappear!"

"I—I'm sorry," I stutter. "I didn't mean to mess anything up. I'm trying to make things better. To make things perfect!"

She glares at me, and the look in her eyes makes me wither.

"Please just listen," I beg. "Haven't you ever thought about how different things would have been if you'd made different choices along the way? What you majored in, where you moved, who you married? Parallel realities are the result of quantum junctions. There could be an infinite number of junctions."

Mom is quiet.

"And in these parallel universes, our lives are playing out

differently," I say. "There are forks in the road that our parallels have taken."

I don't know how to tell her that she's dead in so many universes. Mom, you have a tendency to get in car accidents. If you go back to Universe Four, you might be destined to die.

"Is it like that Robert Frost poem?" she asks, sounding vacant, far away. "Two roads diverged." She's talking mostly to herself, lost in thought. And I'm suddenly seized with a thought of my own, a blazing idea.

"You can come with me to Universe One!" I blurt. "We're just a few clicks away. You'll be safe there!"

"Where's Universe One?" she asks. "I'll be safe from what?"

The word won't come to me at first, but then I whisper, "Death."

Mom puts her hand to her chest. "What do you mean?"

"You would be safe because that path has already played out there, eleven years ago. That fork in the road is behind us now."

"Ruby," Mom says, her eyes growing wide. "I *was* in a car accident eleven years ago. That's how I got this chipped tooth."

"What?" I gasp.

"I hit my mouth on the steering wheel. And a windshield wiper grazed my throat." She pulls the collar of her shirt away from her neck. "I have a faint scar."

"You survived?" I'm relieved. And then I'm outraged. "Why didn't you survive for me? In my universe? It's not fair!"

"It was a minor accident, but the doctor said it was a matter of inches. If I'd had my seat a little less reclined, well, then . . ."

"Come with me," I beg. "Come with me to Universe One!"

"I can't, Ruby. Think about it. Think about Patrick," she says. "I can't abandon him. And what about my Ruby? My Ruby. If you keep me with you, now she'll have lost her mother."

I shake my head, sobbing. "But I can't give you up again. I just can't!" I reach out and grab her arm, but she pulls it away.

"And don't you have your father to go back to?" she presses.

I nod, trying to imagine Dad's reaction if I showed up with Mom. He'd freak at the sight of her, wouldn't be able to comprehend where she came from. She'd be some long-lost ghost, returned from the dead. He'd probably end up in a mental institution.

"You're not thinking of anyone but yourself!" She waves her hands wildly toward the tree. "Make this thing take us back to where we belong."

I wipe my face and take a step toward Mom. Her body is rigid with suspicion. She matches my move and steps away from me. "Please don't do this," I say. "I need you."

"Don't you see that you're robbing me?" Her voice cracks. "If you don't take me home, I'll be dead inside, because I can't live in some almost-place with a mangled mess of what could have been."

I turn away, not wanting to hear any more. "Stop it."

"To my Ruby, I'll be dead. To Patrick, I'll be dead. To all my students and friends. Vanished. Kidnapped. Is that what you want? Don't you see that you're killing me?"

"Stop it!"

Kidnapper. Identity thief. Interloper. Impostor.

Murderer?

A menacing crack of lightning sends a jolt of adrenaline through my already overtaxed nervous system. Too close for comfort.

"Let's get going," she orders. "Did you decode the inscriptions?"

I take a deep breath, trying to get myself together, needing to think straight. No matter what we do, we can't stay here. We have to move on to the next world. "I figured out the one above the door, but it was useless. 'Who are you seeking?'"

"Well, the code inside the tree is slightly more helpful," Mom says, unfolding a piece of paper.

"How did you crack it? Did you find the key?"

"No. I used the process of elimination. It seemed pretty obvious it was an alphabetic shift," she says. "I thought it might give me a clue as to where you were, so I worked on it awhile."

Thunder in the distance. A nearly incessant rumble. Mom flicks on a key-ring flashlight and shines it onto the paper. "Can you see? Your glasses are a mess!"

"I know." I pull them off and inspect them, the frame bent, one lens missing. "Your Ruby had LASIK, but I didn't." I slide them back on and read.

Massive solar flare 1864 = Atmospheric electric surge. Tree retained power 87 hours. Sufficient surge reoccurrence incalculable.

"So a solar flare triggered an atmospheric electric surge," I say.

"I guess that's what's powering the tree."

That explains the dangerous weather patterns. Explosions on the sun's surface can shake the Earth's magnetic field. These plasma assaults cause all sorts of problems: blackouts, flight delays, bad cell phone reception. I can hear Chef Dad's voice in my head: *There's been a record number of lightning strikes the past few days. The weather people can't get over it.*

"I think we can assume that the tree works for eighty-seven hours," she says. "Or until the solar storm lets up?"

"Okay. So help me think this through," I say, shifting the crutches under my armpits. "The first time I went through the tree was something like two p.m. on Friday, and now it's what?"

"It's Sunday." Mom looks at her watch. "No, now it's Monday, two fifteen a.m."

"So it's been about sixty hours."

"But that's from the time you first went through the tree. What if it had been up and running for a while?"

"Good point," I say. "It was vibrating on Thursday, late afternoon, like the motor was on. So if it had already been running for twenty-four hours—"

"That means we're down to our last hour or two!" Mom says. "And the code says that the next sufficient surge is unknown."

"Mom, this must be the next sufficient surge. Ó Direáin used the tree in the year 1864, and he didn't know when it would work again. He couldn't tell when another solar flare would charge the atmosphere. We're being bombarded by solar plasma right now. These are the conditions he couldn't predict."

"Ó Direáin? The man who founded our city?"

"He was an inventor. A scientist," I say. "He was a genius. He built the portal, and housed it—hid it—inside the oak."

"What about those line drawings on the floor? Do you know what they mean?"

I shrug. "They mark the names of the universes somehow. They're runic symbols, I think, but I'm not sure it matters. I have my own numbering system to keep track of where we are. I started in Universe One, and you're from Universe Four. Right now we're in what I'm calling Universe Seven. I know where they correspond with the positions under the steering wheel."

"Steering wheel?"

"The disk inside the tree."

"Okay. Then let's go." Mom touches the doorknob and an arc of electricity leaps. She snaps her hand back, like she's been stung by an angry wasp.

"The charge is getting stronger," I say.

She straightens her blouse and clears her throat, trying to gather herself. "Come on. Get in the tree."

"You sure you're all right?"

"Go. Hurry."

We wait for the door to seal shut, then Mom clicks on her key-ring flashlight. She struggles to twist the slippery wheel. "I hate this thing."

"Hang on." I dig through my backpack and grab Chef Dad's gardening gloves. "These help."

"Why didn't we use these for the doorknob?" Mom asks.

"The metal there needs skin," I say. "A charge exchange. Otherwise nothing happens. The door doesn't open."

Mom turns the disk and it clanks into the next position. Universe Eight. The door opens automatically, and we step out.

"Okay," Mom says. "Let's get back in. We only need to turn it three more times and you'll be home. Then I'll continue on."

It's raining lightly, though it doesn't penetrate the tree's dense canopy. Distant lightning illuminates the cemetery.

"What do you think this place is like? It looks a lot like Universe Six."

"It doesn't matter."

It does matter. Because the Mom in this world might have a chipped tooth and a faint scar on her neck too. She might have dodged death. The colorful gingerbread houses could be a quarter mile away, and Mom would be happy to see me. Patrick too.

In this universe, maybe there's no Ruby I'd be displacing. Maybe I can just fit right in, without disrupting a parallel life.

"Come on, Ruby," Mom says impatiently. "The clock's ticking."

"I have to look around. Half an hour. That's all I need." I step away from the tree and into the drizzle.

"Ruby! This thing's only going to work for another hour—or less! Let's go."

"We could have more like three hours left," I say, calculating the window again. "Don't you understand? You need to go ahead without me so I can see what's here."

"I thought we'd gone over this! I thought you realized that you can't." Mom motions to the sky. "It's the middle of the night. You'll get lost in the dark, and if you stay too long, you'll be trapped here forever."

She's right. But I'm drawn. I'm pulled forward by force that feels inescapable, gravitational. And it comes, once again, to basic physical laws: an object in motion will remain in motion. I'm heading for another try at Mom, in this universe, wherever she might be.

"Stop!" Mom heads me off, takes me by the wrists. "If this tree stops working, you can't follow a yellow brick road. There's no tapping your heels together."

I think of my alternate Ruby and her Oz collection. There's no place like home. "I just need to see if this world will work for me," I say. "Please!" My skin is still slippery from the rainstorm in Universe Seven, and I easily wiggle out of Mom's grasp.

"There's no such thing as perfect, Ruby,"

"Wouldn't you want it? What I want?" My hands are tight fists, fingernails digging into my palms. "You would! Anyone would!"

"Let's go. Back to where you belong, and where I belong."

"But it might work out here. What if the Ruby in this universe has some terminal disease, or was abducted, or ran away, or has a horrible drug addiction? I'd be doing her family a favor by stepping in."

"No. No. That's just nonsense."

"Maybe someone actually needs me here," I say. "Someone might be happy to see me. I'd be wanted." I hoist myself onto the crutches and start hopping. "I've applied the scientific method."

"The what?" Mom chases me again, grabs my shoulders, and locks eyes with me. "This is insanity."

"No, Mom," I say. "Infinity." I walk down the path and open the gate to enter the cemetery. I look around and point to a headstone on the other side of the iron fence. "That gravestone? It's speeding along right now, faster than you can imagine."

"Ruby!" Mom clenches her teeth.

"It's moving because the entire planet is moving. We're spinning on an axis, we're orbiting the sun, and the universe is expanding." I'm close enough to see that the veins in her neck are strained and popping, just like Patrick's were when he found me in downtown Ó Direáin and hauled me off to the ER. Do the veins in my neck do that, too, when I'm mad?

"You're scaring me." Her voice is laden with desperation. "What's your point?"

"This is real," I say, spreading my arms around me. "I didn't invent this portal to parallel universes. It's a natural phenomenon, plus Ó Direáin must have discovered a gravitational anomaly, and somehow added electricity—"

"Don't you understand?" She keeps pace with me, following me down the path. "We're in danger!"

"Mom, listen. Sometimes things aren't what they appear. Isn't that what you used to say? Things aren't what they appear? With the naked eye you can mistake a comet for a planet."

"Exactly! What appears to you to be a parallel universe might appear to me to be an elaborate, advanced, virtual reality game. And it might appear to someone else to be magic. Someone else might manipulate the facts to claim that aliens put this thing here!"

"That's absurd!"

"Is it? Is it so much more absurd than what you're saying? Maybe a crystal that was recovered from the lost city of Atlantis is powering the tree," she goes on. "Maybe this is some sort of Dickensian fantasy, and we're visiting the ghost of Christmas Present."

"That's ridiculous!" I say, but my heart is sinking because I see her point.

"You're force-fitting your ideas. This isn't about string theory, Ruby."

"What do you mean?"

"You're wearing blinders," she says. "You only see what you want to see."

Her words dig in, all claws and teeth. She's painfully right. I've picked and chosen supporting data, and thrown out the rest. It's a scientist's worst crime: I've lost my objectivity.

"Then what's it about?" I ask. The ground rumbles, and I'm reminded of my original hunch—that there could be a source of power under the tree. I'd asked Willow about caverns, wondered about underground caves and rivers.

My mind flashes to a passage I read at the library, from one of the string theory books:

> *Discovering a wormhole would require a long journey through outer space in search of a black hole. Scientists agree that we currently lack the technology to traverse those gateways.*

Maybe I've been looking in the wrong direction. Up instead of down. Left instead of right. *The important thing is not to stop questioning.* That's what Einstein said. But that's exactly what I didn't do. I stopped questioning. I assumed I was right about string theory and wormholes and parallel universes.

"It doesn't matter what it is!" Mom screams, sounding like she's been pushed to the edge.

I look around at the tombs and obelisks, the birth dates and death dates, the cherubs and Virgin Marys.

"What are you looking for, Ruby?" Mom asks. "Who are you seeking?"

"You!"

We stand silently. The rain patters. Our clothes are soaked. My leg throbs.

"Voici mon secret. Il est très simple: on ne voit bien qu'avec le cœur. L'essentiel est invisible pour les yeux."

"What does that mean?" I ask. "Is that the same thing you said back at the apartment?"

She nods. "Here is my secret. It is very simple: it is only with the heart that one can see rightly. What is essential is invisible to the eye."

"Exactly!" I say. "Dark matter, vibrating subatomic strings, invisible worlds."

"No. You're still missing the point." Mom turns and walks back toward the tree. "My heart sees rightly that it's time to go home," she calls over her shoulder. "I've been searching for you all day. I'm so exhausted I can barely stand. And now I find out that you're not even my daughter."

"Yes I am!" I turn and rush toward her, my crutches catching on tree roots. "Look at my face! Look at me. What does your heart see?"

Her face softens into a look of pity. She bites her lower lip and slides my broken glasses off my nose. Her gaze goes from my eyebrows to my cheekbones to my lips. Finally, softly, she says, "Yes, somehow, you are."

She puts her arms around me, and we hold each other for a long time. "Ruby," she says, pulling back to look at me once more, "we both need to get home."

It feels like I'm disappearing, my body hollowed out. I'm evaporating into nothing. Without Mom, what's left of me? "I don't want to lose you all over again," I whisper.

She hands me my glasses and reaches into her pants pocket to retrieve a piece of paper. She unfolds it and reads.

"Dear Mom," she says. "I have gone to the ends of the earth for you."

It's the note I gave to George to deliver to the school secretary, so she could pass it along to Mom. I tremble as she reads the words I wrote just yesterday morning. "Yes," I say. "I've gone a long way."

She continues. "Thank you for the soft couch, the pizza and breakfast, the conversation. Thank you for being my mom for a short time. I loved you for every single minute, and I will always love you, no matter where we are, no matter what dimension we're in, separate or together."

I drop the crutches and double over, sobbing. "I wish . . . ," I say between gulping breaths. "I want . . . but, but like you said, there's no such thing as perfect." I look over my shoulder, squinting to see through the cemetery and beyond. I wonder what kinds of houses there are in this universe. I wonder who lives in them.

"That's right," Mom says, following my gaze. "What if something terrible has happened here? What if both your father and mother are dead?"

Lightning crackles and thunder claps. Mom picks up the crutches and takes my elbow, steering me toward the oak tree. Rain and tears stream down my cheeks.

"I know you're right. I just . . ." I wipe my face and sigh. "I just want you."

"You had a mother for four years. And you had me these past couple days. That's all the universe could give you," she says. "The universes."

"It's not fair," I say. "It's not enough." I slip my hand into hers as we walk toward the tree.

"But it's better than nothing."

I nod, trying to reassure myself. "I'm lucky for the time I had."

We near the tree and feel the ground beneath us roar with an engine-like voice.

"Let's get moving," I say, and I touch the ruthless metal doorknob.

chapter twenty-one

The smell of the ocean is unmistakable. The air is humid, and though it's too dark to see, I can sense that we're enveloped in a dense, jungle-like world. Verdant by day, pulsating with unseen life by night.

"Did you hear a seagull?" I ask as we step out of the tree and into what feels like soft soil, sandy and loose.

"Yes," Mom says. "And a lot of mosquitoes." She mumbles *hurry, hurry, hurry* under her breath, waiting for the door to close behind us.

She offers her little key-ring flashlight, but I tell her I have a better one and fish it out of my backpack. I aim the light at the portal, half expecting it to be a palm tree in this universe, rather than an oak. But its massive trunk and gray bark remain the same, though it's covered by a veil of fungus. The canopy of leaves make their blanket overhead.

"Maybe there was a meteor strike here, and it changed the atmosphere," I suggest.

Mom doesn't comment. The moment the door seals shut, she's ready. "Get back in," she commands. No nonsense.

She makes the mistake of grabbing the knob with her entire palm, rather than touching it with the tip of a finger. For several terrifying seconds, she's bound to the knob, convulsing from the electrical current. Suddenly, she's released. A jolt propels her, and she's thrown onto her back.

"Mom!" I toss my crutches aside and drop to my knees, pressing my hand against her cheek. She's sprawled across the ground like a wounded bird. Wings splayed. "Mom? Can you hear me? Can you move?"

"Yes." She rolls onto her side and slowly sits up.

"Can you stand?" I brush the sand from her hair, then drape her arm over my shoulder and try to pull her up with me. My good leg quivers; it isn't strong enough to lift both of us.

"Stop," Mom says. "You'll hurt yourself."

"I'm already hurt. Can you use my crutches? Hey! Don't lose consciousness!" I gently slap her cheeks. Her face is cold, despite the greenhouse temperatures. "Look at me!"

"I'm okay," she says. She crawls toward the oak.

"Take your time." I tuck the flashlight into my back pocket so I can get the crutches under my armpits and go ahead of her. Between the darkness, the blizzard of insects, and my broken glasses, I'm blind. I feel my way back to the opening in the trunk, patting my hand along the rough bark.

"We don't have time," she calls to me.

I step inside the portal, drop everything, and extend my arms.

She's walking on her knees and is halfway through the door when she collapses backward. Swearing under my breath, I kneel next to her and put my finger to her neck to find her pulse. I put my ear to her mouth until I feel her warm breath.

Then the door starts to close in its relentless, steady way.

"Get inside!" I scream at her, pulling on her legs, her pants wet from all the rainstorms she's been through tonight. "Try, Mom. Anything. Come on!" Her eyes jerk open, and with a hint of awareness she struggles to move forward.

I yank on her waist, and she sits up, wrapping an arm around my neck. The open space diminishes. Twelve inches, six inches. I shove my backpack into the sliver that remains, trying to buy an extra moment, trying to get the last of her inside. There's a sickening crushing sound, Mom's screams, and the tree seems to spit both Mom and my backpack into its interior. Swallowed. The door seals shut. We pant and shiver in total darkness.

"Mom?"

"My wrist." She moans in agony. I find her head and run my fingers through her hair.

"It's going to be okay," I say. "We're almost home."

"You're almost home. I've got farther to go." She presses something into my fingers. It's my flashlight. Though I really don't want to know, I click it on and shine the light on her mangled hand.

"Your wrist looks okay," I lie to Mom, and myself. "I'm sure it's just a couple broken bones. No biggie."

"Liar," Mom says, and the word stings. I have been a liar, a fake.

Posing as her true daughter, trying to step into her parallel life with the intention of stealing it for myself.

The tree's engine seems to growl at me, angry, threatening. I pull myself to my feet and point the flashlight at the wheel. I wipe my hands on my jeans, but they're slick with sweat. "I need those gardening gloves," I mumble, digging into my backpack. My fingers don't find the gloves, but I do find socks. I wipe the one remaining lens of my glasses clean, then put my hands into the socks to use them as mittens. I turn the disk and—*clang!* The disk suddenly drops a foot.

"What was that?" Mom asks, alarmed.

"The steering wheel just slid down the pole!"

"Is it broken?

"I don't know!"

Before I can assess the damage, the door opens upon Universe Ten, marked by a runic symbol that looks like a capital *H* but without the left-hand stem.

At first I think I'm seeing large snowflakes, suspended and swirling through the air. But the air is hot and smells sulfuric. I squint into the darkness, and add a little logical deduction. Yuck. It's ash and soot, not pristine snowflakes.

"What's it look like?" Mom asks.

"The apocalypse," I say, squinting harder. The landscape is an indistinct, glowing blur. But even with my bad vision, I can tell that the world is burning.

"What's that smell?"

"Fire," I say. "I think it's been all lightning and no rain here."

I shine the flashlight on Mom, flat on her back. There's no way she's getting up. "You've gotta stay in here while I go out," I tell her.

"No, Ruby," she says. "Stay inside with me. Maybe the door will close."

"I haven't tried that," I admit. "I always get out, the door closes, then I have to touch the knob to get back in." The tree's engine hums, surges suddenly, stutters, then regains its steadiness. I don't like the sound of it. At all.

"Let's wait it out." Mom's voice is a weak whisper.

I sit next to her and hold her hand. Smoke blows into the tree and into our sinuses, but the air is thick and warm, and the heat feels good.

I pull my shirt over my nose and mouth to filter the smoke. Mom hacks.

"What's going on?"

"Nothing. The door hasn't budged."

"Try turning the wheel."

"Okay."

It's now at knee level, so I lean over it, into it, but it refuses to turn. And it's not just slippery; it's stuck. No give whatsoever, even with the socks over my hands.

"It might be broken," I say, hoping I don't sound as frantic as I feel. "I'm sure it will turn once the door is closed."

Mom hears me straining and tells me to stop. "Save your strength," she says.

I stand on one leg inside the doorway, looking out. I'm not sure, but that might be Ó Direáin High School burning, throwing plumes of flame and smoke into the sky.

"It looks like primordial earth," I say.

"Volcanoes?" Mom mumbles.

"Right."

Universe Ten is disintegrating into ash. I imagine downtown Ó Direáin crumbling. Shanghai, Sweet Treats. All the books in the library, consumed by flames. Mom's apartment. Her denim couch, her messy bedroom.

Mom coughs and coughs and can't stop. I sink to the floor and gently shake her. "Mom, the air is poisonous. We've gotta get the door shut. I'm going to step out, wait for the door to start closing, then jump back in with you. Maybe it will finish closing, and we can move on."

She's silent, motionless.

"Mom?"

I press my finger against her neck and find her pulse. Her breath is warm against my cheek. But she's unconscious. Her fingers are icy, so I press them between my palms, trying to rub some warmth back into them.

"Mom?" I bury my face in her neck. "Please wake up. Please, please, please. I promise to take you back to Universe Four, back to your home." I wait for her to respond, but she says nothing. "I'll do whatever you want. I'll take you wherever you want. I'll get you there."

Her silence is more than I can bear. "Back in ten seconds," I say before limping out of the tree, backpack in hand in case I need to wedge it in the door again. The moment both feet are outside the tree, I expect the door to start closing. But it doesn't.

I force myself to count to thirty before giving up, then step back inside. "It's okay, Mom. Let me try the wheel again."

A gust of wind carries a cloud of smoke into the tree. Horrendous. My eyes sting and water; my throat is seared with hot pinpricks.

Of course the disk won't budge. "Go!" My muscles strain and fatigue. I abandon the wheel and proceed to kick and spit at the door. "Close, you stupid thing!" I grab the edge and lean backward, trying to pull it to get it moving, but I can barely get my fingers around its massive width. Futile.

"I don't think the wheel's going to advance until we're both out," I tell Mom, though she's silent. "It might not work at all anymore, but we have to try."

We need to hurry, to escape this stew of carbon monoxide, hydrogen cyanide, ammonia—unbreathable air. Desperate, I look at her slumped body. It will take every molecule of strength I have, but I'll get her out.

I sit on the ground just outside the tree, hook my arms under hers, then press my heels into the ground and tug. Once we're mostly outside, the door starts closing again. There must be some sort of internal sensor, a mechanism in the floor, that can feel when the tree is empty of passengers. The only problem is, Mom's legs from the knees down are still draped over the threshold.

We only have moments.

"Wake up, Mom!" Coughing and gagging against the sooty air, I'm barely keeping pace with the door. If I don't get her out—now—she'll be crushed. A massive explosion booms behind me, and a sudden rush of flames casts an orange light on the tree. Mom's ankles are still inside. I scream again, pull once more, and she's out.

The door seals shut.

"We made it, Mom." I pant, gulping in toxic smoke, willing myself to stand up and touch the doorknob. The shock of electricity is momentarily paralyzing; it throws me back onto the ground. The tree door opens again. I gather my senses, hook my arms under Mom's armpits, and then reverse the procedure, screaming and tugging on her, until we cross the tree's threshold and are back inside. The door closes behind us.

Retching and dizzy, I try to turn the wheel. Universe One is only seconds away. But it won't advance to the next position. I twist and twist, but it simply won't go.

"Turn!" I scream, shredding my vocal cords.

It's stuck. My lungs are collapsing. We're suffocating inside this dark and unforgiving chamber. This coffin.

"Mom," I sob. "I'm so sorry. We're going to die in here."

Is this what destiny had in mind? Is this my fate? To die with Mom? Maybe I should have been in that car when I was four. Maybe I'm the one who's been dodging death all these years and it's finally caught up with me.

I hold Mom's hand, waiting to black out. It will only be a matter of minutes. I lay my head on her chest so I can feel her heart, still beating.

She squeezes my fingers. "Ruby," she says in a raspy whisper.

I press my ear to her lips so I can hear. "I'm here, Mom."

"Please," she says. "Undo what you've done. You have to go back and reverse it somehow."

"Mom," I say. "I can't—"

An idea jolts me, resuscitates me.

"Reverse!" I scream, crawling back to the wheel. "I need to try it in reverse."

chapter twenty-two

The wheel slides counterclockwise, returning to the position of Universe Nine. Fresh air blows into the tree, clearing the smoke from the interior of the trunk. Sand darts across the threshold, and the salty, seaside air seems to rouse Mom.

"Are you awake?" I ask, shining the flashlight at her face.

She nods.

"I think you're okay," I tell her, brushing a mosquito from her nose. "You passed out from the pain."

She tries to sit up, holding her wrist limply in her lap.

"Steady." I wrap my arms around her, trying to offer support.

"What about you? Your leg?"

"Bad," I admit. "It's seeping through the bandages and sticking to my jeans." I think of Dr. Leonard warning me about pus.

A chill shakes me despite the balmy humidity here. I'm sure I have a fever.

Mom shifts her weight, pressing her back against the inside wall. "Where are we?"

"Universe Nine. We're going in reverse now."

"Good," she says.

"We hit a roadblock, so we have to double back." I shine the flashlight at the wheel mechanism, and inspect the pole. There's the horizontal groove we'd been traveling along. But after Universe Nine, the horizontal groove ends and gives way to a vertical groove going down. So when we reached that point, the disk plummeted a foot, and then settled into place—at the start of another horizontal groove. Poised to rotate in the opposite direction.

"Can you stand?" I ask.

She says yes, and I help her to her feet. "Crutches?" she asks.

"They're gone. I left them inside the tree, and they vanished."

"Thank goodness you didn't leave me," she says.

"The tree wouldn't let me," I say. "Thankfully." Maybe the tree has a way of distinguishing human cargo from inanimate objects.

We hobble and lurch getting out of the oak, and then we turn to face the dreaded knob. With every touch, it delivers more amperes, more current, more impact. At some point, it will be deadly.

Mom reaches for it, and I slap her away. "No way. I'll do it." The electricity tears through me, but I remain on my feet. "Piece of cake," I say through vibrating teeth.

Mom holds her wrist against her stomach, her shoulders slumped, looking weighed down by exhaustion, pain. "How much time do you think we have left?"

"Zero." The tree's humming, engine-like noise has gone up in pitch. It's straining.

"So let's keep moving," she says, determination in her voice.

Back inside the tree, Mom steps toward the wheel. "Maybe we don't have to go one at a time," she says. "See if you can spin it all the way to four. All at once."

I wipe my hands dry on my jeans. "I'll try," I say doubtfully, gripping the disk and turning it. It settles into the notch for Universe Eight, but I keep applying pressure. Surprisingly, I can feel that it's not completely resisting. It doesn't seem locked into place.

"Is it working?"

"Maybe," I say, wishing I still had those gardening gloves. "Do you know what happened to that pair of socks?" My knuckles ache and my shin burns, but there's some movement, a hint of possibility. And then it goes. "We're at seven!"

"Good," Mom says.

"It has momentum now," I say as it slides from six to five. When it lands on four, I let go of the disk. "Yes!" I yell, but my excitement is quelled as the engine makes a grinding noise, like rusty gears wrenching. "That's not good," I say.

Mom doesn't reply. She seems to be holding her breath with anticipation. When the door opens I notice that she straightens her posture. "This is it?" Excitement and relief lift her voice. "We're behind the school?"

I nod. "Welcome home." We step outside. The portal door seals shut behind us, and we're greeted by the rumble of thunder. A low, growling warning. An earth-shaking. "This is Universe Four."

"Ruby . . . ," she says, her voice trailing off. "I . . ." She doesn't know what to say.

"Do you have your phone on you?" I ask.

Mom looks confused. She pats her back pocket. "I do," she says.

"Think it still works?"

She slides it open and the screen lights up. "Seems to," she says. "I've got bars."

"Call Patrick to come pick you up."

Mom nods and holds the phone to her ear. When I hear Patrick pick up on the other end, I take the phone from her. "Hi, Patrick," I say into the phone. "It's Ruby."

"Ruby!" I have to pull the phone away from my ear. "Where the hell are you? And where's Mom?"

I laugh. "It's good to hear your voice," I say. "Mom's right here. She needs you to pick her up in front of the high school." I give Mom a look. "She'll explain everything."

"I will?" she mouths.

"You were just here!" Poor Patrick. The last time I popped into this universe, he was riding bikes with Ruby, and she—poof!—vanished. One minute she was pedaling behind him, the next there was an abandoned bike lying on the ground. "Why do you keep disappearing?"

I lock eyes with Mom. I could tell Patrick about the science, that it's quantum physics, but instead I tell him the truth. "I don't know," I say. "I honestly have no idea."

He sighs, sounding frustrated. "Look. It's about time we hashed everything out," he says. "No bullshit, once and for all. I set up an appointment with that therapist that the ER doctor recommended. For the four of us. You, me, Mom, and Dad. All of us in the same room at the same time."

"Listen, Patrick. I want to tell you something."

"What?"

"You're going to make an awesome dad someday. You're just . . ." I search for the right word. "Good. Thanks for looking after me. For caring so much. It means a lot to me."

"I wouldn't know how to act any differently when it comes to you, even though you're a royal pain in my ass these days," he says. "I need to find the Jeep keys and then I'm on my way. Hang tight."

I end the call and hand the phone back to Mom. "You'd better go. He'll be here in a few minutes."

She looks stunned. "This is good-bye."

"Yes." I can see she's searching for words. "Just don't bust into an eighties song right now, okay?"

She laughs. "Oh, but there are so many that come to mind."

"I bet." I try to force the smile on my lips to stay, but it quickly erodes.

"Ruby, please know that I wish I could go back in time, in your universe, and save myself from that car accident for you." She takes a step toward me and cups my chin in her hand. "For both of us."

"Okay." I can feel my face tighten.

"We've been on quite an adventure, haven't we?"

"Yes." Tears streak down my cheeks, and I wipe them away. "I'm sorry if I caused you any trouble."

"Sweetheart, you didn't build this contraption, but you need to get home before it stops working."

"I know." Mom hugs me, and I whisper in her ear. "Even though I can't have you, it makes me feel a little better, knowing you're still out there somewhere."

She pulls back and puts her hands on my shoulders. "I was thinking of that Robert Frost poem earlier," she says. " 'Two roads diverged in a yellow wood, And sorry I could not travel both, And be one traveler, long I stood, And looked down one as far as I could, To where it bent in the undergrowth.' "

" 'Then took the other, as just as fair,' " I offer.

Mom nods, and with that, she reaches toward the knob and gingerly touches it with a finger. The spark is alarming, but she remains standing.

"You didn't need to do that for me."

She straightens her blouse with her good hand and kisses me on the forehead. "That's what mothers do. And now you need to go."

A streak of lightning punctuates her words.

"I love you, daughter," she says.

"I love you, Mommy."

I limp backward into the tree, so I can glimpse her during that one final moment before the door closes. Before the door seals shut, and I'm without her once again.

chapter twenty-three

The wheel resists and my hands slip off, landing me in Universe Two rather than One.

I mutter a long string of swear words to myself. Why didn't I take a minute to find the socks first? They must be in my backpack, or maybe they disappeared along with the crutches. I wipe my palms on my jeans and try to finish turning it, one more notch. But it's already clanked, so I wait for the door to open. But it doesn't.

Please work, for just a few minutes longer.

The tree shudders violently, knocking me off-balance. I sink down and sit on the damp floor of the trunk, in darkness.

"Open!" I shout at the door.

I wrap my arms around myself, shivering, waiting. Minutes tick past, and I click on my flashlight, pointing the beam of light on my right leg. It's so swollen the denim is stretched across my calf, the pant leg filled with what I can only assume is infected flesh.

I close my eyes and try to remember what the East Bay Café's golden brownies taste like. I try to conjure the flavor, the sensation of sugar and butter and caramel unfurling across my taste buds. But all I can taste is the stale interior of my mouth.

The emptiness of my heart. The racing of my mind. Take all of it, and add my failed attempt at perfection. The sum of it is nothing but the bare truth: I am motherless, and I don't know if I'll ever find anything big enough to fill this vast space.

Right now, though, the inside of the tree feels like just the opposite. Small. Like it's closing in on me. "Open, door!"

It finally obeys, with a jerking motion. Stuck, then unstuck. As soon as there's enough room to get around it, I crawl outside, into Universe Two, knowing that Ó Direáin High School is just a short walk away, and so is Patrick's house on Corrán Tuathail Avenue.

Patrick. He's big enough to fill the emptiness. But I know I can't stay here and intrude again. He's already got a Ruby to take care of, and she needs his help navigating a divorce, and maybe a mother moving to New Mexico before she succumbs to karaoke. Besides, Patrick's got his own happiness to pursue, without the distraction of a not-quite sister. I wouldn't want to detract from the glory of his senior year, his last season of football, college acceptance letters. And maybe—if Universe Two is like Four—he'll buy a clue and realize that a vixen cheerleader is dying for him to notice her.

No. I can't go running to Patrick. It's up to me. To figure out how to make my life complete. To add some new element to the equation, so it all adds up to more than zero. Start a science club at Ennis High or volunteer at the library. Maybe I'll ask Dad if he wants to take a cooking class together. Maybe I'll start a math tutoring business and save up for a high-powered telescope, and take advantage of the fact that Ennis has no city lights. Or, better yet, I'll use the money for a ticket to California to visit George.

Flickers of forked lightning illuminate the sky, and I can see the spire of Ó Direáin High.

This is the last time you have to touch the knob, Ruby. The very last time.

I reach up from the ground and let the tip of my finger—the slightest pad of flesh—connect with the metal. This time the wrath of the electrical shock is exponentially worse. My spine feels pulled in five directions, my head feels split in half. The current rages on, ripping through me. I'm attached to the metal by a lightning arc, then I'm released with a vengeance, crashing to the ground, twisting my bad leg under me.

I'm going to die.

I lie on the ground, aware that the tree is open, waiting for me to reenter. I look up at the canopy of branches, a roof of leaves. Above that, the sky is pulsating with lightning. I think of Dad, and I can hear his voice, calling me downstairs for dinner. I can see him standing at the end of the driveway, pacing, looking for me. I'm almost home.

Hurry, Ruby. Roll over and crawl.

The ground is rough and bumpy, littered with bark. Knuckles of tree roots are like fists in my stomach; they bruise my ribs, assault my kneecaps. I writhe in agony, belly crawling back toward the tree, dirt in my mouth and under my fingernails as I claw my way. The tree makes a whinnying noise and the ground beneath me trembles.

Back inside the tree, I make my way to the center of the hollowed-out trunk, to turn the wheel one last time. With a reassuring clank, it settles into the position of Universe One. To the position marked

Home.

But the door isn't opening again.

Hum-hum-mmm. Loudly, insistently. Waves of vibrations shimmy through the tree, and the droning becomes stronger, more alarming. It reaches a crescendo, and I press my ears closed against the deafening din. The tree quivers, then shakes violently. The humming gives way to a *zzz-zzz*—the sound of electrical shortage. Snaps and sparks leap from the inner walls, lighting the chamber like fireworks on a summer night.

If one of those little flares happens to land on me, my clothes could catch fire. Dozens streak through the interior darkness of the tree. A flickering shower of nascent flames.

chapter twenty-four

I'm lying on a bed of grass. It's wet, cool against my cheek. The smell of earth—Earth—is a realization that I'm still alive. N_2 and O_2 in, carbon dioxide out. Breathe, Ruby. Breathe.

Oh, but the horrific odor. Burned hair, singed flesh. Smoke, soot.

I roll over onto my back and look up at the oak, the ancient portal tree—devastated, torn apart by lightning. Its magnificent canopy is a crooked tangle of black limbs. My breath catches in my throat. It cannot possibly mend itself.

My tree is dead.

I'm not.

Though I don't remember, the door must have opened one last time, and I managed to crawl out before the tree was completely ablaze.

I close my eyes.

Someone is kneeling over me, shaking me. "Ruby!"

"Patrick?"

"It's me! It's your dad."

My tongue feels too big for my mouth. "Dad?" My voice is gravelly, hoarse.

"Oh, thank God you're alive. You're alive!" He grips my shoulders. "Where have you been? What happened?"

"Dad?" My cracked lips tear when I speak, and I taste the blood.

"Ruby, can you open your eyes?" He caresses my forehead, my cheeks. "Oh, my baby! I'm so glad you're alive. Open your eyes."

"No," I whisper. "The sun. It hurts."

"Okay, okay," he says. I can feel him slide his arms under my body, like he's trying to scoop me up.

"No!" I scream. "My leg!"

"Okay, okay," he says again. "Help is right behind me, on the way."

"Promise me something, Dad."

"Anything."

"Promise."

"Yes, Ruby, I promise." His silent tears drip onto my dry lips, and I taste the saltiness. Like seawater. Like Universe Nine. Like the Pacific.

"Take me back to California."

Silence. The wind rustles something nearby. The cornstalks.

"Oh, Ruby," he says.

He misunderstood. "Not to live there," I say. "To visit Mom's grave. I want to plant fresh flowers. White impatiens."

He cries even harder, his tears streaming down my cheeks, finding their way into my ears. "Okay, okay," he says. "We can do that."

"Know something? About Mom?"

"What?" Dad says.

"She's beautiful. So, so pretty."

A noise gathers in the distance, moves toward us. Voices, panting, barking. I open my eyes and squint through the early morning sunlight. The cornfields sway. People wearing fluorescent-orange shirts break through the tall stalks. Dozens of people. Dogs pull at their leashes.

My eyes seal shut again. They need to stay closed for a long, long time.

"She's over here!" Dad calls.

"You found her?" It's Willow's voice, strained with joy.

"Finally." This voice sounds irritated, put out. It can only be Kandy.

chapter twenty-five

Linda Bell's brass nameplate is dangerously close to the edge of her desk. I nudge it back, away from the tug of gravity.

"Are you comfortable?" she asks. "Let's sit by the window." She motions to two oversized leather chairs.

I carry my cane, not needing to use it for such a short distance.

"How's physical therapy going?" Linda asks once we're settled into our seats.

"I walked ten minutes on the treadmill today," I say.

"Great." She follows my gaze out the window. "The mums are beautiful, aren't they?"

"Yes."

"Though they're a reminder that it's autumn, and the weather will be turning cold," Linda says, leaning forward. Her blond bangs are cut precisely. A straight line, underlining the brim of her hat.

"Not many people wear hats." In the corner there's a rack, loaded with feathery, lacy, or jeweled caps. "Older women, mostly."

She nods. "I like hats, and you like science."

"Yes."

"Physics? Chemistry? Biology?"

"All of it."

We sit in silence. A wall clock ticks. I stare at the mums, orange and yellow.

"Do you remember our session on Friday?"

"Yes."

"But you don't remember the hats."

I glance at the hat rack. Of course I remember them. "I guess not," I say.

"Have you been sleeping?" Linda asks.

"Yes."

She waits for me to elaborate, but I don't.

"Is it hard to motivate in the mornings, to get out of bed?"

"No."

"I hear you've been to Cleveland, and you had a delicious steak dinner." She says "delicious" like she's in a commercial for the steakhouse.

"Yes."

"How's your appetite?"

"Look, I get it. You want to know if I'm depressed, if I'm sleeping all day, not eating, still interested in the usual stuff."

Linda smiles. "Well? Are you depressed?"

"My head feels like it's full of helium."

"How do you mean?"

"Detached. Floating above my body."

"How so?"

"Never mind."

"And how does your leg feel? Does it feel detached, too, or are you getting used to it using it again?"

I tap the cane against my atrophied leg, finally free of its bandages and brace. "I'm lucky I didn't lose it."

"That's a positive attitude."

She waits again for me to say something. I admire the mums, notice a bowl of chocolates wrapped in silver-and-red foil.

"Ruby, we have a lot of time to talk. As many hours as you want, over the next month, or even year." She opens her hands, palms up. "What we need to know now, for the police, is whether there's someone we should be looking for."

"Nope."

"Your story . . ." Her voice trails off. "It's missing a few pieces."

"Of course it is. I got struck by lightning. I'm a little messed up. I can't remember everything." I cross my arms across my chest.

She sighs. The clock ticks. Outside, a truck backs up—*beep, beep, beep.*

"You don't remember where you were? You don't remember where you slept, or what you ate?"

Yes. But you're the last person I'd tell. Do you want me to land myself in a mental ward? No thanks! "Sorry," I say. "It's all blank. The doctors are calling it post-traumatic amnesia."

"Is it possible you're pretending to have memory problems?" she asks.

"Not that I recall."

She flutters her eyelids, stifling an outright eye roll. "Do you remember where you were going?"

"I was boldly going where no one has gone before."

"Ruby." She spits my name out, like it's a gulp of sour milk. She's lost her patience, same as last session when I used my "boldly going" line. It's just so hard to resist.

"How many sessions have we had?" I ask.

"This is our fourth," she says. "You were in the hospital a week, in a rehab center a week, and you've been home for two. Last week you started school again."

I nod earnestly, like she's telling me something I don't already know.

"Please answer my question," she says. "When you left home on Friday, the twenty-first of August, did you have a destination in mind?"

I shrug. "It's too bad my digital camera got fried by the lightning. I bet that would've provided some clues."

"Oh? Like what?"

"The face of my kidnapper."

"Are you joking? I can't tell."

"I'm joking."

Linda closes her eyes, takes a deep breath, and blows it out slowly through her mouth. I can smell the morning coffee on her breath. "So you ran away. You'd had enough of the stepmother and stepsister, and the move to Ennis. You were heading back to Walnut Creek, California."

"You figured it out!" I slap my hand on my knee. "Eureka!"

Linda bites her lower lip, looks out the window. There's something familiar about that gesture. Ah, yes. That's what Mom does when she's worried. Dad rubs his temples, Mom bites her lower lip.

Linda takes a moment to regroup. Then, with startling enthusiasm, she tries, "I must know where you got that grape shampoo. It's so much nicer than the brand I've been using. It's wonderful. Do you know where I could buy some?"

"Not offhand."

Linda strums her fingers on the arm of her chair. "We can't trace the manufacturer. We'd like to know who carries that product so we can get some geographic clues as to where you were."

I shrug. "I can't help." It's the same sequence every session: she asks her rehearsed questions, I get annoyed and cop an attitude, she gets huffy. Repeat, repeat. I wonder how much she charges per hour.

"And what about that book of codes?" she asks. "Where did you get that?"

"At a used bookstore," I say. "Back in California." This is what I say whenever Ó Direáin's journal comes up. "When do I get my stuff back from the police, anyway?"

"When they decide to stop the investigation," she says.

I fold my arms across my chest and glower.

"I understand that you're angry," she says. "The way your father uprooted your life. You must miss California. What was it like?"

"Can we just skip the psychobabble?"

Linda straightens her posture and glares at me. "Fine. Then tell me about the photo. The one of you and your father, and the boy, and the woman who looks like an age-progressed version of your mother."

"You can do anything on a computer. Photoshop is amazing."

"Why would you want to create a family photo like that?"

"For fun?"

She smiles. "It's not complicated. It's a fantasy you're trying to actualize. You want an ideal family, something you've never had."

"I'm fine with the family I have," I say emphatically. "Right here, right now."

At least I'm working on being fine with it. I have to admit, autumn in northeastern Ohio is spectacular. I've added fall leaves to my list of jaw droppers conjured up by Mother Nature. Man, what George and his sketchbook could do with all those colors. And Willow took me to an apple orchard a few days ago. For the first time I tasted real, fresh, apple cider. I can't get it out of my mind.

She goes on. "Tell me more about your magic tree. You believe the tree was mystical somehow."

"I never said that."

"You did," she insists.

"I was confused when the search party found me. I was in medical distress. You can't take what I said seriously."

"So you don't think it was a magic tree?"

"Magic? No," I say. "But in the end it doesn't matter what I think."

"Why not?"

"Because theories are just that—theories. And because it's gone now. Burned to a crisp." I picture the tree, what's left of it: a sizzled, dead mass of skyward blackened fingers.

"You sound disappointed about the tree."

"I think that everyone's a little disappointed." I reach into the glass dish and find a piece of chocolate labeled DARK.

"In what way?"

"You were hoping for a Satanic kidnapping. Something juicy." I peel the foil wrapper off the chocolate, roll it into a ball between my fingers. A tiny bit of aluminum, a decent conductor of electricity. I look at the wall outlets, the ceiling fan, the computer on Linda's desk. Electricity flows all around us. Strands of Linda's hair jut at angles along the edge of her hat. Static electricity. Outside, in the atmosphere, the electromagnetic force. The ionosphere is pulsing with it. So much is powered by the invisible.

"Hoping for a Satanic kidnapping?" Linda almost lets an excited smile turn her lips. "Why would you say that? Is that what happened?"

"Did you know that electric eels can produce a five-hundred-volt blast?"

Linda smiles with a look of barely controlled patience. "How interesting. A science fact. Are you studying eels at Ennis High this week?"

"No." I shake my head, close my eyes, savor the melting chocolate in my mouth. Chocolate is made of atoms. Atoms are made of electrons, neutrons, and protons. Protons and neutrons are made of quarks. Quarks are made of vibrating loops of string. Vibrating and warping the fabric of space, producing black holes, tunnels, and shortcuts from universe to universe.

But of course, string theory is just that. A theory. An idea, a hypothesis, a big fat maybe.

"What did you say about strings?" Linda leans in.

"Oh, was I talking out loud? I didn't realize."

Linda nods. "Of course you didn't." She scribbles something on her legal pad.

The clock ticks, and ticks, and ticks.

"If you're not in the mood to share," Linda finally says, "I'll see you Wednesday."

I stand up too abruptly and lose my footing. Linda lunges forward to help, and I get my cane underneath me just in time.

"Are you steady?" she asks.

"I'm fine. I did ten minutes on the treadmill today," I say. "Did I mention that already?"

"Yes," she says. "You did."

chapter twenty-six

Locker doors slam shut, and within seconds the hallway clears. I can't remember the room number—again. Is art class in 106 or 109? I stare helplessly up and down the hall at the closed classroom doors. I heave my new backpack off and search through folders, looking for my class schedule. It's not post-traumatic amnesia. It's my seventh day of school, and I don't have everything memorized yet. Ennis High has this crazy rotating schedule, and an army of substitute teachers. It's a little disorienting.

"Over here," Kandy growls impatiently. She's behind me, a wave of perfume. "Hurry up before the bell rings."

Ever since I came back home through the tree, Kandy has been civil. Not friendly, but at least I don't feel like she's ready to disembowel me with scissors. Yesterday, after I'd showered and was heading to my room in my towel, I caught her staring at my bare, skeletal leg with a look of pity, or maybe disgust, or guilt.

The bell rings as I sit down and hook my cane onto the back of my chair. Mrs. Gambier flutters in, a commotion of file folders, wrinkled clothes, and a stained mug, which I sincerely hope is for cleaning paint brushes and not for drinking. She can't find room on her desk for everything, so she dumps the folders onto her chair. Papers spill onto the floor.

"Give me a moment!" She's breathless, as usual.

I sneak a glance at my phone. Contraband. But Principal Mather and Mr. Burton made an exception for me for the time being, so my caseworker can keep tabs on me. Or in case the police need to reach me with questions or information regarding my kidnappers. Here at school people don't even bother whispering wild theories behind my back. I can hear them in the halls: She disappeared, was tortured for information with electrocution. Mafia, I'm telling you.

Yeah, that's the running theory. The mob is after us.

No new text messages. I'm due for one from George; he's been sending at least two a day. Faithfully. And I've been responding. Happily. While I was in the hospital, Dad called to tell him I got struck by lightning, but I haven't said a thing about the tree or Ó Direáin or quantum physics, because I still don't know how to explain.

I stick with safe stuff: hygiene-impaired lab partners, football pep rallies, and did-you-know science trivia. A cockroach can live a week without its head. I tell him that the themed cafeteria lunches aren't so bad after all. One of the lunch ladies is Greek, so every once in a while we get a feta and spinach dream wrapped in phyllo dough. George's replies are super-quick, which makes me love him all the more. He tells me about what's going on on his end: the East Bay Café is changing ownership and they're taking the couches out. Aliens abducted coffee shakes & put pinot noir in their stead. I'm not fooled. He's bombing chemistry and wishes I were there to help him. Back in 1789 chem class had to memorize 33 elements. Instead of 118. Screw progress!!!

Of all the things I want to tell him, I wish I could tell him we kissed. We kissed! On a park bench in downtown Ó Direáin, in Universe Four. And again outside Shanghai, after talking about LEGOs and wildflowers that only grow on Mount Diablo. And once again, in Universe Seven, under a ceiling painted with glow-in-the-dark stars. A love-buzzed feeling surges through me just thinking about his biceps.

My phone lights up, but it's only a text from Willow. All okay today? She sends the same exact message, every day. Yep, I respond and tuck the phone away.

Mrs. Gambier claps her hands. "Attention!" She finally has her supplies precariously arranged on her desk. "Just yesterday, I had a wonderful conversation with Mr. Manning about something called dark adaptation. Has anyone heard of this phenomenon?"

Sure, I've heard of dark adaptation. I raise my hand, but she's too excited to stop.

"When you go star gazing, you have to let your pupils adjust. After about thirty minutes, they go through dark adaptation." Mrs. Gambier opens her eyes wide, as if to illustrate. "There's a pigment called visual purple that builds up in the retina, and then you can see. You can see thousands of stars. Millions!"

I was under the impression that this was art class, not science. For a second, I wonder if Kandy was screwing with me, and I'm in the wrong room after all. I smooth my class schedule across my desk and eye it warily, though I'm sure Mrs. Gambier is the art teacher and Mr. Norton is AP physics.

"Today," Mrs. Gambier announces, "we'll be splatter-painting a large canvas. Everyone will be responsible for finding three shapes that we'll call constellations. The longer you stare at the canvas, the more you'll see. You have to give it time for your pupils to adjust, so to speak. Your constellation-shapes will then be the starting points for smaller oil compositions. Any questions?"

The class breaks into noisy chaos for a few minutes, until Mrs. Gambier raises her voice above the din. "One at a time!"

Kandy squirms, probably worried about ruining her designer jeans and shoes. "What about our clothes?" I ask.

Kandy glances at me, and for a moment our eyes meet, and I swear I see a glimmer of humanity. The same way I've been looking at her lately, now that I understand. She's still counting days until she can change her name to Amy or Jennifer or something ordinary. Much to Willow's chagrin, she's got the countdown posted on neon paper on her bedroom door: 250 DAYS TILL LEGAL NAME CHANGE. Below that, the other sign remains: GET LOST, GO AWAY, DIE.

I suppose that Kandy's also, always, doing a reverse countdown. Calculating how old Maddy would be if she hadn't miscarried, or aborted. I haven't asked what happened. I'm glad that Maddy is out there, in another universe. But Kandy will never know.

There's a knock at the classroom door and then the door opens slightly. It's Dad. He peers into the room, leaning in from the hallway.

"Forgive the intrusion." He scans the rows until he sees me. He winks.

"Yes, Mr. Wright?" Mrs. Gambier says. "Everything all right?"

"Could I see Ruby, please?" He waves me toward him.

I stand up and start toward the door, leaving my notebook open on my desk. "Get your stuff," he says. So I go back for my cane, and gather my books and pen and toss them into my new backpack.

When we get out into the hallway, I close the classroom door behind me. "Why are you here?"

"I already signed you out," Dad says. "I thought we could go to Cleveland today, to the Natural History Museum."

"Really? Don't you have to work?"

He shrugs, strokes the stubble on his face. "I finalized some catalog copy last night, and for some strange reason my email and cell phone aren't working today. I can get calls and messages from everyone except the office." A mischievous smile plays across his lips.

For a second, I'm worried this isn't my real dad. Am I in the right universe after all?

"You never blow off work."

"Never say never." He gestures to the closed classroom door. "Are you missing anything important in there?"

"Nah. Kandy will fill me in later. I think."

He hands me a postcard. It's a view of the Golden Gate Bridge, shot from Juniper Campground on Mount Diablo. I flip it over, already knowing it's from George.

> Rubes—I'll be in Columbus for a wedding the last week in April. Can you drive down for a day? Miss you.
>
> George

"Can I?" I ask Dad.

"Sure," he says. "Get the dates so we can put it on the calendar. I'll drive you. We can spend the night, maybe check out the sights."

"Thanks," I say, grinning. Now I have a countdown of my own. Seven months till the end of April. That's about 210 days.

"Seems you two are meant to be friends for the duration," Dad says, taking my backpack for me.

We're meant to be. Destined.

"Willow told me about a great Chinese restaurant in downtown Columbus," Dad says. "Maybe we should take George and his parents there for dinner one night."

"We'll order pork buns and Peking duck, and the barbeque assortment platter."

Dad puts his arm around me, and I lean into him. "I'm glad you're home, Ruby," he says. "Safe and sound."

We walk down the hallway together. He pushes open the double doors, and outside, the Ohio sky is a stunning shade of blue.

Not a cloud in sight.

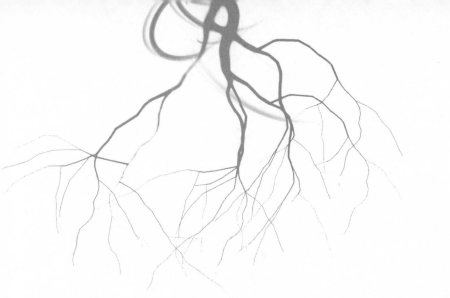

author's note

This is a work of fiction, but string theory is real, as are the theoretical physicists mentioned in this book (Hugh Everett III, Brian Greene, Michio Kaku, and Lisa Randall) and their respective publications. As of this writing, there are no books entitled *String Theory 101, Fluid Universe, String Theory Basics,* or *Parallel Places & Peculiar Physics.*

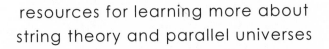

resources for learning more about string theory and parallel universes

Brian Greene's website, www.briangreene.org; his NOVA series, based on his books *The Elegant Universe* (New York: W. W. Norton & Co., 2003) and *The Fabric of the Cosmos* (New York: Alfred A. Knopf, 2004); and his book *The Hidden Reality* (New York: Alfred A. Knopf, 2011).

Dr. Michio Kaku's website, www.mkaku.org; his TV show, *Sci Fi Science*; and his book *Parallel Worlds* (New York: Doubleday, 2005).

Lisa Randall's book *Warped Passages* (New York: HarperCollins, 2005).

acknowledgments

My heartfelt thanks go to:

My editor, Emily Easton; Laura Whitaker; and the entire team at Walker Books for Young Readers and Bloomsbury.

My agent, Minju Chang, who has been my guiding star throughout the publishing process.

Everyone who critiqued this story along the way, especially my Fort Myers, Florida, and online groups.

SCBWI Florida for the inspiration and networking they provide. Attending their conferences helped lead the way to this book's publication.

Carrie Dunn, MD, for answering all my questions about Ruby's injuries and visits to the emergency room.

My parents, for keeping a house full of books, and for not

batting an eye when I skipped law school to get an MFA in poetry instead.

My husband, Terry, my true love in every imaginable universe.

My smart, funny, beautiful girls, Maeve and Rose. My love for you is so profound it could bend the fabric of space-time.